NAKED DJ

Before we hit PLAY ...

This is a work of fiction. No one character is based solely on a particular individual. I've drawn on my former career as a radio DJ, as well as liaisons of varying degrees with musicians and songwriters, to tell a tale that's as close to the truth as I can get without being sued.

—Jo Maeder

Lyrics to *I Married the Stripper (The Tip)* © 2016 Jo Maeder
Lyrics to *Hustle Wit' It (The Stripper)* used by permission
© 2005 Chris Henry

Cover design by Ploy Siripant

ISBN 978-0-9855482-6-1

Also available in ebook and audiobook
Audiobook read by Rachel Butera

A Message from the Publisher

If you love a book, word-of-mouth (and mouse) keeps it afloat in the vast sea of reading choices. Leave online reviews, tell your friends, alert your local bookstores. It does make a difference in what others decide to read. Thank you.

1. Radio broadcasting — Fiction 2. Female DJ — Fiction
3. Music business — Fiction

I. Title: NAKED DJ/by Jo Maeder

The "Femcees," the first "all-girl" DJ line-up,
WHER, Memphis, Tennessee, who started in 1955.

Alison Steele, "The Nightbird," New York City.
Heard from 1966-1995.

NAKED DJ

1

Darn Shaky Business

Another move? Big deal.

After nine of them in seven years, I had low-maintenance living down to a science. I left behind whatever wouldn't fit in my banged-up, neon-yellow FJ Cruiser. Rarely bought new clothes. No one in the next town would have seen me in the ones I had. Cheap furniture came from yard sales and thrift stores. I stayed off Pinterest so as not to explode with envy over the bright, shiny world it threw in my face that was about as attainable as me hosting a network TV show.

I allowed myself two Starting Over indulgences: the tallest, strongest, most sinfully delicious coffee that Starbucks made while I stayed up all night and packed, and a new mattress in my next place. It was a clean slate thing (plus my mattress wouldn't fit into the Cruiser). Cheaper than hiring a mover, my accountant father would argue.

"But get a Prius," he said when I called my parents with the news I'd been downsized out of a job again. "The Cruiser is a gas guzzler. And would you buy a home already?"

"The Cruiser is paid off, Daddy," I replied. "Even a used Prius won't save me a car payment a month in gas. As for why I keep renting, it's the radio jinx. Whenever a DJ buys a place the odds are pretty good he'll be out of a job soon."

"But you're out of a job anyway! Forget about throwing away money. Throwing away your life is worse."

"And staring at Excel spreadsheets all day is living life to the fullest?" (You'd think by now he'd give it a break.) "Eating yourself into an early grave is living life to the fullest?"

"That's enough!" My mom was on the other line. "You know you can always come back home, Patty. You were such a star here."

"That's because I was *with* a star. And it's Jeri now."

"You and your damn names," Dad said.

Seven years away from Richmond, Virginia, still wasn't long enough.

After bouncing all over America, I'd landed in Houston five months earlier to work for a Hot AC station — upbeat adult contemporary music like the Go-Go's, Bee Gees, mixed with Taylor Swift "oldies" (yeah, I know). I'd looked for a furnished place in a nice neighborhood because I couldn't take another shitty apartment filled with someone else's castoffs while smelling my neighbors' greasy cooking, which set off triggers from my past. Or hear them fight over what bad TV show to watch and then watching it. Worst of all, hearing them showin' the love.

I'd felt like a stagehand at a theater. One set moved out. A new one moved in. The show had had its run. Next. Enough already with being a rolling stone that gathered no moss, like a barnstorming stunt pilot in the 1920s breaking a few hearts along the way.

Never my own, though. I'd paid my dues there.

On the east side of Houston, just outside the 610 Loop, I'd found an apartment over a three-car garage at the upscale home of the Westwoods. It was beautifully appointed if frou-frou is your thing. With a starter home in the neighborhood running a million dollars, I felt like a trespasser, or a spy. A DJ living in the lap of luxury somehow didn't seem right. Still, it took me all of two seconds to be down with it.

About the same time it took to do a Jeffersons with Ree ("Movin' on up! To the Eeeeast Side!" Richmond style).

These Houstonians had *real* money, though. Most of the women worked out every day at a health club that cost $15,000 to join, plus another $400 a month.

"Rich women going from workout class to workout class," a sales exec at the station told me. "No wonder they look fantastic. Nice life."

If you say so.

I had picked up decent side money pet-sitting for the Westwoods' neighbors and friends. I was damn good at it and wanted a pet of my own. With all my moving around and it being hard to find a rental that would allow one, I kept putting it off — like a lot of things. Sometimes it seemed like I got along better with animals than with people, especially dogs. Whoever said dogs have owners and cats have staff was right.

I remember telling my landlady Lau*rynne* in our initial conversation what I did for a living.

"A DJ on the radio? Well, isn't that *fuuuun!*" she'd said in her Texas drawl. With grown kids, she had to be in her forties, at least, but she had the body of someone my age.

She was mixing herself a gin and tonic at three in the afternoon when I broke the news that I'd lost my job.

"That's a darn shaky business you're in."

She did not offer me a drink and I could have used one.

"What business isn't?" I said.

"Government jobs. I started at NASA in the mail room right out of college, became a secretary to a bigwig and retired at age fifty-two."

"You're in your fifties? I never would have guessed."

"Honey, I'm *sixty*-two and a grandma! I have terrific benefits and a nice pension. Steve and I have traveled all over the world since we retired. China, Machu Picchu, and Europe *seven* times."

She daintily sat on the edge of her regal Louis XIV chair and swirled her tumbler around before taking another deep swallow. That Pinterest-beautiful, easy-living bullshit began to pulse in my temples. It was the effortlessness that enveloped her that got me. Like she didn't even have to try to stay thin or be wealthy or look way younger than she was.

"What are you going to do?" she asked.

"Find another radio job. Here, I hope."

"How old are you now? Late twenties?" Her Botoxed face didn't change expression.

"Twenty-eight."

"Jeri, darlin'. You can't keep dressing like that and living like a gypsy." She waved her hand at me. "Do something with that hair. Grow it out. Men *love* long hair. You do love men?"

"Unfortunately, yes."

"Then settle down with one." She looked around her sumptuously decorated living room. "It's not so bad, is it?"

Window treatments on top of window treatments? I would have done a spare, mid-century modern, vintage thing. A huge peace sign on the bottom of the pool. A lava lamp by the bed. Not a water bed, though. They're fun to frolic on ... once.

"You're still young enough to get a job at NASA."

"Doing what?" I was incredulous.

"I could see you in the PR department. Maybe you'll meet a smart, handsome astronaut. Or a nice scientist like I did. Have kids. *Enjoy* life!"

"I *do* enjoy life!" I eyed her drink, feeling like I was in the final stages of dehydration.

She did have a point, though. My next relo would put my mattress purchases in the double digits. There was something about that I couldn't shake. But what company put "former radio DJ" in its skill-set search?

"Could you open a door for me there?" I was startled to hear myself say that.

"Let me talk to Steve. Will you still be able to pay the rent without a job?"

I didn't want to lose this place. "Absolutely. And I do have a job. Pet-sitting, remember? I can take on more clients now."

I was also pretty good at squirreling away money when I was making it, and I was a wiz at applying for unemployment (another skill set you don't see a company looking for).

"What is it they do these days?" she asked. "Voice-something. Where the person on the radio isn't there at all?"

"Voice-tracking. Someone in one city pretends they're on the air in another by recording themselves, then sending it to a computer in yet another city that puts it all together. That's why I'm out of a job. A woman in Tampa is taking over my show."

"Saves the station a lot of money, I bet."

"They're spending five grand a year instead of thirty-five, and no extra benefits to pay." I couldn't stop what sounded like a sigh mixed with a grunt from escaping. "Most listeners don't even know the person isn't live."

"Hmmmm." Her eyebrows barely narrowed.

I'd tried voice-tracking once. It was like the episode of *I Love Lucy* when she worked in a chocolate factory. I couldn't remember what city I was talking to or the station name, much less what to say. Not being live sucked the energy out of me. It felt like dead air, lifeless. Yet I totally respected anyone who could do it. They were bringing home a steady paycheck. I wasn't.

I gave Laurynne a big smile. "Maybe I'll hang up the headphones and work for NASA."

She glowed approvingly. "Would you like to join me in a drink?"

I opted for straight vodka (managing not to laugh when she offered me Candy Cane and Maple Syrup flavors) with a splash of orange juice. Before it was finished I was confessing that my first love had been a rapper with a number one hit. As soon as I said it, I regretted it. I knew what her next question would be.

"What was his name?" She reached for her iPad.

Great, she was going to Google him. "Reginald Roberts."

She tapped in his name, then rocked back. "You mean 'The Stripper' singer, Mr. Ree?!" Slipping on her reading glasses for a closer look, "Oh, yea-ess. A fine specimen of his race."

She seemed impressed — *and* like she was suddenly having second thoughts about being my NASA fairy godmother.

"Well," she said, "we all do silly things in our youth. Were you ever in *jail*?"

"No!"

I'd been lucky in that department.

Three drinks later, I was stumbling past my old Cruiser and up the stairs to my garage apartment that sat above a pair of Mercedes and a *stunning* '60s T-bird convertible for joyrides.

Maybe finding a nice NASA scientist wasn't a bad idea. Maybe I did need to quit radio.

I didn't feel like I'd fit in anywhere I worked. Not here, not Atlanta, Cleveland, Detroit, Miami, Phoenix, Richmond, Sacramento, Salt Lake City, or lovely Yakima. That one was market 198, but it was morning drive. I thought for sure it would lead to a better job and better pay. With three listener calls an hour, mostly from the same person, it was more like *mourning* drive.

Did I just need to be someplace hipper, like Boston or Seattle? Miami filled the bill, but I'd landed there just after leaving Richmond and Ree, and was soon replaced by syndicated programming. For a long time, those despondent days came back to me at the mere sight of a palm tree. Eventually I conquered that and tried for jobs in cool cities like L.A., San Fran, and New Orleans. No takers.

Nigel kept saying I belonged in New York, the most exciting city I'd ever visited, and the ultimate challenge. I knew I was a good DJ, but was I *that* good? Besides, all the stations there were unionized, and no one ever left a union gig unless they died.

Nigel. Just thinking of him brought a ray of sunshine into the room, like it always did. He was a promo guy, I reminded myself. Being charming to everyone and pumping up talent was his calling card. So what? Right now, that was exactly what I needed. Where was my cell?

Do not call him. You've been drinking.

I flopped on my bed. A second later I bounced back up to find my phone. I hadn't brought it with me to the Westwoods'. I'd thought I was only going to be there five minutes.

I'd missed a call: a number with a 212 area code. Manhattan? Must be Nigel. He'd heard the news I'd been canned and was calling to console me.

I held the phone to my chest. "Oh, Nigel," I said in a dramatic swoon, adding an exaggerated sigh and giddy giggles.

I played the message. Instead of Nigel's crisp British voice I heard the low, smooth sound of someone who was no stranger to talking into a microphone.

"*Heeeey,* Jeri B. It's Rick Rivers, PD of WBRR in New York City. We met at the Marconi Awards in L.A. a few years ago. Hear you're on the radio beach. Ever thought of taking a bite out of the Big Apple? We could use fresh, sassy talent like yours. Call my assistant Olivia in the morning if you're interested. She'll fly you out here. But *not a word to anyone.*"

WBRR? *The* WBRR? Holy crap!

I slapped my face a few times to make sure I wasn't imagining this.

The station wasn't just any old classic rocker. It was the mother of them all. It debuted the same day the Beatles released *Sgt. Pepper* in America (June 2, 1967). It had broadcast live from the original Woodstock. When John Lennon was shot, it was the station everyone turned to and grieved with. Their DJs had once been as famous as the rock stars they interviewed. Being a radio geek, I'd streamed some of their airchecks from the last century on a site dedicated to great rock radio stations. This was one of the few still standing.

Barely. It was no secret WBRR's ratings were now pitiful.

The station had just changed ownership from one of the last smallish companies in the market to the mega Sonic Broadcasting. A bloodbath was brewing. I could smell it.

I couldn't bring up Nigel in my phone contacts fast enough.

No. Rivers had said not to tell anyone and I had to be careful what I said to Nigel under any circumstances (especially inebriated ones). Record promo people were tapped into the radiosphere like the CIA in the Middle East. They could circulate a rumor faster than a virus on the Internet.

Which meant Nigel was the perfect person to know when I *did* want something leaked.

He might very well have whispered in Rivers' ear on my behalf. It wouldn't have been the first time. And now we'd be in the same city. Had he arranged it that way? It thrilled me to think he had. Excuse me while I put on my "He's A Player" blinders.

To hell with NASA, at least until I had my shot at the shiniest brass ring of them all. New freakin' York! The number one market in America.

My high crashed with a thump right to the solar plexus. The one person who would know what this moment meant to me and guide me through the landmines was out of my life forever.

"Ree, I finally made it to the top," I said.

If only we could have reached it together.

2

THE DANGLING CARROT SOCIETY

The Internet had armed me with plenty of ammo to pretend I was a true New Yorker, such as knowing the stars of the major sports teams and how to pronounce their names. Or the most likely place to get hit by a vehicle if you're walking (Amsterdam Avenue and 125th Street). I was up on my rock stars, too. Did you know Jimi Hendrix and the very un-rock star actor Joe Pesci were in the same band? Joey Dee and the Starliters. Not at the same time. Trivia like that made me wonder where I'd be in forty years.

Where would Ree be? There are some people you can't imagine getting old. Like Hendrix. James Dean. Amy Winehouse. Tupac. Anna Nicole Smith. Michael Jackson. Prince.

Ree was like that.

My cab was just a few blocks from the restaurant where Rick Rivers and I were meeting. I cut through my Zen deep breathing to conjure up Ree's formula for seduction: flash your target a look that says *I'd rip your clothes off this instant if I wasn't so busy.* Then split.

In the case of Rick Rivers, seducing him to offer me a job without giving him the wrong idea would be tricky. I *had* to pull it off. I was done with changing my name, hair color, and address. If WBRR didn't work out, I swear, I was really, truly, one hundred percent done with radio.

The last time I'd seen Rick was after I'd lost my job at a Sacramento station due to a format flip. I spent a bundle hitting the Marconi Awards in L.A. to network. As soon as people found out I was out of a job it was as though I hadn't bathed in a week, like I literally had the stench of failure on me. I swore I'd never do that again. But here I was in New York City because I went to that, so you never know. Rick's hair had been long and straggly then, and he was wearing a stained Staind tee he thought was funny. He had just turned around a dying heritage rock station in Philadelphia and was riding high.

My cell rang. It was Nigel, causing my pulse to race a bit.

"Just calling to give you a last-minute pep talk before you meet Rivers for dinner."

"How did you know?"

"Hard to get anything by me in this biz, love. You'll be terrific! They flew you in. You practically have the job. Here's a tidbit for you. Rivers married a barely-legal exotic dancer he picked up on that L.A. trip where you met. Now there's a man bursting with self-confidence."

We placed a gentleman's bet as to how long it would take him to bring up Ree's hit about a stripper. Nigel predicted after we ordered. I said before.

"Speaking of Ree," he said, "his new one is about to drop. The MGX machine is in overdrive."

I'd known for a while that Nigel was in charge of Ree's comeback album. Over and over I'd pushed it out of my mind, like a deadline on a distant horizon.

"It's a smash!" he said. "Worth the wait. I'll play it for you tomorrow night when I take you out."

I was glad Nigel couldn't see my reaction. It was somewhere between exhilaration for Ree and feeling like I was about to step into the crosswalk at Amsterdam and 125th. Shit. I had to get my game on this instant. I was about to face Rick Rivers.

The door to Boba 47 was made of intricately carved, weathered wood. Beyond it the atmosphere radiated nouveau hip extreme. Slinky music and subdued lighting easily put me in the Hire Me Hustle groove.

I did a double take when I saw Rick wave to me from the bar. He sported a buzz cut, gray suit, yellow tie. His last vestige of hipness was a goatee the size of a postage stamp.

"Lookin' like a rock star, Jeri!"

"Thanks, Rick. It's Jazmyn now. You look *great*."

"Nice tat," he said as we settled in at our cozy table and he eyed my upper left arm. A grapevine wrapped around the inside but not the outside. "Never seen anyone do half. Didya chicken out?"

"I vowed to finish it when I made it here."

"A beautiful segue, Janice."

"*Jazmyn*." I spelled it for him.

"Right. You're from Richmond, aren't you? I was on an alt rocker there once." In a trying- to-be hip voice, he oozed, "Cody Cooper rockin' through the night on XL102."

"Why'd you change your name?"

"Rick Rivers works in any market. Cody was too Southern, too DJ. Also, I wanted to move into management and back to the Northeast."

Rick Rivers didn't sound "DJ"? I didn't ask for his real name. I'd have to reveal mine.

"It's weird," he said. "I still think about that tunnel tragedy sometimes."

It was hard to forget. In 1925, a work train entered the Richmond Church Hill Tunnel (that had been built in the 1870s) and never made it out the other side. The tunnel collapsed, killing four men. There's speculation that there were many more casualties but since they were probably poor African-American workers hired on the cheap with no documentation, there was no way to know how many, nor their identities. Efforts to dig out the bodies were too dangerous, especially after a couple of houses collapsed into it. The tunnel was sealed. Concerned citizens kept trying to get the bodies and train recovered. The History Channel was going to do a show on it, but more tests revealed it was still way too dangerous. A historical marker finally went up in 2012.

"I used to have nightmares about it as a kid," I said. "Terrible ones. They finally ended when radio saved my lost soul."

"Another radio redemption. Amen, sister."

"Then the radio nightmares started."

I didn't need to explain to Rick what I was talking about. It's a phenomenon all DJs share. The song playing on the air is running out and you're locked out of the studio. Or you don't know how to work the equipment. Or the program log makes no sense or is in a language you don't speak. Or you open your mouth and gibberish comes out.

"I still have them," he said, "and I've been off the air for years."

We perused the menus quietly for a moment. I did my trick of lightly tapping my left wrist with my right forefinger (out of sight under the table) to curb my appetite.

When we decided on our orders, he said, "I couldn't believe how stuck in the past *some* people were in Richmond. They called me a Yankee. I'm from Baltimore. I even heard a co-worker refer to the War of Northern Aggression. I had no idea what he was talking about."

"The Civil War," we both answered.

"I bet you ran into problems with Mr. Ree," Rick said, now that we'd bonded.

"A few."

"Still in touch with him?"

"No!" I leaned back from the table. "Absolutely not."

"Yeah, I've known a few recording artists. What a crazy life. What egos."

"DJs are bad enough."

Rick had only been at 'BRR for two months. Like me, he hadn't been born when most of the music was made. Now his ass was on the biggest line of all. Just a half a rating point in the Tri-state New York City market can mean millions in lost or gained revenue.

His eyes shifted to my boobs. "Is there a significant other back in Houston?"

What difference should that make?

"No one is moving here with me, if that's what you're asking. How's your wife?"

That got his eyes off my chest.

"She's fixing up our place on Long Island and couldn't be happier. Our boy is almost four." I saw my chance to win my bet with Nigel. "Is it true she was an exotic dancer?"

He grinned. "Now she only strips for me."

He slipped into a perfect white person's thug rapper imitation of Ree, arms moving in downward motions.

"Who hustle wit' it for a piece of that pie? The stripper, the stripper, the stripper!"

I plastered on my default smile and did not point out the correct pronunciation was *strip*-ah.

"Man, I love that song," he said. "It still tests well. What, ten years later?"

I was glad Ree was making money off it. Too bad I had to hear it for the rest of my life.

"I hear MGX is giving a huge push to his new single," Rick said.

"Can't do better than having Nigel Hamilton-Jones in your corner. So, back to 'BRR."

Damn, I loved saying those call letters. Also that Ree's rap music would never be heard on a rock station.

"You've never worked at a rocker before," Rick said, "but I think you'd be great. You've got a hip sense of humor and a youthful edge."

"I'm ready to rock and roll, baby."

He shifted a bit in his chrome chair. "Nix 'rock and roll.' Screams oldies. Just say 'rock.'"

"Oh." With a puzzled expression, "Doesn't 'BRR' stand for best rock and roll?"

"Good evening!" sang out our waiter. "Would you like to hear our specials?"

Rick ordered the $25-an-ounce Kobe-style Washugyu beef. I asked for the low-cal sashimi.

As soon as our had-to-be-gay waiter walked away, Rick got down to business.

"What do you think of the station?"

I had my line ready. "It's like an old pair of faded jeans you can't part with."

"But rarely wear, right? In other words, it sucks. But the brand loyalty is through the roof."

"The average age of the DJs is what, a hundred?"

Rick had a nervous habit of picking at his postage stamp. "Cat Cruz is far from that."

Catalina Cruz posed for *Playboy* when she was in college and had been holding down middays for almost twenty years. At forty, she was the youngest of the jocks. She also ran one of the sloppiest boards I'd ever heard in radio. Dead air all over the place. But she was gorgeous, loved by her listeners, and a Latina who sounded Caucasian. Getting hired in radio is as much about reflecting the demographic you're trying to reach (while meeting EEO quotas and not having your FCC license challenged) as it was your on-air style.

She would have to kill the general manager's dog to get axed.

It was true that most minorities in this business work as hard, if not harder, than their white team players. Who was dubbed The Hardest Working Man in Show Business? James Brown. But I'd seen a few get away with so much shit I couldn't believe they kept their jobs. I'd seen white people, too, get away with shocking unreliability and bad behavior. Like, who are they fucking? Who are they related to? Who have they blackmailed? It's just the way it is sometimes. Cat Cruz already seemed like one of those divas I wanted to punch in the gut.

The waiter set down before us a vertical metal thing the shape and size of an ice cream cone. Inside it were a few pieces of bread. I begged off. Rick dug in.

"The station has unbelievably strong recognition as *the* spot on the dial for rock. P1 listeners up the wazoo. Jocks are like family members to listeners."

P1, I was once told, stood for Preset 1 on a car radio dial. Cars are where the majority of radio listening takes place for most formats. P1 listeners were the most coveted listeners because they spent the most time listening to the station and that increased ratings.

"The problem is they just don't tune in and leave the radio set there like they used to. Streaming live numbers aren't great either. Too much competition out there."

"Yeah," I said, "you can never see too many viral pet videos."

He laughed too hard at my joke. Of course, being a DJ, I also loved that he did.

"So we need to renovate. *Slowly.*"

What did that mean? Was he going to offer me overnights? The radio equivalent of Siberia. Could Ariella, the woman doing it now, be in her *seventies,* as rumor had it? I'd streamed her show, awestruck. She didn't sound that old. Maybe she was retiring.

"Our challenge," he said, "is to turn around the *Titanic* before it collides with the iceberg. For starters, we're renaming the station." He paused for effect. "WBRR now stands for *The Bear.*"

"Like a polar bear? Or like wearing no clothes?"

"Actually, a little of both, *kinda*. But B-E-A-R. What's wrong?"

"Well …" I ignored the *kinda* part and tried for tact. "Sounds great for a station in the Rocky Mountains. Wall Street hates bears. If they're going to name it after an animal, call it the Bull."

"Too much like bullshit."

Exactly.

He unleashed his pitch like a windup toy. "We'll play the best rock of yesterday *and* today. We'll have fresh talent that brings *energy* to the airwaves and gets it out of its time warp. The expensive oldsters will go as their contracts expire. Do *not* repeat that."

As if they and the world wouldn't know.

"You'll be a star in the new regime. Hell, you may end up in mornings or afternoons. I know a woman in drive time is rare in this format."

In any format.

"If you rack up better numbers …"

Rick might be a card-carrying member of the Dangling Carrot Society, but he had me. Bear schmear. Bring it on.

"The Dick and Dork morning show are going to have 'Bare it on The Bear Thursdays' where girls come in and take off their tops for major prizes."

Done to death already.

"Real theater of the mind, Rick."

Twirling his wine glass as though he were grinding it into the table, he said, "Chopper's giving away a tricked-out Harley with a big grizzly on it. We're going to have people dressed as bears handing out station stuff all over the place. And Madd Maxx will have the Barenaked Ladies do an acoustical concert on his afternoon show."

I admired Rick's do-or-die outlook. Nigel was the same with the records he promoted, forging on with a winning attitude whether he loved or hated the product or artist.

"That brings us to the lovely Cat Cruz and you."

I sat up straighter.

"I'm going to leverage the Barenaked Ladies connection by calling the midday show ... The Barenaked *Radio* Ladies and have *two* hot women on instead of one. Would you have a problem pretending you were doing the show nude?"

A laugh got caught in my throat.

"Cat might actually take her clothes off," he said. "She's still smokin' hot and an exhibitionist. You wouldn't *have* to." He pulled at his chin some more. "Unless you wanted to. I'm sure a pictorial in a major men's magazine could be arranged."

I clutched my folded arms.

When I'd started in radio, I was asked to slather myself with honey and have hundred-dollar bills stuck all over me. Selected listeners would then have five seconds to grab as much money as they could. Ree intervened. The station had no problem talking the traffic-reporter into doing it. In the madness that ensued, one of her breast implants ruptured.

Our cheerful server appeared with our food. I flashed him a charming smile. "Would you do your job naked?"

"Only if you left me a *really* big tip, honey." He flitted off.

"It's pretend, Jazmyn."

"A pictorial isn't."

"A suggestion only."

The more I turned over the Barenaked Radio Ladies idea in my mind, the more I hated it. The only thing I hated more was not being on New York radio.

"Rick, you could pair me with the Wicked Witch of the West. I have to be on the air here at least once in my life."

As for the show itself, he wanted me to run the soundboard.

"I'd run a tight one," I said, "but that means Cat's the star."

"No, it doesn't. Howard Stern runs his own board. It puts you in *control.*"

Rick's offer was 100K, just above union scale. It was triple my last salary, but New York was three times as expensive, even by Houston standards. On the other hand, I had no income at all.

"And you're asking me to pretend I'm naked?" I shook my head. "Please."

"I'll throw in a bonus based on an increase in ratings."

I had lingering doubts about Cat, but we shook on it.

My sashimi had vanished. He still had half of his meal left.

"Miss lunch?" Rick asked.

I pushed the plate away.

"We'll put you up in a hotel for two weeks," he said, "but would you mind moving to a less-expensive place?" It wasn't really a question. "Parker Meridien's too rich for our blood."

The seduction was over. I was now in that new gainfully employed state of mind: a mix of gratitude, terror, challenge, and enslavement.

3

BRIGHT AS EINSTEIN

I walked up Fifth Avenue after dinner, taking in Manhattan. Being hired at WBRR was like being inside a space capsule and landing on another planet eleven years after it was launched. I'd started in Richmond and ended up in the city of cities, the backdrop for so many movies, TV shows, and books I loved. I wanted to memorize every street, every person, every sound. Yes, I was a speck on a speck. I swooned anyway. I even loved the smell of gas, concrete, and tar that hung in the air.

Eight years ago, Ree and I had spent a long lost weekend here about midway into our doomed romance. We instantly dreamed of becoming New Yorkers. I could see changes in the city since then. There were now digital signs that counted down how many seconds you had to cross the street, adding even more of a rat race edge. Go, go, go! Time's running out. The skyline was dotted with new super-tall buildings — One World Trade Center the tallest.

It reminded me of a mythological hydra that if you cut off its head, grew back five.

New Yorkers strode past me as I stopped and gawked at the top of the Empire State Building lit up in white lights. It was an Art Deco oddity next to its sleek, glassy neighbors.

I passed a few people walking dogs and fought the urge to run over and bond. Did you do that in New York? Probably not. Or at least not with professional walkers. As soon as I spotted their earbuds and a vacant expression I knew to stay away.

A cute preppie guy and I walked in sync. When we stopped at a corner for the third time, I smiled. He smiled back. Not everyone here ignored you, I thought. I moved over to a store window to gaze at a cool outfit, reminding myself that I needed to upgrade my wardrobe ASAP. I sensed the preppie guy had moved next to me. What would his opening line be? I turned.

He was pointing down at something.

He was *exposing* himself. He had a look that said "I can't help it."

Welcome to New York.

"Fuck you, asshole."

I hailed a cab.

Embarrassed, angry, then laughing over my baptism-by-flashing, I thought about the wacko dudes I'd encountered in my line of work. At the top of the list was Krazy Karl, an engineer who climbed thousand-foot towers as if they were a playground jungle gym. He had tracked me down in every market I'd worked in since we'd met in my hometown. I thought he'd given me a pretty good antenna for nut jobs. I'd have to raise it a few more feet here.

"Where are you from?" asked the cab driver.

He stared at me in his rearview mirror, not watching the road. His car was too old to be a smart one that drove itself. Was he navigating by sonar?

"I'm a New Yorker," I answered. "It just took me a while to get here."

"Very good, very good, yes."

I loved his accent and pastel turban. I would've been disappointed if my first cabbie wasn't a foreigner, but could he please look where he was going?

"I guess it's obvious I'm not from here," I said.

"From the way you stood on the sidewalk instead of in the street to get my attention."

Photos of his smiling family taped across his dashboard filled me with a vague unease and emptiness; that loamy-earth-not-being-tilled feeling I'd had before. Shit. Why was my biological alarm clock going off now? I just got to New York! When I'm thirty I'll do something about it.

Maybe.

I leaned forward. "Aren't you afraid of crazy people getting in your cab?"

"I had one long time ago. He robbed me." He reached underneath his seat. Out came a .357 Magnum. Pointing it in the air, he said cheerfully, "No worries!"

The radio yanked me out of this bizarre moment.

Who hustle wit' it for a piece of that pie?
The strip-ah, the strip-ah, the strip-ah!
What you do when she do how she wobble that thigh?
I tip-ah, I tip-ah, I tip-ah
Keep two for that chest, give me change for this twenty
I need the best brew, fresh made in Germany
Stay cool when it drop cuz it about to blow
That booty is hot bouncin' off the flo'
The rule No Touch, what the hell I might
I don't care about cellulite

With glee, the cabbie shouted out, "Hustle wit' it shortie for a piece of that pie!"

Ree had written "The Stripper" when he was a high school senior, as a joke, in five minutes.

We never imagined it would become so big, so fast.

"The future's bright as Einstein, Patty!" he'd said. "*Our* future."

A warm current rushed from my tatas to my turquoise toenails. To have experienced that song exploding like it did, to have played a part in making it happen, was an incredible feeling.

Until I remembered what happened after.

The bubble didn't burst so much as deflate in one big long ugly mess. One week he blew ten grand on drugs and partying. Soon he was flat broke and on crack, and I was taking Percocet to keep my weight down. I'd been given a prescription when I had my wisdom teeth pulled. I discovered the pills not only killed my pain but my appetite as well, and I could still function on them. Boy, did I love that superb, drifty feeling at the end of a long day and night of doing my show, voicing commercials, and appearing at station events all over town.

Most of all, whatever I was mad about with Ree vanished.

Ree's record company always said a check would be coming the next quarter while I paid for most everything. I blamed our woes on the evil executives and his manager, not him.

When Ree said, "I don't even *like* strip joints," I believed him.

When he said he was completely faithful, I believed him.

When he said he wasn't a drug addict, just a light user, I believed him.

Then I caught him stealing money from me to buy drugs. I won't even get into the phone calls from *Ruby Heaven* he swore was just a friend.

I had to leave Ree. To survive.

Back at the Parker Meridien, I kept going to the window, staring down at the traffic, the people, the lights. The city that never sleeps. It had been a long day, starting in Houston, and yet I was too excited to wind down.

And scared.

It's one of those strange facts of life that people you'd think have no reason to be insecure often turn out to be the biggest blobs of quivering self-doubt you'll ever meet. Like DJs. They warm up crowds at concerts and interview the hottest celebrities. They never met a stranger. They must have been born with bullet-proof confidence, right?

Not only was I now in New York, I hadn't shared the mike with anyone before.

I Googled Cat Cruz. She looked like one of those naturally lean people who could eat a bucket of KFC chicken twice a day and not gain an ounce.

Hated her.

She'd called herself the Cat Woman, I read, until the Batman people served her with a cease-and-desist. She was a widow and mom. I Googled her husband. He was *seventy-five* when he died? And rich. Why did Cat even work? What on earth would she and I have in common?

Curled up in bed wearing a leopard print slip, I tossed and turned and tossed some more. I was on the 35th floor with the windows sealed tight and could still hear a dull roar outside. I tried to imagine I was near the beach and the ocean was rhythmically pounding the sand in the distance.

At two a.m. Ariella came on WBRR. Born Shirley Murkowski, she was a middle-class Catholic girl from Fort Lee, New Jersey, and a pioneer for female DJs. A legend. Nigel had said, "A night without her voice drifting through it would be unthinkable."

She sounded like sitting in that chair was the only place in the world she wanted to be. I was riveted. Even at this hour all her spots were national: Ford, Home Depot, AT&T. Not one local.

This really was the big fucking time.

Ariella's soothing voice was the aural version of chamomile tea. I was soon drifting off to sleep, straight into a radio dream/nightmare. In this one, I was on the air naked. I hated it at first.

Then I liked it.

4

TOO MUCH TANG

Nigel Hamilton-Jones, VP of pop promotion for MGX Entertainment's music label, was a man accustomed to working with household names and making grand gestures to appease them.

"At last!" he cried over the phone, his primary place of business. "You're in the number one market, where you belong."

His flattery was like water to a dried-out plant on the verge of expiring. I had once read about B.F. Skinner's theory of "variable reinforcement." The rat will keep looking for the cheese if he gets it inconsistently versus having it shut off completely. Nigel was my cheese. His nonchalant you-got-talent-kid morsels tossed my way when I was repeatedly replaced by someone else was enough to keep me in the radio game.

The Nigel game, too.

We were seven years into a flirtatious friendship. It started when he reached out after Ree and I broke up to tell me that he completely understood why I fell for him and why I left.

"Leaving Richmond is a good move," he'd said as I tried not to seem petrified. "You're meant for the big time. I'll do whatever I can to help you. Consider me your stealth agent."

I thought he was bullshitting me but he did turn out to be pretty much the only person to offer me consistent solace or encouragement. "Nigel's a big fan of yours," the praise would filter back to me through an impressed PD (program director). Whenever we bumped into each other at industry events, or when he brought by an artist to a radio station where I worked, I'd be jacked up for days.

He was handsome in a wholesome, Ryan-Seacrest-with-a-British-accent kind of way. I wouldn't have minded in the least if he'd collected his pound of flesh literally. It was rare to have someone totally get what I did for a living. It didn't hurt that he had an awesome expense account and access to every happening event. I was in New York, New York, feeling like the queen of the hill at the top of the heap.

I needed my king.

And there was the fact that the last time I actually had an orgasm with a man anywhere near me was six months, three weeks, and five days ago (but who's counting?).

I'd heard he'd had a serious girlfriend who was divorced and the mother of two children. When did they break up? Two years ago? I didn't know what happened because I never spoke to him about his private life, nor mine.

Was Nigel even interested in a "slap and tickle" with me? I couldn't be sure with a guy who was pleasant and twinkly with everyone all the time.

Also in the Watch Out column was that he was the one promoting Ree's new single, pitching it to radio stations and everywhere else. No matter what had gone down with Ree when we were young and dumb, I still believed in him as an artist. I wanted his new song to be a hit.

Really wanted, as much as I did back then. Maybe more so since this was surely his last chance. Nigel had lots of other artists, many with way more clout, who had songs that needed to be worked, too.

Crap. If moving out of Friendland with Nigel was on the horizon, this was already getting complicated.

About an hour before he was to pick me up, there was a knock on my hotel room door. I opened it to see a bellhop holding a large flat box. "Jazmyn Brown?"

I loved hearing that name. "Yes." I signed for it, then realized after a moment's awkwardness that he expected a tip.

The smallest bill I had was a ten. He had no problem taking it.

The card with the Dolce & Gabbana box said: *Welcome to the Big Apple, Jaz! Try this armor on for your ultimate radio battle. NHJ*

Inside was a stunning black lace (and very short) dress. Were we about to have a date-date or was this typical over-the-top Nigel?

Now that I was employed by WBRR, I couldn't accept the dress. It certainly was worth more than the standard radio station rule of no gifts over $50.

No harm in trying it on, I told myself.

Ohmygod. I felt five inches taller and ten pounds thinner. You can't put a price on that.

I called him. "Nigel, thank you so much for the dress, but you know the payola rules."

"No problem, love. D&G donated it to a *Vanity Fair* photo shoot. Cost me nothing and I'm merely passing it on. That's another thing I like about you. Your ethics." He lowered his voice conspiratorially. "Still not a good idea to tell anyone."

"In that case, thank you."

"Have to jump off for a call. Tell me more in the limo."

Limo?

Nigel beamed when I walked into the hotel lobby wearing the dress. *Buh-bye six months, three weeks, and five days of celibacy.*

"Jazmyn Brown, you look *sensational*."

I threw my arms around him. "What a promo guy."

"I prefer to think of myself as master of the ego massage."

"*Mass*-age," I repeated with his accent. "Knead away."

After our embrace lasted longer than I anticipated, I said, "You look pretty good yourself."

"It's those frequent flyer miles. Being on a plane half of my life stops the aging process."

He gallantly held out his crooked elbow. I took it, feeling like a movie star walking the red carpet. We slid into a white stretch.

"Rivers loves you, by the way."

"I didn't think you'd be talking to him since he doesn't play your records."

"Love, I talk to everyone."

I looked at him sitting across from me in a casual beige suit, no tie. He exuded all the power and pizzazz a top exec in the New York music biz should. His brown hair fell into his face just so, the dimples in his rosy cheeks showed when he smiled (which he did constantly).

"It's so nice to be in the company of a handsome man whose middle name isn't Drama."

"It's Diva Whisperer."

He reached for the unopened Dom chilling in a bucket.

"Speaking of names, Jazmyn's a keeper." He looked at me curiously. "What's your real name? Or is that a deep dark secret?"

It was definitely in the Off Limits folder, along with a lot of other things. I told him my middle and last name.

"Mary Brown? Perfectly dreadful. But Jazmyn Brown has a nice ring to it, and it's versatile." Ver-sa-*tile*. "Works for rock, urban, pop." Nodding at my short, platinum haircut, "I love your new look, too."

"I love that I'm in New York."

He took a beat before saying, "So do I."

The cork popped out and ricocheted off the window, landing in my lap. I tossed it at him playfully. We were in our own private limo world, a divider between us and the driver, with the seductive lure of Manhattan (and that D&G dress I couldn't stop caressing) kickin' it up several spine-jangling notches.

Nigel poured the golden bubbly. "Here's to twenty million potential listeners."

"Take that, Bobby David," I said.

We grinned, sharing the memory of one of my classic firings, from a country station in Atlanta called The Hoot. Its logo was an owl dressed like a Hooters waitress.

We clinked glasses, shouting, "Too much tang and not enough twang!"

"Now tell me, Jaz, what's the skinny with WBRR? It's not making enough money for New York and the presentation's from the Stone Age. I'll bet you this limo you won't be playing 'Hocus Pocus' by Focus for long."

"Who?"

"Consider yourself lucky you don't know."

I told him about The Bear. Though it would hit the trades any second, I warned, "You didn't hear that from me."

"The *Bear*. What the bloody hell are they thinking? And teaming you up with Cat Cruz? I hope you negotiated a bodyguard."

The notion of a catfight pumped me up. "It wouldn't be the first time I took on a woman."

"You've been in a tussle before?"

When I was Fatty Patty and got picked on constantly. He didn't need to know that.

"Knocked a girl's front teeth out once."

He sucked in his breath while his eyes widened.

"I mean, tooth. It was just one."

"You are a *goddess*."

"The Bear's going to start playing new music," I said, knowing that would get us on another topic.

He pressed back in his seat as though pinned by a gale-force wind, then lurched forward. "I have a new mission. To be the first label to get a new record added on 'BRR in three decades!"

We clinked flutes again.

"To WBRR, however long it lasts," I said.

"How about to *us*?"

I hesitated. "Why not?"

He cocked his head. "Is your heart still in Houston with a cowboy named Tex?"

"Hardly. And you? Surely you have a girlfriend, or three."

"I'm all business. Work is fun, but it's still work. Most women don't understand that."

"I know the feeling." I crossed my legs nervously. "Look! One World Trade Center!" I said as the limo rounded a corner and headed right toward it.

"And soon your voice will be bouncing off its antenna."

For a few minutes he rhapsodized about my brilliant DJ skills, quoting word-for-word a funny phone call I once aired. If that wasn't enough to win me over completely, he never referred to me as a *woman* DJ. I was a great DJ. Period.

"Enough about me," I said. "Tell me about you. Where are you from in England? How did you end up in the States?"

He told me he was born outside London and came to America to attend N.Y.U.'s business school. After he did a research paper on the media conglomerate MGX (the letters stood for Mickey Green Xtraordinary), they hired him for their record label. He rose quickly through the ranks.

"My family runs a bed and breakfast in Devon, a manor house we've had forever. They expected me to be involved. I had a boringly non-dysfunctional upbringing, I'm afraid."

"I call that a refreshing change. Tell me more."

He seemed uncomfortable talking about himself. When Zeppelin's "Rock and Roll" came on WBRR, he cranked it up. We bounced in our seats and sang along. During Page's guitar solo I told him the term "rock and roll" was now verboten on WBRR and why. He had a good laugh over it.

"Does it mean they won't be playing this song anymore?" I said. "It's a classic."

"There's got to be a consultant justifying his fee behind that one. You'll be using it again one day."

We pulled up to a restaurant in the Village just as the song ended.

"We're early for the rez," he said. "Would you rather wait here than at a crowded bar?"

He must want to make out. "Absolutely."

After he told the driver to circle around a few more minutes, he moved next to me. Instead of kissing me he picked up his black carbon fiber ZERO Halliburton briefcase and took out an iPod.

"Before we go inside, I'd love your opinion of Ree's new song we're promoting—or rather, *trying* to promote. He's being so difficult we may not put it out at all."

"Ree's being difficult?" I said in mock surprise.

"It's a sequel to 'The Stripper' called 'I Married the Stripper.'"

He was *married*. I was surprised to feel my heart pounding.

Sliding the iPod into the limo's port, Nigel cranked the volume. A loud bass riff started in almost the same way "The Stripper" had ten years before. Goose bumps covered my arms. It was his music getting to me, not him. Just his music.

> *I said "I do" when I said I never would*
> *Thought you'd stop strippin' and life would be good*
> *You kept on grindin' 'til your last trimester*
> *I said That's it, now it's time to sequester*

Your body from men, you the mother of my son
You popped him out, the next week you'd gone
Strippin', strippin', strippin'
They was tippin', tippin', tippin'
Where were you last night? Your cell wuz off
I made you and the boyz beef stroganoff
I'm the cook, the maid, and the soccer mom
While you out shakin' dat, shakin' dat bomb.
Now I'm workin' my act, change my name to Jack
When I drop my G, women will attack
I'll take 'em in da back, make 'em hot and bothered
My lap dance gonna send our kids to Harvard.
Yeah, I'm strippin', strippin', strippin'

"It's fantastic, Nigel! He's nuts for having a second thought about it."

"He says if we release it he'll never get beyond the stripper pigeonhole."

"It beats *no* hole."

"Welcome to my world. Ree refuses to hire a manager. Although after the last one plied him with drugs, I see his point."

"And royally ripped him off," I said.

"And it being hard as hell to make a buck in the music biz now. But he'll be getting one hundred percent of nothing rather than eighty percent of something if he doesn't get a reality check. You love it? Tell him. He'll listen."

"What makes you think that? I haven't spoken to him in years."

"Because all the songs on the album are about you."

Shit. I grabbed the champagne, bringing it to my lips. "That's crazy. What's marrying a stripper have to do with me?"

"He said you wouldn't stop being a DJ any more than the stripper would stop stripping."

I nearly spit out my bubbly. "I see. It's okay for *him* to be totally devoted to his work but not me?"

"Easy!" Nigel backed away. "He's in town re-mixing some of the other songs. He told me he'd love to see you again but wasn't sure you wanted to see him."

I scanned the soft white leather ceiling of the limo, searching for a response. How could I make *So who did he marry?* not come out like I cared.

Whoever he was with now, and he was certainly with someone, does she love his music and laugh at his jokes as much as I did? Does he kiss her the same way, make her special meals for no special reason, give her the best damn foot rub on the planet, make love to her till her thighs shake and her voice turns hoarse?

Did he bring the best and worst out in her?

I couldn't be alone when I faced Ree.

Nigel reached over and lightly rubbed the back of my neck. I closed my eyes.

"Mmmmm. That feels good."

What better person to have at my side, it occurred to me, than the man who "held him where the hairs are short," as my dad would say.

"We can talk about it later," Nigel said softly. He moved closer. "I'll never forget the day I met you."

I leaned toward him. He wrapped his arms around me. My resistance ... what resistance?

"I was so nervous, I barely noticed you," I said.

I was in my early twenties and filling in for the afternoon guy on Y-100 in Miami (just missing the station's decadent days when the air studio was plastered with wallpaper of naked women). Nigel brought Pink by the show. I challenged her to an Inuit throat-singing contest. It was an Eskimo sport, like female sumo wrestling but you threw strange sounds around that sounded like dogs fighting. I can't do it anywhere close to Tanya Tagaq, queen of the form.

It was great fun and great radio. Pink said on the air that it was one of the best interviews she'd ever done (which made the afternoon guy a real pain to work with after he heard about it).

I snuggled closer into Nigel and was feeling all warm and woozy when I heard, "I have to make sure you're over Ree. You'll never know until you see him again."

My eyes opened, wide.

"If you can get him to agree to release that song as the first single, I'll do something very special for you."

I jolted from his arms.

"You don't have to do anything," I said. "I love the song and have no problem telling Ree he's being an ass for not putting it out there immediately. Is that why you gave me this dress?"

He looked bewildered. "What the hell, Jaz. We've been flirting for how many years?"

"What happened to the woman everyone thought you were going to marry?"

He paused as he shifted mental gears. "You mean Susan?"

"Did she have children?"

"Yes. She thought the music business would be a bad influence on them even though they loved going backstage and meeting their idols. Not a good match for the long term."

"Oh."

"Now that we're finally in the same city, don't you think it's time to ...?" He crossed his arms. "Unless you've been playing *me* like a violin all along, eh?"

"No! You think that?"

I moved back to his side and tried to kiss him.

He only let it get as far as a quick peck. "Not here. I want our first kiss to come with a bit extra, love. Memorable, you know?"

He said it a little hurt and oh-so-sweet. Resting my head on his shoulder, I clasped his hand. There was something about Nigel that made me feel safe and adored and free to be myself. Isn't that what everyone wants?

"Okay," I said softly. "But do we have to see him tonight?"

"Whenever you're ready, love."

A few hours later I was sprawled on my hotel room bed turning my cell over and over in my hand. Fatigue and curiosity won. I texted: *Hey mystery man.*

Mr. Ree sounded like mystery, hence my term of endearment for him.

My phone rang almost immediately.

"What's goin' down, Miz Brown? Heard you grabbed your brass ring."

A funk track thumped behind him but I could still hear aloofness in his tone. Fine. I could play that game, too.

"And you grabbed a wedding ring," I said, as if I were commenting on the weather.

"Hardly."

Relief converged with the mental image of Ree with a harem of women around him.

"'I Married the Stripper' is a smash, Ree. Congratulations."

"It's stupid silly. There are much better songs on the album. Yo, Trey, hold off," he called to someone. The music disappeared. "What are you doing on a classic rock station? You're hit radio."

"It's New York and I can play Dylan, so it can't be that bad."

"True dat." I heard the smile in his voice.

"It was Jones," I said, as if we'd had the argument yesterday about which street in Greenwich Village the cover of *The Freewheelin' Bob Dylan* was taken.

"Fourth."

"*Jones.*"

Suze Rotolo, the girl walking with Dylan on the cover, was seventeen when they started dating, twenty-one when they broke up. I had no idea then that my relationship with Ree would span almost the same period.

He lowered his voice. There wasn't a trace of aloofness in "Get your fine frame down here right now."

There went my heart pounding again.

"Maybe Nigel and I will stop by."

"You and tut-tut-cheerio Nigel?" he said with a British accent.

"We've been friends a long time."

"Yeah. *Friends.* So why do you have to come with him?"

"I hear your album is about me. You're leaving out a big part of the story."

"Am I?"

"Like your turning into a raging asshole once you made it big."

"It wasn't until people started calling me a one-hit wonder that—oh, shut me up. It's in the past now."

"Don't shut *me* up. I've waited seven years to speak my mind. You think my leaving was about work? You weren't the guy I fell in love with anymore."

"You're right. I was a batshit crazy kid and an addict."

He hadn't lost his touch, disarming me.

"Why do you think I stole money from you?" he said. "It was a cry for help. I wanted you to kick my ass into rehab. Now I know I'm the only one who could have done that. I've been clean for years. I read every self-help book and addict memoir I could find and never stopped praying. Come see me. Can't *we* be friends, too?"

Why did I suddenly want to cry?

"I've seen your photos on the net," he said in his honey-coated voice. "You're more beautiful than ever. But I thought you were gorgeous even when you were a kid, didn't I?"

When my mother met Ree, the first thing she did was bring out a family photo album that had photos of me when I was fat, hoping to discourage him. I was furious, embarrassed as hell.

"You must be an excellent cook, Mrs. Brown," was Ree's comment.

I thought my heart would explode from how much I loved him.

"He's a lost little boy," Mom had said later. "The kind you want to take care of."

And I did. Traveling down a one-way street with a dead end. And yet, before all the hell went down, I was a whole and happy person for the first time in my life.

"I'm glad you've got your life together and your career back on track," I told him now as I turned on my side and rubbed the empty hotel bed. "We're both living our dream. I'm afraid ..."

"Stop being afraid. Stop playing old tapes. Think of the future. Come see me."

"Maybe."

"No maybe. Yes or no?"

"Yes. But not today."

Before he could pin me to a time I hung up.

Hurt and angry, I stared at the ceiling. It felt like our break-up was days, not years, ago. I was also proud of Ree. Conquering his addictions was a lot like me stepping on a scale, seeing 245 and vowing it would never hit 250. And it never did.

So far.

Fatty Patty was still in me, though, always threatening to come out. Was batshit crazy Ree still there as well?

5

THE OVERCOMPENSATING BOOGIE

Cat Cruz lived at 25 Central Park West, a gorgeous Art Deco building near Columbus Circle. I wasn't sure if arranging our meeting there instead of at the station or someplace public was a gesture of friendliness or hostility, it being her ritzy turf and all.

I was dripping with sweat by the time I got there. I'd known the red pleather pants were a mistake the moment I walked out of the hotel into the heat. And again when Cat's doorman ushered me into a lobby that reeked of money.

Pleather.

I figured it was the most rock and roll piece of clothing I owned. I mean, *rock.*

The elevator softly opened on the 25th floor. A middle-aged woman in a black uniform with a white apron answered the door and escorted me to a living room overlooking Central Park.

"Ms. Cruz will be with you shortly. May I get you anything?" She sounded Jamaican.

"A glass of cold water would be nice, thank you."

The apartment was decorated in Upscale Hotel. A beautifully framed photo of Cat, her son, and her really old husband was the only indication we were in someone's home.

I'd found an interview on the net where someone asked her why she wanted to be on a rock station, since she was Hispanic.

"Are you saying Latinos only like Latin music? I grew up in America," she'd said. "I also love breaking stereotypes."

Fair enough, but I didn't see any signs here of what she did for a living. Any station I worked for, I always kept their promo coffee cup and refrigerator magnets in plain view, part of my mental cheerleading exercises.

The maid emerged from the kitchen with a silver tray bearing a glass of water. A small plate held half a lemon covered with a fitted white cloth to prevent the seeds from escaping. I picked up the glass. It was lead crystal, judging by its weight. I held it to the light, admiring its beautiful, intricate etchings of angular snowflakes.

"Very pretty," I said to the maid.

"Family heirloom."

She disappeared down a hall. I could hear a TV blaring a high-energy daytime chat show.

After five minutes, no Cat. After ten, I walked toward the sound of the TV, woke up the maid who was crashed in front of it, and told her I was leaving. On cue, her cell vibrated. It was Cat texting she'd be there soon.

"So, so sorry, I thought she was here," the maid said. Her musical island accent made it impossible to be mad at her. "It's hard to keep track of her. Oh!" She jumped on her remote and turned up the TV's volume. "They're about to find out who's the daddy!"

I headed back to the living room.

Poking my head into the impressive kitchen, I quietly opened the fridge. Cat had several bottles of champagne, energy drinks, bottled water, and Styrofoam boxes of takeout. I peeked in the vegetable bins. Clean as a whistle, as though not even an onion had ever been stored there.

As long as I could hear the TV blasting, I checked out her cupboards. There were more beautiful glasses, dishes, packaged cereals, and lots of Parmalat milk. No wonder she was so thin. She obviously didn't spend much time thinking about food.

How can anyone be wired that way?

I was sitting down in the living room when Cat walked in the front door with her son. She stifled a laugh when she saw what I was wearing.

She was pretty short, which made me more wary. I'd yet to meet a tiny woman who wasn't a ball of all-consuming fire if you pushed the wrong buttons on her.

"We ran into a good friend who owns restaurants all over town. Lost track of the time."

Like I didn't know she was well-connected.

Her voice was deep and sexy, somehow both hip and classy. Her son Marley eyed me up and down too. He looked to be around ten, the spitting image of his mother, right down to the snooty attitude.

"I heard you were from Texas," he said. "Where are your cowboy boots?"

"I left them in my pickup truck."

That got a crooked smile out of him. He took off for his room.

Cat looked casually chic in a Yankees baseball cap, trendy jeans, and a snug white V-neck tee that looked great against her amber skin and also showed off her cleavage. She looked my age and unquestionably rocked.

She took off the cap. Her dainty French-manicured hand released her ponytail. Long, dark, wavy locks with expertly applied auburn highlights cascaded around her shoulders.

I felt like mall trash.

The living room was silent. My pleather pants squeaked when I breathed.

"Your hair looks great," Cat said. "Reminds me of Clairol Arctic Blonde, one of my favorites when I was poor. I was so daring then. Had nothing to lose." This said with a smile.

I smiled back. "I can't imagine you as a blonde or poor."

"Fortunately, I married well. Vee died when Marley was a child. I don't *have* to work, but I'd be bored if I didn't."

Lah-di-dah.

"How'd you get into radio and on WBRR so quickly?" I asked her.

"I was broke and living in a rundown loft in Brooklyn with four other people." She rattled it off as if she'd told it a million times before. "Occasionally we had hot water and heat. I paid my N.Y.U. tuition with financial aid and by posing for *Playboy*."

She stopped abruptly, eyed my legs, which squeaked when I moved.

"I did a show on the university station so I could have access to a studio to make demos for voice-over work. I wanted to be an actress. One day the PD of 'BRR called and asked if I'd be interested in being a disc jockey. That was it." She tossed her head again when she said, "I've never worked for another station. Ever."

Another dig.

"What happened to acting?"

"I did some off-Broadway shows for no money and was about to jump to TV but I married Vee instead. Eventually I had Marley. Then I became a widow, and my priorities changed. I'm very happy with how it worked out. I love being on the air, going backstage, giving autographs. I'm not recognized *everywhere* I go. I know enough famous people to know how grating that is."

So she had used radio as a stepping-stone to stardom and only made it to the first rock.

Cat leaned in, studying my face. "You're the perfect age to do TV. All you need is a chin implant, cheek implants, and a little collagen in your lips."

I set my jaw, replied evenly, "I'd rather have breast implants like yours."

She sat back, "I'm completely natural."

"Uh-huh."

"I'm trying to help you," she said. "Don't you want to explore other avenues where there's more money to be made?"

"Not if I have to do all that."

"Go ahead and be proud. You're limiting yourself." She pulled out her vibrating cell. "How did *you* become a DJ?"

"When I was a kid, listening to the radio was the only time I felt alive."

She started texting someone.

"I thought DJs were the happiest, funniest, coolest people on the planet," I said. "My eleventh-grade class took a field trip to my favorite radio station. I then knew my purpose in life."

Too late I realized I was scratching the thick arms of my chair. Two of my new red acrylic fingernails snapped off at the same time. Damn! They'd cost me.

"I'd offer you some glue," she said, "but I haven't had fake nails since Loverboy was at the top of the charts."

I slipped my hands into my lap. She eyed my foot. I hadn't noticed it was tapping up and down.

"I suggest you lay off the caffeine or whatever it is that's making you hyper."

"I'm energetic."

"My show is laid-back. I keep talk to a minimum."

Since *I* would be running the board on *our* show, we'd see about that.

I shifted, making my pants squeak deliberately.

"Tell me, Cat. How do you see the Barenaked Radio Ladies concept working?"

She made a dismissive motion with her hand. "They once teamed me up with a comic to add humor to the show. It just added a lot of talk people didn't want to hear. And he didn't understand the basic rule of dancing with a partner. One person always leads."

Oh, brother.

She smiled, curling her legs under her. "Tell me about the *rapper* you married."

"We audited marriage. Three years. So what about you and me pretending we're naked?"

"Rock stars ask me out all the time. I always say no, even though they're probably great in bed. Scrawny men often are. Overcompensating."

"Ree's not scrawny."

"Why'd you break up?"

"Landed a gig in Miami, big step up from Richmond. Now, can we talk about our show?"

"I bet his not having another hit had a lot to do with your leaving."

I stood up. "It's been a real barrel of laughs."

She walked me to the door. "When do you start?"

"Monday." I didn't extend my now imperfect hand. "Guess we won't be road testing this."

"I'm sure it'll work out fine."

For *her*.

Closing the door, she made an attempt to be nice. "I like your bag. Whose is it?"

"Walmart. Fifteen bucks."

"Very funny."

"I'm serious."

She inspected it approvingly. Maybe we should go on a shopping/bonding trip, I thought. If we didn't come off as friends on the air I doubted it would work. *She* was the one with acting experience.

Nah, I just wanted to get the hell out of there, rip off my fake Loverboy nails, and buy some new clothes.

6

SWAG AND STATIONALITY

WBRR was in the kind of beautiful old, ornate midtown building they haven't made in ages. Its gargoyles laughed at the bland glass monolith across the street. Or were they staring at their reflection?

I strutted toward a door emblazoned with the station's call letters, hoping that what was on the other side would be more like a club buzzing with excitement than a doctor's office.

It felt like a museum. Even the receptionist was right out of a time capsule. She looked like she hadn't changed her hairstyle in forty years.

"I'm here to see Rick Rivers," I said. "I'm Jazmyn Brown."

"Have a seat. I'll tell him you're he-ah," she said in the gravelly voice of a lifetime smoker.

I took in the black-and-white photos of the DJs doing their coolest poses on the wall near me. Most wore leather. Real leather, I'm sure. I went over to the picture of Ariella.

She looked great, like a sexy mature woman in a Cialis ad getting cozy with a handsome older guy. I wondered how old the photo was.

What age would I be in my last station head shot?

A Hasidic Jew appeared, wearing a long black coat. Gray tendrils fell in front of each ear.

"I'm Ben, the comptroller," he said. "There's some paperwork you need to fill out."

The line for my name brought me up short. *Patricia Mary Brown.* I was so not that person.

"What will my paycheck be after taxes?" I asked Ben quietly when I was done.

His fingers danced around the kind of calculator I'd only seen at flea markets. He wrote out a figure. My mouth dropped.

"Where did it go?"

"You're paying city taxes on top of everything else and have no dependents or deductions," he said in a rush of heavily accented words. "New York is a hard place for a single person. Especially a single woman."

Was I imagining the judgment in his voice? As if there was something wrong with not being married at my age?

He brought me over to my new boss.

Sitting at his desk, Rick Rivers eyed me up and down, picking at his goatee. I sat across from him and sought out a way to divert his attention.

"*Dark Side of the Moon!*" I took a closer look at the platinum record on the wall.

"Anyone who's ever mattered in rock has walked these hallways," he said, as if he'd built this mothership.

He gave me a tour of the facilities. Every single hallway was lined with gold and platinum records by the biggest names you can imagine. Next to the air studio was a wall covered with signatures. Rick pointed out Jimi Hendrix, Jim Morrison, and Jerry Garcia. I nearly lost it when I saw all four Beatles' signatures.

In that instant I felt different about WBRR. It would rip my heart out if it didn't survive.

At a quarter to ten, as Dick and Dork neared the end of their show, we slipped into the studio and Rick introduced us. I detected an underlying tension and wasn't surprised. What did a young PD bringing in a young DJ *really* mean.

The studio had a view of monstrous buildings and hardly any sky. The room itself felt more like a college dorm, with posters of nearly naked women and the words "Eat Me" (and worse) plastering the walls. I'd never seen anything this blatantly ... I wasn't sure what to call it. Sexist or just juvenile?

Seeing me eyeing the décor, Rick said, "This isn't the jock studio."

"Welcome to the WBRR Way Back Machine," said Dork.

I assumed that with Cat, Ariella, and the part-timer Mandy, the jock studio would be the same equipment as Dick and Dork's minus the pin-ups. If this was the atmosphere that got them in the mood to be nine-year-olds on the air, so be it.

Dick had dark circles under his puffy eyes and a "studio tan" — pure white skin. He was the one with the pipes. Dork's voice was high-pitched and scratchy.

Since the photo in the lobby, Dork had put on weight. He'd built his reputation on doing crazy things like taping himself to a telephone pole during rush hour traffic (and getting arrested), and ambushing celebrities and asking them embarrassing questions (and getting punched).

Neither of them were spring chickens.

Their young producer and board operator, Pig Boy, was styled pure '70s, with a gigantic Afro, striped bell-bottom pants, and a polyester shirt with long pointy lapels. How could he let them call him Pig Boy? In interviews he claimed it was his childhood nickname because he loved pork so much. No one forgot it, that was for sure. Between that and being the only African-American on the staff, his job was as secure as Cat Cruz's.

I asked where Judy, the traffic and news headline lady, was.

Dick pointed to Pig Boy hovering over the sound mixer and pushing buttons. "Somewhere in Jersey. We only see her at events."

Another sign of the ruthless cost-cutting times.

The words ON AIR lit up in red near the door. Dick cleared his throat over and over, then signaled Pig Boy to pot up his fader on a fairly new soundboard. The really old ones had big knobs you turned called potentiometers, hence the term "pot up" or "pot down."

"We have a hot babe in the studio, Dick."

"I'll say. Check out those tight jeans and Laurie Anderson hair."

"What do you mean? Her hair's long."

"Not Pamela, ya idiot. Laurie. Lou Reed's widow."

"It's more like Madonna in her '80s *True Blue* phase when it was white blonde and short," said Dork. "I like long hair on a woman. When it's short I feel like I'm with a guy."

"How could you think *she* was a guy?"

I leaned into the guest microphone. "Maybe you're secretly gay, Dork."

"Secretly?" Dick said.

"You've got a sexy voice," Dork said, panting.

It was the usual radio guy banter, but with a big difference. Their audience was humongous and heard, through syndication, way beyond New York City. It was nothing short of electrifying.

When we broke for commercials, Dork said, "Welcome aboard. You've gotta be something to take on Cat Cruz."

"*She's* taking on *me*."

Rick, who had been sitting in the back of the room texting furiously, motioned for me to clear out of the studio with him.

On our way out, he nodded to Pig Boy. "Code Cat."

"Not again," he whined. "Don't I have enough to do?"

"Just go into the folder with the generic stuff she's recorded until Mandy gets here. Prophet will take care of the rest."

Prophet was an automation program that saved stations a lot of money. (Should've been spelled Profit.) One way was by letting them go on remote control for voice-tracking.

"Cat's not coming in," Rick said to me. "Again."

Her behavior baffled me. Not once had I given up a chance to be on the air.

Rick brought me to a conference room where the jocks had assembled around an oblong mahogany table. The smell of men's cologne was thick.

"Will Ariella be here?" I asked Rick.

"With her hours, she's excused."

"I'd love to meet her."

"Trust me, she's as unforgettable as her voice."

Slowly they trickled in. The only other woman was Rick's young, hip assistant, Olivia. We shook hands.

"Were you the one who booked my flight?" She had. "You couldn't have picked a better time. The sunset was on one side, New York on the other. I was blown away before I even touched the ground."

She looked at me like I was a hick from the sticks. "I didn't give it much thought."

I noted she had a nice voice. Why wasn't she on the air? That could be about to change.

"Ms. Cruz won't be joining us today," Rick announced to the jocks.

Dork called out, "How many say she ate bad shrimp last night, raise your hand." About half went up. "How many say her kid is sick." The other half went up.

Everyone's head turned toward Rivers.

"Bad shrimp."

I checked out the other DJs while Rick ran the meeting. It was cool to see old rockers like Madd Maxx and Chopper with their deeply lined faces. Maxx's hair was dark brown and fake, according to Howard Stern. (Teeth, too.) Chopper's was gray and braided down his back.

Maxx was an afternoon drive legend. He was always marrying younger women back when he had people like Roger Daltrey and Bruce Springsteen at his weddings. Chopper, another radio icon, was an honorary Hell's Angel with a collection of vintage Harleys. He was on after Maxx from six p.m. to midnight. His son had been born with cerebral palsy and he was a major fundraiser for the disease. I'd hate to see him lose his job.

Rick introduced me to everyone. When he revealed the Barenaked Radio Ladies idea, the room erupted into whooping.

"Let's give Jazmyn a round of applause, guys," Dick said. "She's got guts."

What the hell was I getting myself into? I wondered again.

Olivia didn't join in the applause. Maybe she didn't like losing her status as sole Young Bitch On The Premises.

The mood in the room soured as Rick unveiled 99 The Bear in all its glory.

When he added, "Don't say 'rock and roll.' It screams oldies. Just say rock," every pair of DJ eyes grew in size.

I looked down, putting myself in their skin. The room was stone silent.

"Have fun with it!" Rick said, the words every DJ has read in every memo from every boss.

The guys brightened when he announced that Olivia was taking on the title of music director, a position that had been eliminated many years ago, to deal with the new music The Bear would be playing.

"Swag City!" Dick and Dork yelled.

"It's about fucking time," Maxx said in his deep voice. "You know how embarrassing it is to have to *buy* music?"

"You cheap bastard," Chopper said. "You make a friggin' fortune and you can't support the artists whose music helped make that fortune? You'll probably sell the CDs on eBay."

Maxx puffed out his chest. "What if I do?"

Rick made a sign for time-out. "Guys, you'd be lucky to get a keychain out of a record company today."

This met with grumbling.

Chopper said, "Just get some Chili Peppers on my playlist. Calling myself a rock and roll DJ and not playing them? Now *that's* embarrassing."

"Uh, rock, Chopper," Rick said. "Just rock."

Chopper sat back, crossed his beefy arms, and glared at him.

Rick nodded at Olivia, who passed out a document several pages long.

"The new Employment Standard Practices Agreement," Rick said. "This is the last time it'll be printed for you. Please read it and sign it by Friday through your new employee portal or your paycheck will be withheld. I know a lot of you haven't created an account yet. We'll be paper-free in a week. It's the only way you'll know what's going on."

Maxx snorted. "Employee *portal*, my ass. The union won't let you get away with holding our paychecks."

Rick pulled at his goatee. "I've already cleared it with them. Time to enter the real world. Also, get your head wrapped around the idea of a new studio. It's coming."

I didn't understand the bellyaching that came out of these guys over that. I loved new studios. It was fun to learn new equipment; kept me from getting bored. True, something was always lost in the old system that I liked, but overall, I'd rather be working with the latest than with relics.

After that, the meeting wrapped up quickly. Dick and Dork headed out the door, singing Bowie's "Ch-ch-ch-ch-changes!"

Rick called me over. "I'll take you to meet Shane and cut some promos."

Shane Riley was the creative services director. He did what was called "stationality," creating a distinctive sound through whooshes, beeps, and bangin' rock chords mixed with his ballsy announcing style, so that anyone tuning in would know instantly where they were on the dial. It was rare to find someone with a kick-ass voice who could also do the sound wizardry.

"Great guy. Insanely busy," Rick said. "He's imaging all over the world now."

High-tech toys formed a cocoon of metal around Shane while green and red digital lights did a rhythmic dance. The usual big fat Neumann microphone was suspended over his soundboard.

Rick quickly introduced us and left as Shane's recorded voice thundered through the studio like Zeus calling down from Mount Olympus.

"Ninety-nine the Beeeeear."

Shane faded down the volume and turned to me. "Welcome to New York, Jazmyn."

He had a nice smile, a friendly vibe. And that voice! Unlike a lot of macho-sounding male announcers—Madd Maxx, for one—he didn't seem full of himself. He looked to be in his thirties, with a nicely trimmed beard, small black rectangular glasses that made him look smart (he probably was), and brown hair that reached the top of his collar. In jeans and a tropical Hawaiian shirt of pineapples and palm trees, he reminded me of a Jimmy Buffett Parrothead.

Wherever I worked, I ended up getting pretty close to the production guys. They tended to be sensitive and trustworthy, gave me the 411 on what was going down at a station, and threw money my way through commercial announcing gigs (voice-overs). Also, their darkened studios were a refuge from the craziness on the outside.

Shane moved his scripts off a stand so he could see me. "My advice, for what it's worth, is 'Don't sign any leases.' There's no telling what's going to happen here."

"I'm not leaving New York if The Bear goes under. This is the last stop for me."

He grinned. "That's the spirit."

He gave me a quickie course in renting an apartment in New York City. Apartments advertised as "no fee" would still be pricey. "That's to lure you in. They factor that into the rent." Many brokers used bait-and-switch tactics. "An apartment will look perfect online but it'll be rented by the time you see it. Suddenly you're looking at places that cost way more than you intended to spend." He said a lot of brokers would drop me if I didn't grab something the first time out. But the real shocker? "Expect to pay at least 15% of your first *year's* rent to them when they do find you something, plus at least two months' rent upfront, sometimes three."

For a moment I wished I was back in that garage apartment at the Westwoods'. It may very well have been the nicest place I'll ever live.

"You can move to another borough or beyond," he said, "but then you'll be in the commuter grind. You need to be really sick of Manhattan before you can handle that. You're not even close."

Right. I'm a New York City woman now.

"I can steer you to a few hotels that cater to people from the West Coast or abroad who use them as a second home. The hotel bill will work out to what you'd pay in rent. It's already furnished. You can leave any time." He leaned back in his black leather swivel chair. "That's what I did when I first got here. Then I got married, moved to Westchester."

"But it's so transient." I sounded like a lost little girl when I said, "I want a *home.*"

He quickly swung back to his control center, fiddled with a fader. The lights brightened above me. Nodding toward the guest microphone, he said, "Let's carve this turkey."

I looked over Rick's scripts.

HI. THIS IS JAZMYN BROWN. I'LL BE KEEPING YOU COMPANY EVERY WEEKDAY FROM TEN TO TWO WITH CAT

CRUZ ON [very sexy] THE NEW BARENAKED RADIO LADIES SHOW.

I made a face.

"Need a pen and paper?" Shane asked.

I crumpled the lame script and tossed it in the garbage, then picked out a pen from a cup holding several. I noticed what it was advertising.

"Zoloft? Wow. Anti-depressant swag," I said in a light tone.

Shane didn't seem to find it funny. Maybe it wasn't from a sponsor.

I now had to create something provocative enough to make a listener hesitate before pushing the "seek" button on the radio. It was Pop Art. It was business. It was payin' da bills.

THIS IS JAZMYN BROWN, ONE OF YOUR BARENAKED RADIO LADIES ON 99 THE BEAR EVERY WEEKDAY FROM 10 TO 2 — THE OTHER LADY BEING CAT CRUZ. THAT'S RIGHT. WE'RE NAKED <u>ALL FOUR HOURS</u>. JUST ASK DICK AND DORK OR MADD MAXX.

Shane nodded his approval. "Nice how you worked in the cross-promotes for the other shows."

I scribbled some more.

IT'S BEING DONE <u>TASTEFULLY</u>, MOM, AND NO ONE CAN SEE BUT THE MILLIONS OF PEOPLE WATCHING 99 THE BEAR'S WEBCAM.

"I wonder what Ariella thinks of The Bear idea," I said.

"She could rise above anything."

FROM ARIELLA AT NIGHT TO THE BARENAKED RADIO LADIES IN THE DAY, WHO'S BETTER COMPANY THAN 99 THE BEAR?

When we were done, Shane asked if I had an agent. They were necessary for the big-bucks VO work, he said, but some would want a cut of my WBRR salary, too. He had one who wouldn't.

"Get me your voice-over demo," he said. "I'll help you get it into shape if it needs work."

"Thanks, but what can I do for you?"

He pushed his glasses up his nose. "Don't turn into another Cat Woman."

"Level with me, Shane. How does she keep from being fired?"

He sipped from his WBRR mug emblazoned with an electric guitar logo. "She's beautiful, a minority on a white station, a beloved brand name among our core demo, men. And she shows her tits occasionally."

I gathered up my things. "I show my wit occasionally. Think that's enough?"

It felt good to make him laugh. At least I had one person in my camp.

7

RENDEZVOUS WITH REE

Nigel's limo (this one silver) slowed down in front of an old ware-house in Brooklyn. It looked grimy and desolate, like the set for a gangster movie.

"We're here," he said. "Better not let Ree know anything's going on with us yet. No reason to piss him off right now."

I nodded. Nigel and I still hadn't had a real kiss yet, but hearing him say that confirmed I wasn't imaging something was percolating.

"I'll be up in a few minutes," he said. "I have to make some calls."

"You're not coming with me?"

He squeezed my now damp hand. "You'll be fine. You need to see him alone first."

It took a moment to see he was right.

When I reached the fifth floor, the elevator opened into a brightly colored lobby. An inflatable monkey riding a bicycle hung from the ceiling. The air smelled of popcorn and caramel. Was this a recording studio for kids, or was it meant to bring out the kid in its customers? With musicians, it didn't take much.

I looked around for the posse of losers hangin' in the studio, a jealous woman clinging to her staked-out territory. All I saw was an engineer with a head of dreads.

And Ree. Six-foot-two of solid muscle. He'd shaved his head. His baby fat was gone, making his cheekbones more pronounced.

He was a real man now.

Flashing his beautiful smile, he looked me up and down. "Well, ain't we uptown cool. About time you wore sexy outfits like that."

I was wearing another gift from Nigel. Not as revealing as the D&G, but still eye-popping.

His strong arms embraced me. Ohhh, how I missed those arms.

"So great to see you, hold you, baby," he said as he stroked my neck.

I debated whether to jump back or hold him tighter. I froze instead.

"Where's my man Nige?"

"In a limo making calls."

"As usual."

"He'll be here soon."

"No one works a hit like he does. Don't think I'm not counting my blessings."

I pulled back and looked at the engineer in an attempt to stop the white heat zapping back and forth between us.

Ree introduced Trey, who shuffled toward the door with a knowing smile. "I'm out a few." His right hand rested on a back pocket where he probably kept his pipe.

"Don't go too far," Ree said.

I sat on the black leather sofa, studying the new and improved Ree. He pulled off his loose sweatshirt so I could see how buff he was in his tight white tank. His grapevine tattoo remained unfinished. My stomach tightened.

"I'm older, wiser, and completely clean, Patty. Haven't touched a cigarette in six years, much less anything else. I even drink tea instead of coffee. Man, it made me irritable as all hell and I didn't even know it."

He put the cup of mint tea he was drinking to my nose. I also got a whiff of *his* scent.

"I want to have at least one more hit song, save my money, and make a life with the woman I love. None of it means a thing without her."

I put on a brave smile. Of course he had moved on. "I'm sure she's quite a woman."

"She sure is."

He seemed puzzled by the devastation written across my face I had tried in vain to hide.

"I'm not getting married to anyone except *you*. Baby, let's pick up where we left off, before I acted like a badass."

Oh shit to the 10th power.

"I don't know, Ree. I don't know." I shifted to business mode. "You're not back on the charts yet. And then, how will you handle it? Release 'I Married the Stripper' as the first single. It'll be huge. Huge!"

"Okay, Miz Tough Stuff. You know how to challenge me. I like that. And the song is called 'The Tip.' As in, I'm giving guys a tip to keep their fantasy woman a fantasy."

"Why not call it 'I Married the Stripper' and put 'The Tip' in parentheses after it?"

"I'll still be a rap cartoon."

One of his rants was about to launch. I'd loved them once — until that was all he did.

"Booty, booty, and more booty. It's objectifying women! I was trying to make the guy in the song look like a jerk but they thought *I* was a skin-deep hustla."

His words lacked the volume and intensity of his past rants. I tried not to smile.

"I was forced to put out 'The Tip' because some rapper was passing himself off as *me*. The lawyer I hired to sue him said I needed to put out a new album to support my case. I wrote the song, sold it for a lot of money in Japan to use in a commercial so I could pay his ridiculous bills."

"Ree," I scolded. "Stop complaining."

"I'm not complaining. I'm explaining with conviction."

I stifled a laugh. "You're lucky that rapper tried to rip you off. It was the kick in the butt you needed. The new song is a role-reversal send-up. If anyone can't see that ..."

He eyed me suspiciously. "Nigel's using you to get to me, isn't he?"

I'd completely forgotten about Nigel.

"This is what *I* think. The song's a hit. I've always been honest with you about your music. I'm urging you to do this for *your* sake."

Our eyes locked again. Our bickering had always led to incredible sex.

No, no, no.

"It's really good to see you, Patty."

"I'm Jazmyn now, *Reginald*."

He registered surprise. "J-A-Z-M-Y-N? The name I suggested?"

"Would have used it sooner but program directors wouldn't let me. 'It sounds too, uh, *jazzy*.'" I said, putting on a deep voice. PDs were often ex-DJs. "'We don't want people mistaking us for the *smooth jazz* station.'"

"Now they're all gone from terrestrial radio."

"Don't look at me like that."

He came closer. "Like what?"

Like he could melt both polar ice caps.

"I just want to give you another friendly hug." He opened his arms.

I put up my hands to push him away. "I'm sure you have plenty of women you can hug."

He lowered his bedroom eyes, giving me his sexy half-smile. "I'm not interested."

What harm could one little *friendly* embrace do?

I put my arms around his neck, turning my head so I wouldn't kiss him. I still felt an electric shock dance over my lips.

"Let me get this straight," my voice sounded soft and sexy. "You needed me so much that you stayed away for seven years?"

"You made it clear that's what you wanted."

"That's a cop-out." I resisted running my palm over his smooth head.

"Don't you get it?" His hands moved to the ultrasensitive spot in the curve of my lower back he knew so well. "You were the successful one. I had to be able to support *us* to feel I deserved *you*."

How did a jagged piece of glass suddenly get in my throat?

He rubbed my covered arm. "Is your tat unfinished, too?"

I nodded.

We'd been living together three years when Ree took me to the Media Mart where we met and proposed over the P.A. system. He knew I was completely fed up with him, but I said yes.

I never did see a ring. "Too predictable," he'd said.

We had gone straight to a tattoo parlor and picked out matching grapevines to wrap around our left biceps. We asked the tattoo guy to give us half of one each. We'd finish them when we got married, we decided.

We broke up for good six weeks later. I was so young. What did I know?

I ended our embrace with a tiny sniffle. "Let me hear what else you're working on."

He texted Trey to come back. I moved to a chair, not the couch. Ree asked about the station.

"You're supposed to pretend you're butt nekkid?" he said.

"Yes, *pretend*."

"You shouldn't have to do that."

My eyes traced the well-defined muscles in his arms as he talked, my mind trying not to picture the rest of his body.

"See what happened with my first hit?" he said. "I was *putting down* guys who were into strippers and everyone thought I loved them."

"Do you think I've forgotten about Ruby Heaven?"

"You'll never believe I was faithful to you, will you? Just because some woman called you claiming we were knockin' boots while you were on the air … "

The truth was I'd never know the truth.

"Success comes with a price tag," Ree said gloomily. "And the money I had to spend to keep it all goin', I should've been set for life with that hit." He did that high voice men do when they're imitating a nagging woman. "'*What about the money you spent on drugs, Ree?*' That was pure stupidity. But it's unbelievably easy to slip into that world with the pressure that's on you, especially when you're in your teens and the *Nigels* of this business do nothing to stop it."

Nigel had once told me he was "straight as a gate" when it came to drugs, but if an artist he was promoting was into them he had to look the other way or they'd be impossible to manage.

"It's their choice," he'd said.

"Your leaving me is what I needed, Jaz. I owe you for that."

His words were good to hear, but they also made me sad. Why couldn't he have gotten his shit together when I was there?

"Where are you living now?" I asked.

"Richmond. It's my home," he said. "Remember how we always dreamed of buying one of those beautiful old historic houses? I finally saw the money from that lawsuit over my mom's accident and bought one that needed a lot of work."

His mother had died in a six-car pile-up on the Interstate caused by an unlicensed truck driver just before we'd met. He was living with his cousins in the projects then. It was one of those weird disconnects. He would come into enough money to turn around his life but the price was losing his mother, his biggest champion. He felt blessed, punished, and a lot of survivor's guilt.

The case dragged on for so long, and he had been lied to by his manager, music lawyer, and record company about royalties that were coming, I didn't believe he'd ever see a dime.

"And you know what?" he said. "As the house got fixed up, so did I. One of my first concerts is going to help raise money for the stodgiest historical society I can find there. I want to see the faces of those little old white ladies!"

The notion was pretty funny, but I couldn't imagine going back there to live. "What I remember is our dreaming about owning a place *here*."

"New York's nice to visit, but not worth what it costs."

I fidgeted with the bottle of water I'd taken out of my bag. "You've been doing this renovating alone?"

"I broke up with someone about six months ago."

"What happened?"

His expression changed. Was he about to cry? He must have really loved her. I wasn't sure if I was jealous or feeling sorry for myself for not having moved on too.

"I didn't love her," he said.

Not sure how to react, I grabbed his sweatshirt and threw it at him. "I'm sure your true love is out there."

He put his top back on, grinning. "I *know* she is."

Trey and Nigel walked in, preventing me from saying something stupid like, "Take that sweatshirt off now."

"Yo, Nige." Ree and Nigel patted each other on the back.

"Hello, Ree."

"That's fifteen minutes off my time," Ree said to Trey, whose eyes were glassy. He reeked of pot.

"Yah, man. It's cool."

No more letting other people eat into his budget. This was new.

"You're crazy to be spending your money on dope," Ree told him, to my surprise.

He made a few notes as Trey mixed the tracks and we listened to eight songs about unrequited love and opportunities missed.

I sat between Nigel and Ree on the couch.

They tried to sling their arms behind me on the back of the sofa and ended up touching each other. Nigel popped up and paced. I scooted away from Ree.

No two ways about it, he turned me on, up, out, and sideways.

I lost myself in the songs, in Ree's voice. He could always sing. Hearing him in our apartment harmonizing with Nat King Cole, Bob Marley, or Dylan took the edge off anything. But the public wanted a rapper. That's what they were getting for this new album.

> *You were my pearl. You made me proud*
> *I let you down. I was a coward*
> *I slipped into a haze of black*
> *You had to leave to get me back*
> *Just take me back*
> *Take me back*
> *Take me back*

I felt exposed, flattered, and something else that made my heart feel heavy and waterlogged: Ree's pain. And mine.

Why were the majority of the world's greatest love songs written by men? Was it because they were raised to hide their emotions and ended up feeling more deeply? A man opening his heart and laying it bare turned me to putty.

When it was over I said to Ree, "It's a *great* album. I hope you can slip in more of your singing on the next one." If there was a next one.

"What do you think of the lyrics?" Ree asked.

"Accessible to a wide audience, memorable hooks. 'Take Me Back' would be my pick as the second single."

"Why not make it the first?"

I looked at Trey. "What do you think?"

He slowly scratched the side of his face. "I wish I'd written 'I Married the Stripper.' You can fart in the wind after that and they'll buy it."

"It's 'The Tip,' and don't talk like that in front of a lady."

"Sorry, mon."

Ree held up his hands. "All right, I surrender. I'll put it out first. I don't care what they call it. They were right about 'The Stripper.'"

Trey and Nigel clapped. I threw my arms around him. "You won't regret it, Ree."

He held me tight. "There's only one thing I regret," he said softly in my ear. "Now when am I going to see you?"

Nigel said brightly, "I'll give you two privacy."

"Thanks," Ree said, "I'll get her back to the hotel."

Nigel looked at me. "Okay with you?"

"Uh, sure."

Off he went. He really was testing me.

I hung around a few minutes listening to the music. Memories of the hundreds of hours I'd logged in studios with him came back. I couldn't take it.

I walked to the door, grasping the handle I knew would need a good yank to break its airtight seal. "I'll get a cab."

"Do your thing, Trey. You don't need me here. Let's go somewhere, *Jazmyn Brown*."

When we hit the street, I glanced around for Nigel's limo. Nowhere to be found.

Soon we had our arms around each other as we walked down the nearly empty Brooklyn street. It was like we'd never been apart.

"How are your parents?" he asked.

"Bigger than ever."

"Does Nigel know …?"

"Not yet. Let's keep it that way."

He dropped his arm. "I knew there was something going on with you two."

I wasn't surprised he'd picked up on it. Nigel and I had acted too cold to each other.

"We're not *together* together. Just thinking about it. Where can it go with you and me anyway," I asked Ree, "with you touring and wanting to live in Richmond?"

He narrowed his eyes. "Ever hear the joke, 'The key to success is sincerity. Once you can fake that you've got it made'? That's Nigel Hamilton-Jones."

"You just hate anyone who gets along with everyone," I shot back. "You know why he does? Because *he's* secure with himself."

"He's paid to be that way."

"You took it personally when your label didn't pull the stops out for your follow-up song."

"And I didn't have the right material because I didn't listen to you. I *know*. I should have gone with the producer and manager you suggested instead of the one with the better drugs. I was an idiot! How many times do I have to say it? I did listen to you about the elephant, though."

Ree had been so angry at his record label for their creative bookkeeping with his royalties, he'd threatened to hire an elephant and ride it in front of the record label's office until they handed over what he was sure they owed him. I told him doing that would end his career.

It still made me laugh. And maybe I was wrong. His career stalled anyway. What harm could it have done, really, to have been known for that? It probably would have gone viral and landed him his own TV show.

"Let's see how Tut-tut feels when he meets your parents and finds out you used to be supersized."

"You said you didn't care if my butt got as big as five hippopotami in July as long as I was happy, but you didn't think I would be and *that's* what would turn you off."

"Right." He pulled me to him. "I'm forever imprinted in your brain, your DNA, your soul, Jaz. Stop fighting me."

Our kiss started out sweet and slow, then gathered steam. If there had been a bed right there ... No. I couldn't sleep with him.

Why not? Because ... um ...

"The end is near, so fuck your brains out! Fuck your brains out! Spare change?"

We jumped back from a homeless man, hand outstretched. It wasn't only what he said but how he smelled. Ree gave him a dollar.

"Maybe that was a sign," I said as we walked on. "The end is near?"

"I was focusing more on the fuck-your-brains out part."

"Forget what just happened, Ree. I only want to be friends. I need to go. I have to be up early to meet a real estate broker."

I heard a kind of barking/whimpering noise behind us. A forlorn dog had emerged from an alley where the homeless man was now standing. The man was putting out a handwritten sign on a piece of cardboard and settling down next to the dog. Was it wrong to feel sorrier for the dog?

At the corner was a grocery store. "Ree, I'm going to buy that dog some food."

"You still haven't lost your love of animals," he said with pride.

Upon my return, the dog jumped all over me like I was her savior. Who knew when she had last had her shots, if ever. I kept my distance. The man did nothing more than utter a flat "Thanks."

"What's wrong?" I challenged him.

"I need money, man."

"Maybe you shouldn't own an animal then."

"It would cut down on the money I do get."

I angrily ripped open the bag I was carrying and scattered nuggets of food on the ground. The dog sucked it up with the force of a vacuum cleaner.

"You play on people's sympathies with an animal?" Ree said. "You should be ashamed."

"Ashamed?" He cocked his head up. He wasn't that old and had a lot of teeth missing. "Ever hear the Temptations' 'Ain't Too Proud to Beg'? That's me, man. No shame, big gain."

I put a plastic salad bar to-go container down and poured water into it. She couldn't drink it fast enough. What was I going to do? I didn't even have a home myself at the moment. I mentally said a prayer for both of them and we kept walking.

8

STICKER SHOCK

Buying an apartment in Manhattan was out of the question. A shoebox was half a million. I called every online rental that didn't have a broker involved. They were already taken.

I gave in and started calling brokers.

Five messages saying I was looking in the $2,500 a month range yielded not one response. I upped it to three grand.

$3,000 a month for *rent?* Most of the ads stated NO PETS. Just as well or I'd be saving every dog in distress I laid eyes on.

Even in a sharp business suit and tie, the one broker who called me back couldn't disguise that he was barely out of his teens. Eight-thirty in the morning, Jeremy and I began a nonstop jog around Manhattan, jumping in and out of cabs, starting in Washington Heights and working our way downtown.

The apartments quickly blurred into an unappealing blend of bad smells, dungeon-like darkness, views of a brick wall across a narrow alley, and so little square footage I'd have to go outside to change my mind.

Jeremy was impressed I was going to be a DJ on WBRR.

"They must pay well."

"Not bad."

"You're a star. You should look in the five to six thousand range. Four minimum."

"I was raised by a man who believed the key to happiness is low overhead."

He punched the elevator button again, forcing a smile. "Must not be from New York." His bobbing up and down on the balls of his feet increased. "I see a lot of out-of-towners who land jobs here for a hundred-fifty grand and think they're doing great," he said. "I ask them, 'So what else do you do?'"

By his standards I was broke, but pride kept me going. Maybe Ree was smarter than I thought, staying in Richmond.

More sticker shock: a Manhattan parking garage was a minimum $500 a month. For a car I wouldn't even use that often? Crazy. But I couldn't do appearances outside the city without my own transportation. No radio station would provide that. I couldn't sell my car until I knew for sure what the future held. In three months I could be back in Virginia living with my parents and unable to get a car loan without a job.

One place in Chelsea was quite livable at $4,600.

"I'll give you a break at a fifteen-percent commission instead of our usual seventeen," said Jeremy. "And it's only first month's rent and one month security. A deal!"

I took out my cell calculator. The final move-in figure: $17,480. Before I even bought a doormat. Another $50,600 to shell out over the rest of the year. Then they could gouge me with a rent hike for the following year. My dad had taught me to never spend more than 25% of my income on housing. This was more than 60%. I would have to lie to him about what I was paying.

I snapped a photo.

"What are you doing?" Jeremy asked.

"Taking pictures so I can keep the front-runners straight while I think it over."

He rocked so far back on his heels I thought he was going to topple over. "This'll be gone by the end of the day! If you like it, you have to grab it now."

My instincts said to slow down. The station was covering my new depressing hotel room with thin walls for another ten days. How bad could commuting be? I also calculated Jeremy had easily spent over a hundred dollars on cab fares.

"Let's call it quits," I said. "I need to rob a bank."

He didn't hide his irritation.

I felt guilty for wasting his time and money until he gave me his card and said, "Play me some Led Zeppelin."

All would be forgiven if I said his name on the radio.

The trick to being a great radio DJ is to convince the listener that everything is off the cuff, what you say as well as what you play. Imagine you heard a DJ say, "Tony in Wherever, USA, called for the new one" from so-and-so. That DJ didn't decide on a whim to play it for that guy. A log generated by a computer, possibly thousands of miles away, had dictated that he or she play it.

If you heard a caller talking to the DJ and requesting a song, then the song magically appeared and the conversation ended right as the artist started singing, that bit could have been recorded the week before. The DJ waited for that song to show up on the music log in a position that allowed for banter before it. The call was timed, then woven together with the intro of the song.

On Seventh Avenue near 23rd Street I found a place to eat. A turkey sandwich, beer, cappuccino and tip set me back almost thirty dollars.

The energy of Manhattan soon lifted my spirits. I was on an invisible treadmill set at a speed just below jogging. New Yorkers had a way of ignoring you and checking you out in one second — that is if they weren't looking at their cells. And how do women walk in stiletto heels while texting?

How do they walk in them at all?

That thought, along with all the gorgeous items in store windows with astronomical price tags, had a familiar I'm-not-worthy bile rising inside me. And yet, I didn't want to be anywhere else on earth.

At the famous Hotel Chelsea, where Sid Vicious of the Sex Pistols had murdered his girlfriend Nancy Spungen, and rockers from Patti Smith to Janis Joplin had lived, I slowed, remembering Shane's suggestion to stay in a hotel for now.

The Chelsea was booked solid.

I sat in the lobby, watching the cool people come and go, wondering what they did, who had broken their hearts, what drugs they were on. It hit me that I was surrounded by millions of people and felt strangely alone. I was tired of spinning around like a whirling dervish. I wanted to be in one place with one person. Nigel? My father would love him, unlike Ree.

If only Ree wasn't hovering around. Oh, right, he hadn't sent me a single text. I *did* tell him to leave me alone. Could we be friends? Really?

Howzitgoin I texted him.

A pinprick of sadness hit me when I didn't hear right back. I let it slide. Ree was a busy guy right now. And I was a busy girl. I had to find a place to live. I'd already turned down Nigel's offer to stay at his place until I found something. That was too much too soon.

And what if Ree and I ...

No!

I strolled in the summer heat, soaking up the sun and whatever else my senses could detect.

A coffee pot that had been on a burner too long. Hot dogs. Sugary sticky cinnamon buns.

By the time I reached the Village I was craving something sweet. I'd walked enough to earn it. I saw a sliver of a store, MarieBelle, selling ice cream, sorbet, sherbet, and something called granita. Oh, and chocolate. Lots of chocolate in adorable deep turquoise boxes with brown ribbons. These morsels were far from ordinary. Some were tiny delicacies an inch square in dozens of flavors and emblazoned with different colorful images. Each one was a work of art and cost a couple of bucks. Why would you eat something so beautiful? It was impossible to pick one anyway.

I sampled the rose petal gelato. There was no need to try anything else.

Oh. My. God.

My rapturous state upon leaving the heavenly store lasted about five minutes. I passed a newspaper stand displaying a black button the size of a dinner plate with bright yellow letters that screamed: FUCK YOU.

I called Nigel, meaning to sound disapproving. When the words came out of my mouth I laughed.

"Soon you won't even notice things like that," he said. "Did you find a place to let?"

"At these prices, I should be looking in New Jersey."

"A hotel's not a bad idea for now. I'll get you a good rate at the Gramercy Arms." It felt good to be with a guy who had my back.

I took a photo of the FUCK YOU button.

I almost sent it to Ree.

9

GILDING THE LILY

Outside my hotel a sleek black limo waited, with Nigel and another gift. This time it was an awesome MGX leather bomber jacket. Like the dresses, it had to be worth a lot more than the radio station limit of $50. I said nothing. My disclaimer was officially on record. Besides, Madd Maxx had been wearing an Eagles tour jacket at the jock meeting.

"Just one condition," Nigel said. "Please don't wear it to the Rolling Stones party or people will be slipping you their music."

"But I like helping struggling artists if they're great. That's how 'The Stripper' happened."

"So do I, just not when I'm in the presence of a beautiful woman like you. I get interrupted enough as it is."

I softened.

"If you get cold," Nigel said, "put on my jacket. Now I have to make a couple of calls to the West Coast before offices close out there. Won't be long."

I snuggled next to him as I eavesdropped.

"He wouldn't know a hit if it went down on him!"

The next call, his voice went from happy to defeated. "Sure." He hung up, shaking his head with a deep sigh. "There was a bloody bidding war for her!"

He filled me in, though I had a sick feeling I knew what had happened.

"We paid three times what we normally would, that was the problem. Well, that and the fact that female artists are just harder to break. There are *still* a few program directors out there who worry about playing two female artists back to back."

He didn't hear my "What?!"

"Expectations ran high and the top brass didn't think she'd deliver. Probably a wife or one of their kids had a lukewarm response. Or she was just too close to twenty-five instead of fifteen."

The idea that I was three years beyond "old" in the music business did not go unnoticed.

"Does she have to pay back the advance?" I asked.

"Probably. Or some of it. The worst part? It'll be next to impossible for her to get another deal now. Damn!" He slammed his fist into the soft seat cushion.

Every recording artist who isn't a superstar is in danger of being kicked to the curb. When it happened to Ree I was doing my radio show in Richmond. The station program director came into the studio to express his condolences, assuming I knew. I had two more hours to get through on the air. Whatever I said felt like sawdust in my mouth.

"Oh, well." Nigel put on a brighter tone. "When there's uncertainty at the top, my job is a lot harder. Survival of the fittest, Jaz. Darwin would've had a field day studying the music biz."

Like a flat tire instantly refilled with air, he made another call as though nothing bad had happened. I couldn't block out how this dumped woman, who probably worked a long time and spent untold thousands of dollars to get her mega deal, had gone from being high as a kite one day to toxic waste the next. The same thing happened to Katy Perry when Columbia records dropped her, I reminded myself. A miracle and oh-so satisfying revenge *could* happen.

The music on WBRR gave way to the DJ talking. Despite being on the phone, Nigel turned *up* the volume, lowering *his* voice so I could hear the break. To the listener, Chopper sounded fine. But I could hear the air of detachment signaling he knew a tractor-trailer was hurtling toward him.

"Keep your willy up," Nigel said to his caller. "It's a hit!" He put his cell in his jacket pocket. "I'm done. Where were we?"

A peck on my cheek sent a whiff of spicy cologne my way.

I eyed him suspiciously. "With all the payola rules, is it okay for you to date a DJ?"

He laced his fingers through mine. "As long as you aren't involved in deciding what music gets played, there's no problem."

"For the record, if I was given the opportunity to do that, I'd take it."

He grabbed my hand more tightly. "Jazmyn, you're an *artist*. Talent. A management job would make you terribly unhappy. Endless bullshit. Believe me, I know."

The Museum of Natural History, after hours, was hosting the private Rolling Stones listening party for their new album. The music bounced off display windows filled with stuffed safari animals.

There was no mistaking Mick Jagger's vocals and Keith Richards on guitar. I tried not to act like I was scanning the crowd for members of the band.

Tall, skinny black women in native African outfits mingled with the crowd while effortlessly balancing glass bowls on their heads filled with *live fish*.

"They were flown in from West Africa." Nigel's eyes were alive with excitement.

"The women or the fish?"

"Both." He whispered, "Just kidding. They're local, I'm sure. Probably doing it for free for the exposure. No one, especially the Stones, would spend that kind of money."

Next the women returned with bowls of *fire* on their heads, and began dancing.

Androgynous servers who could have been men or women (really couldn't tell) offered food to be eaten by hand. I imagined dredging my fingers through a bowl of sauce as a stuffed rhinoceros looked on. Who knew what germs were in there already? We passed. So did everyone else.

"Flamboyant yet cheap," Nigel said with admiration.

The Stones were nowhere in sight, but there were plenty of important people in the biz that Nigel made sure I met.

"Tune into her midday show tomorrow on WBRR ... The Barenaked Radio Ladies ... She's going to set New York on fire!"

Nothing like pressure to be amazing and error-free the first day.

More than a few women flirted with Nigel, subtle compared with what I was used to. Women would slip Ree their phone numbers right in front of me.

"Slumming with the record ducks?" asked an unmistakable earthy voice.

Cat Cruz had arrived in a leather vest trimmed with fringe that showed off her boobs and flat tummy, tight jeans so low on her hips I was amazed they stayed up, and pink alligator shoes with extra-high spiked heels.

"Record ducks?" I responded.

"Play my record. Quack, quack. Play my record."

Her crass comment stunned me.

Nigel jumped in. "And where's *your* date, love? In one of the displays? Oh, look, Jaz. It's the editor at *Billboard* who writes about radio. Let's say hello."

"Oh, look, it's Mick," Cat said, darting off. "Let me go say hello."

"Jagger wouldn't be caught dead here," Nigel said. "Is she ever threatened by you."

For the rest of the evening he expertly wove us through the crowd so we wouldn't run into Cat. He remembered everyone's name and personal information about them. His mind had an astonishing storage and retrieval system. Mine worked that way with music, but with people I wasn't so hot. I'd tried those tricks for recalling someone's name, like picturing an object that it sounded like. I'd meet someone named Bob and picture a bobsled only to call him Fred because I thought it rhymed with sled.

At last we piled into Nigel's waiting limo.

"What time is it?" I asked.

"Seven-thirty, love. Shank of the evening."

"I wouldn't mind a quiet night in," I said.

"Oh." His voice fell.

"*Together.*"

"Oh! How about I make dinner at my place? Just a cozy evening to calm your nerves before your big debut."

If this meant what I thought it meant, my nerves would be far from calm.

I have to say, a man doing anything in a kitchen was a turn-on. Probably because my dad cooked for me and my mom on the weekends. The whole house had sighed away the tension of the week when he did that. Come to think of it, Ree had seduced me by cooking for me. I was determined not to sleep with him. I mean, how could this gorgeous guy be into me? Really into me? I thought. I'll never forget that first meal: his mama's barbeque ribs recipe that is still the best I've ever had, roasted sweet potatoes, and a healthy salad. No dessert, as I insisted.

"I thought Brits weren't known for their culinary skills," I teased Nigel.

"Rubbish. One of the best restaurants in the world is the Fat Duck outside London. You haven't lived until you've had their snail porridge."

"No thanks."

"Trust me, it'll put you over the moon."

He described other delicacies on the menu. White chocolate and caviar. Salmon poached with licorice. Smoked bacon and egg ice cream.

"Can I just order the last one and pretend I've eaten an entire meal?"

"I'm not saying my cooking is any match, but how does a soufflé with fresh fruit salad marinated in Grand Marnier, scones with tiny currants, delicious organic jams, clotted cream, and chocolate-covered biscuits called McVities sound? I know it's more of a brunch menu but it's all I can whip up at the moment."

I grabbed his hand. "I can't wait."

"Not to be presumptuous," he said, "but are you an early riser or a night owl?"

I liked where this was going.

"I'm usually asleep by midnight and up by seven. You?"

Nigel, it turned out, was an insomniac who managed about four hours of sleep a night.

"So when I become a pop, *I'll* be the one up changing nappies in the middle of the night."

He saw my wary expression. "I'm not talking about this instant, but someday in the not-too-distant future I hope to be in that situation. Don't you?"

"Sure. Yeah. Of course!"

In the past I would have said: the more distant the better. I wasn't ready yet, but it was a *possibility* now.

He moved in for what I was sure was our first kiss, then pulled away.

Wait, I thought as my winged fantasies came crashing down. Was Nigel a closet case? That happened to me in Detroit with a guy who acted like a boyfriend in every way but one. I figured out why we weren't having sex when I found issues of *Stud* in the cabinet under his bathroom sink when I went looking for a new roll of toilet paper.

"Are you *sure* you want to go back to your place?" I asked.

"Only if you are."

I swatted his upper arm. "Nigel. Do you want to make love to me or not?"

"Yes! If *you're* sure you don't want to make love to Ree."

"I am one hundred percent sure."

"Good. But I can't kiss you here."

"Why not?"

"Because I'll want to do a whole lot more."

We moved slowly through the Lincoln Center traffic, holding hands, our passion at a nice simmer.

He played a song about to come out on MGX. The band, Streaming the Net from North Carolina, sounded like Coldplay with a funky edge.

"Definitely crossover potential," I said.

"I'll bet a Benjamin I get it on 'BRR in a week."

I waved my hands. "No way. I'll lose."

I reached for the button to lower the windows and let in the balmy night air. It was full of music from stores still open, passing cars, and street musicians. At a stoplight we studied a store window for "adult diversions."

"Never felt the need to gild the lily in that department," he said.

"Oh, come on. Everybody tries *something* after awhile."

"You'd look lovely in that number. Shall I buy it?"

I nodded at the male mannequin in a matching spiked black leather hood, collar, and thong. "Only if it comes in pink."

He turned serious. "I promise this is the last time I'll bring this up. You sound convincing you'll stay away from Ree, but do you still have feelings for him?"

I nestled into the crook of his arm. "I hope not."

"That's not a no." He slid his arm over my shoulder.

"He was my first love, Nigel. Sure, I think about him some-times. How can I not when his song's still played on the radio? Don't you ever think about yours?"

He lightly placed his hand on my cheek and turned my face to him.

"I haven't *had* my first love. I've had my share of fun and a couple of serious relationships, but real love goes beyond that. And when I have it, there won't be another. Let me ask again. Do you still love him?"

"*No.* Besides, I'm sure he has women chasing him day and night."

"That's true, but I haven't seen him with one woman."

I tried to temper the acid in my reply. "You mean you've seen him with a constant stream of different ones. That wouldn't sur-prise me."

"He's a star, love. What do you expect?" The limo had stopped. "We're here." He looked at me again, silently, to confirm I wanted to move forward.

I wasn't going to let lingering feelings for Ree ruin this night or my life. Besides, they weren't *feelings*. They were just thoughts. Thoughts.

"What are we waiting for?" I lowered my voice. "It's the shank of the evening."

10

By Hook or By Crook

I arrived at the station the next morning floating on air from ending my dry spell, and with a man I saw as a strong contender for Mr. Forever. I'd get over thinking about Ree. Of course I would.

Then I saw Pig Boy. He was in the state radio morning show producers are always in: sleep-deprived controlled chaos with serious coffee breath.

"Um, what do I call you?" I asked.

"Pig Boy." The shiny wedding band on the hand clutching a WBRR mug probably hadn't been there long.

"That feels weird."

"Then *Mr.* Pig Boy." He pushed open the heavy studio door with his shoulder.

"Wait! I know you're going to be running our board at first," I called out. "I came in early to watch you and pick it up faster so you can get back to more important things."

"Run your board? News to me. Our studio is *totally* different. You'll see. Good luck."

The air studio door closed with a soft thud behind him.

I found Rick at his desk, deep in concentration at his computer.

"Right, the jock studio. You've probably never seen anything like it."

The phone number for the new head of engineering was in the studio, Rick said, but with five stations to oversee there was no telling where he was, or if he could explain over the phone how this one worked.

"Shane can help you."

I soon entered Shane's sanctum sanctorum. He was playing back a liner he'd just recorded for another station. "Ninety-four-seven the *Bone*. Always hard ... *rockin.*'"

"There's a line I should be saying." My version cracked him up.

Shane took pity on me when I told him my dilemma. "For you, I have a few minutes," he said. "You'll need all the help you can get with Victor's Vendetta if you're going to start airing phone calls."

I tried to learn my way around the maze-like station as we walked down several hallways. He told me Victor was the chief engineer from before the day WBRR signed on until he "retired" after thirty years. He was an arch-conservative who grumbled all the way to the Woodstock festival about having to oversee the broadcast from it. By the time Hendrix closed the three-day historic event with "The Star-Spangled Banner" Victor had dropped acid, smoked the best weed on the planet, and cavorted naked.

"He embraced hippiedom like no other," said Shane, "complaining loudly and often that the station and the jocks were sellouts bowing to pressure from Madison Avenue. He couldn't be fired because of the union. Management eventually hired someone younger and cheaper and eased him out. His parting gift was to install the most back-assward studio you can imagine when it comes to recording phone calls. At least you don't have to use a reel-to-reel player anymore."

"For a moment there I thought you were going to tell me I had to pull the music and commercials."

He stopped, rested his hands on my shoulders. "Only the recording of calls is digital."

I found it hard to move until he put his hand on my back and pushed me.

"The jocks revolted when there was talk of bringing in Prophet and computerizing everything," he said. "The company said 'If it's costing us nothing, leave it alone.' The Dick and Dork studio can be used for voice-tracking in a pinch."

The first thing I noticed when we entered the jock studio was the absence of a window, other than a tiny vertical one on the door. The only sign I was in Manhattan was a large photograph with the Twin Towers still standing that was mounted over a rectangular screen that went with the device for recording and editing phone calls.

The second thing I noticed was the faint scent of men's cologne. "Does every guy have to spread his scent here?"

"Only Madd Maxx. Even the phone smells like him."

He hadn't been on the air since the day before. How could that be? I picked up the phone and sniffed it. Whoa!

One wall was covered with posters of every major rock band that ever lived and Polaroid photos taken with them in the studio with the jocks. The ceiling was soundproofed with something similar to foam egg cartons painted black. The other predominant color was tan. The soundboard was a Gates.

"Very late eighties," I said.

"You're too young to know that."

"Between Richmond and here, I've seen a lot. But nothing like this. At least I won't have to do the show standing up."

"Where did you ever have to do that?"

"You've never done CHR?" Contemporary Hit Radio. "You stand to keep the energy up."

There was a wall of CDs, another with *albums,* and several five-foot-tall revolving racks crammed with what looked like eight-track tapes — "carts" with numbers on them denoting commercials. There was a laptop bolted down near where the jock sat that could be used to surf the net for informational purposes.

Usually music and spots were preloaded into a computer. All I had to do was click a mouse and move faders up and down. Now I had to physically find each song on a CD and put it into a separate deck to play on the air.

"This is from the Stone Age!" Panic rose in me along with my voice. "How can it be? This is *New York*."

"It's New York with a very short list of jocks who have a strong following in the format who were fine with analog. Add to that a privately-held company with tight purse strings that didn't care about impressing Wall Street. That's all about to change with Sonic. It's not *that* bad. Donna will pull everything for you, and put it all back."

"Donna?"

"Her title is producer but she's really a glorified gopher to Cat. Now for the really fun part."

He showed me how to record a phone call. I had to take my microphone, and Cat's, out of "program" (live) and into "audition," pot it up, and do the same with the fader for the telephone. I stared in disbelief.

It would be so easy to forget to put everything into audition and end up talking on the air. Or forget to raise the volume, which would mean nothing was recorded. Every station I'd work for before, I hit the record button, started talking, then hit stop when I was done. Simple.

Shane saw my frozen look. "You'll get used to it."

A numbness spread to my fingertips. There went my plan to be flawless out of the box. The variations in equipment were only part of the problem. Each station's programming log — the "script" for any show — looked different. I had to learn that, too.

"Look at it this way," Shane said, "If you screw up, the listeners will think it's Cat's fault."

She and I had no road map as to what we were going to talk about or how we were going to structure the show. She had no intention of coming in early to meet with me.

"It won't feel natural if we do that," she'd said.

Shane cleared newspapers and music magazines from one of the counters. "Wait'll you see this." He lifted a portion of the counter. Hidden below were two honest-to-God turntables. "They're here as a backup in case a CD player fails."

I felt a shiver, similar to the one I'd had seeing the wall of autographs in the hallway.

"I really am working in a museum."

"I call it retro." He reached for a knob that controlled the speaker volume to the large JBLs suspended from the four corners of the small studio. "There's one thing this room has going for it that the others don't."

He cranked what was playing over the air: Aerosmith's "Back in the Saddle." It blasted with such force I could feel the bass thumping in my chest. It was impossible to stand still. I rocked out the way I always did when I heard a great song. Shane did too. It was hilarious to see him let go.

He lowered the volume. "Incredible! You can still open it up as loud as you can stand it. Updated studios now conform to OSHA rules." He turned the volume up two-thirds. "They only go this far."

I'd take lower volume over this radio relic any day. Looking around, "Is there an aircheck machine?" It would record only when the mike was turned on. I couldn't wait to analyze my first show later.

He pointed to a piece of equipment. "Still uses cassettes."

He showed me where the stash of tapes lived. It was a big box filled with old airchecks sent to the station by DJs trying to get a job there long ago. (Subtext: see how many people want your job?) I picked one up. It was coated in dust. *Smokin' Sammy Stevens*, it said. I wondered where he was now.

Shane smiled when he said, "Be sure to *have fun with it*."

The digital clock on the board said 9:33. T-minus 27 minutes and counting.

Soon it was 9:50 a.m. Ten minutes until my very first show in New York. Where was that little elf that was going to pull the music and commercials and screen calls?

Olivia appeared in the studio. I knew something was wrong.

"Cat's not coming in?" For a moment I was thrilled.

"No, Donna Duffries, your producer, is running late. Rick asked me to help you." She was less than overjoyed.

"Thanks. If you could pull the spots, I'll get the music. I need to start familiarizing myself with the CD collection."

"So how was the Stones party last night?" she asked, the first time she'd shown any interest in me.

"It was great. I thought I'd see you there."

"I was there."

"Oh, you were?"

"Nigel was keeping you very busy. Are you dating?"

"Uh ..." I hadn't expected such a direct question. And spending one night with someone didn't mean you were dating, or at least ready to tell the world you were. "We're very good friends. We go way back."

"Yeah," she smirked, "so do we."

So *that* was what her weirdness was about. How far back?

I was too focused on my first show to think about it. Dick and Dork were signing off and Shane's deep voice roared, "The Barenaked Radio Ladies Show on WBRR, New York's ninety-nine the *Beeeear*, the *best* rock. Radio never looked so *good*. Cat Cruz and Jazmyn Brown are next."

I felt like I was on a pair of water skis, pulled up to a standing position that I had to maintain for the next four hours. Every show I'd ever done felt that way, but this time I was going a hundred miles an hour instead of fifty.

The first song on my computer-generated playlist was U2's "It's a Beautiful Day." I smiled. When that song played I couldn't be upset about anything.

Cat breezed in. Olivia darted out. As U2 faded, I followed the playlist and started "Honky Tonk Women" with liner cart number 272 "Keith Richards Dry" going into it. "Dry" meant there was nothing but ole Keef's voice on it, no music or sound effects added. Perfect for laying over intros to songs. I calculated the intro time of the song with the length of the Keith liner, hit the play button on the CD player, turned up the song as far as it would go so the opening cowbells would cut through. Hit the liner cart at just the right moment.

"Hey, New York. This is Keith Richards rockin' with WBRR. The best rock and roll."

Guess it was okay for a member of the Rolling Stones to say rock and roll. I didn't envy whoever had to edit "and roll" out of a ton of artist I.D.s.

The second Keith stopped talking, the rest of the band kicked in.

"Yes!" DJs live for talking-it-up-to-the-post moments.

Looking like a million bucks in a summery dress and strappy sandals, Cat put down her Chanel bag in front of me so I could see its interlocking Cs.

She looked me over. "Don't you get tired of men thinking you're a hooker?"

I almost spit out the warm water I was sipping to keep my throat relaxed. "That's hilarious, coming from someone who posed for *Playboy*."

"I'm in hysterics. Where's Donna?"

"Not here yet."

Perturbed, she said, "Then you'll have to phone in my breakfast order."

"*Excuse me?*" I laughed. "Our first break is after 'Honky Tonk Women.' How about—"

"I need my breakfast!"

"What's the matter? Your finger's paralyzed and you can't make a call?"

"And don't refer to it as *our* break. This is *my* show. You're my sidekick."

"Have you not heard the promos?"

She stormed out of the room. I blasted the music. I was being paid to rock out to the Rolling Stones. *Rise above it, Jaz.*

The digital timer said we were 2:50 into the song. Keith Richards' closing guitar riff smoked and Charlie Watts' drums and cymbals thumped and crashed. I waited for the "cold fade," when it would all come to a halt and hang in the air for a few seconds.

Cat hadn't returned. I cracked the mike and talked over the finish.

"WBRR, ninety-nine The Bear, the best rock, and a classic from the Stones. Ever hear Tom Jones's version? Check it out sometime. This is Jazmyn Brown. Cat's in the ladies' room getting undressed and I'm already naked, but I'm sure you're far more interested in seeing the Rolling Stones in *London*, right? We'll be sending you there in the noon hour. Up next—hey, she's here. The ravishing Cat Cruz!"

Instead of going to her seat on the other side of the control board, she tried to boot me out of mine. I refused to budge. She continued to lean over me while yanking the mike toward her and purring into it.

"Oooooh, it feels so good to take my clothes off. Aren't you going to join me?"

Right there, she'd blown my illusion that I was already undressed.

"Having my shirt off isn't enough?" Before she could blow that too, I said, "Let a listener talk me into taking off the rest." I reeled off the request line number and dumped into spots.

"Get up," she said. "That's my seat."

"How am I supposed to run the board?"

"*I'm* going to."

I'd have it out with Rick Rivers later. I moved to the guest microphone. Cat wouldn't turn my mike on but started pretending she was taking phone calls. I walked around to put my mike in audition and pot up the fader, but she blocked my way.

Between battling Cat and the box of donuts a fan had sent, I was being driven wild.

I was about to march into Rick's office when Donna arrived, upset over a train delay. She had a high-pitched voice, bugged-out eyes, and teeth that lined up perfectly (no overbite). With her curly red hair, she looked like she'd just put her finger in a live electric socket.

The callers were the best part of the show. Not a single one made it to the air, though. Cat managed not to record them.

"Just let me do it," I pleaded. "Callers bring a show alive!"

"Callers bring a show to a standstill. They're clutter."

"Don't pull your passive-aggressive shit on me. We should have talked about this *before* we went on the air."

"My, what big words you know."

We shut up as Rick entered the control room.

"What's the problem? Why are you over there, Cat? We agreed Jazmyn would run the board. I want callers on the air as soon as she has the hang of it."

"She thinks she's co-hosting."

"She is."

Cat leaned back, giving him her best bedroom eyes. "Let's have a drink later and talk about it."

"We've already talked about it, Cat. Jazmyn is to run the board and you're a *team*. Got it? And be sure to say her name so listeners learn it."

She looked ready to slit his throat. I glanced at the log. Only twenty seconds left on Fleetwood Mac's "Over My Head." My sentiments exactly.

She reluctantly got up and we switched places. I gave Rick a nod. There wasn't enough time to prep an on-air break so I hit a sweeper and segued into "Roxanne" by the Police. Shane's voice saying "Ninety-nine the *Beeeeear*" ended right at the post where Sting laughs during the intro.

"Yes!" I shouted again.

Cat rolled her eyes. "Are you going to say that *every* time?"

"I am. It's about time you knew what a tight board sounds like."

"You are *not* going to steal my joy."

"Since when is job spelled j-o-y?"

"Ladies, that's enough! I'll be in my office listening."

While the song played, a dude named Marvin got through on the phones. Judging from Cat and Donna's reaction, I put him on hold.

"No one can figure out what Marvin does," Donna squeaked. "We think he calls every air personality, every day, like a telemarketer. I've heard him turn up on other stations."

I hit the record button again. Sometimes guys like that can come up with a line that's useable. Finding it among their nonstop ramblings can be a challenge.

"Jazmyn Brown!" he said, "I'm lookin' at your picture on the website. Cat Cruz's got some competiiiiiiition. Are you really naked?"

Cat reached for the phone next to her, with fifteen lines coming in, and clicked him off. Over the next few hours we talked to a lot of deez/dem/doze guys, well-educated Wall Streeters in need of their Pink Floyd fix, and kids on summer vacation discovering the Doors. They all asked: Were we really naked?

We played along. It was already old in my book.

The webcam that had been installed on the studio laptop was controlled by Rick Rivers. He had the following message posted: DUE TO THE FULL NUDITY OF THE BARENAKED RADIO LADIES, THE WEBCAM WILL BE OFF DURING THEIR SHOW TO INSURE NO MINORS SEE THEM.

Cat bit into the succulent strawberry and cream cheese pastry she'd had delivered. She caught me wetting my lips.

"I'd offer you some, but I'm sure you're trying to lose those extra Texas barbeque pounds."

I was as thin as I was going to get.

"Don't worry, I'm not going to steal your joy again."

"You didn't steal it the first time," she said. "I didn't let you." Turning to Donna, "Call my manicurist and make an appointment for me when I get off. I'm going to a fabulous dinner party tonight at Kevin and Kyra's."

When Donna reached the door, Cat called out, "And that outfit. You're too short for it. I keep telling you to see my personal shopper at Saks."

Seeing Donna's distressed expression, I followed her out.

"Where's the bathroom again?" I asked her.

"That's where I'm headed."

Once there I told her from my stall, "You look great. Don't listen to her."

"Cat keeps saying she's trying to help me, but she makes me feel awful. Like *I* can afford to shop at Saks! This job pays minimum wage. By the time I shell out for transportation, parking, and the I.R.S., I don't make a dime. I have to live with my parents."

I quickly checked myself in the mirror. (DJs are the world's fastest pissers.) "I want to hit the outlet malls in Jersey as soon as my car shows up. Interested?"

"You mean it? You're so cool. I hope she gets fired and you get the job."

When we returned to the studio, Cat said, "A fan of yours named Karl called." She saw my reaction. "Nut case? We all have them."

"No matter where I go, he finds me."

"Cut him off," Cat said. "Don't even say hello or goodbye."

"He's harmless," I said.

"Unless he's on death row and about to be fried, it's not far enough. Song's ending."

I put on my headphones and turned up the inner flame.

Cat and I made it through the show without strangling each other. Her lazy-ass ways and diva 'tude were one thing, but she hadn't even wanted to crank up "Purple Haze"! What kind of a rock jock is that?

While Donna filed the last round of commercials, she asked, "What's the hook for Queen's 'Bohemian Rhapsody'? I'm doing a new hook tape and can't figure out if it's 'Mama, just killed a man,' 'Scaramouche! Scaramouche! Will you do the fandango?' or 'Gotta get out, gotta get right outta here'?"

A hook tape is a compilation of eight seconds of the catchiest part of a hundred or more different songs. People sit in an auditorium—usually located somewhere like Kansas—listen to it and rate each "hook." Their responses help decide what is, and isn't, played on radio stations across America. Even in New York.

A record company can only get a song a shot on the radio. It's the people rating hook tapes, as well as sales, Internet clicks, and listener requests that decide its fate. The personality and looks of the artist, along with his or her willingness to schmooze radio geeks and jump through endless hoops, count big time. But no matter how much you hate a song, it's stayed on the radio because millions of people who have nothing to do with the music business love it.

"Maybe it's 'Magnifico-oh-oh-oh-oh-oh-oh-oh-oh,'" I answered. "No, 'Mama mia, mama mia, mama mia, let me go.'"

Cat said with certainty. "It's the opening. 'Is this the real life? Is this just fantasy?'"

Then it hit me. "If that song came out today, it'd never make it on the radio because it has too many different parts."

"Same for 'Stairway to Heaven,'" Donna said.

At 1:55 p.m. Maxx barged into the studio, reeking of cologne.

"A thousand dollars to tune up my Jag! What a rip-off."

Cat and I beat a path to Rick. Sitting at his desk, he gave us a wide smile.

"Great show! Sales loves it. How would you two feel about mud wrestling at a club on the Island?"

Cat's index finger flew out at him like a witch casting a hex. "This is not working. Either she goes or I do."

"So you wouldn't be interested in posing nude again for *Penthouse?*"

That gave her pause. "Really?"

"With *both* of you," he stressed.

Her face went through a series of mean changes. "You'll be hearing from Howie."

After she stormed out, I turned to Rick. "Thanks for standing up for me, but you're not serious about *Penthouse*, are you?"

"Just got off the phone with them." He appreciated the fully clothed view before him. "Now I have to get ready for a call from the Howitzer." He was referring to Howie Kamen, renowned talent agent.

"Rick, I'm *not* posing nude."

He pulled at his goatee, knitted his brow. "I'm confused. You dress like you would and you lived with a guy who wrote a song about a stripper."

I looked down at my outfit. "I dress like a *rock DJ*. And Ree's music shouldn't be any reflection on me, especially since we're not together anymore."

"Okay, I'll ask Donna if she wants to do it."

"Fine."

"The mud wrestling gig is a grand in your pocket. *Cash.*"

I shot him a withering look.

"How about three hundred for appearing at a BMW dealer for two hours?"

"Sure."

His thumb and forefinger massaged his hairy chin. "Couple of formatics. Don't use the word *classic* on the air. All music is current music. And don't mention a song we don't play."

I looked at him blankly.

"The Tom Jones reference. Don't give listeners an excuse to jump online."

"Got it." Like that was going to save this station. "I have one question, Rick. What's the hook for 'Bohemian Rhapsody'?"

He sang off-key: "'Mamaaaa, I just killed a man. Put a gun against his head, pulled my trigger, now he's dead.'"

I should have seen it as an omen.

11

KRAZY

Saturday morning, ten a.m., the Barenaked Radio Ladies waited for a crowd of people to appear at Bayonne BMW. Hanging in the air was the usual nervousness that no one would show up. The salespeople made small talk in the showroom that was perfumed with the scent of new cars and tires — an aroma I had not inhaled in a while. After arriving in a limo that Cat said the station always provided for her, it didn't take long for me to consider asking how much a new BMW went for and what they would take for my Cruiser.

We sat at a table decorated with a long banner emblazoned with an angry grizzly bear. Outside, the station van was parked near the busy road with a goofy twenty-foot inflated Yogi Bear next to it. I thought of Victor's Vendetta. Someone in the WBRR promotion department with a sense of humor knew they were about to be fired.

Cat had a stack of 8x10 glossies of herself, and I had Bear bumper stickers to hand out. Rick refused to book a photo shoot for me until I signed a contract, which was "in the works." Donna was earning her usual minimum wage to make sure we did the phoners to the station that the client had paid for.

Freddy, the manager of Bayonne BMW, hovered around the table. "I made the callbacks to be an extra on *The Sopranos*," he told us almost immediately.

We acted impressed.

A family wandered over. Disappointed we weren't from Z100, they were followed by a young couple who were fans of Hot 97.

An older guy said, "Scott Muni. *That* was a DJ. Cousin Brucie. The DJ of DJs!"

Two women in their early twenties said they didn't listen to the radio. They only streamed Internet sites and downloaded iTunes.

"And SiriusXM," said one, "in my dad's car."

"That's radio," I said. "If there's a DJ, it's radio to me."

A few WBRR listeners appeared. After fawning over Cat, getting a kick out of meeting Donna who had only recently been heard on the show (with that squeaky voice she was unforgettable), and polite hellos to me, all they really wanted was a WBRR T-shirt. We could be giving out station sunglasses decorated with diamonds and they'd still crave a simple T-shirt. I know a DJ who, in an effort to keep fans from stealing his pile of station giveaway tees when he wasn't looking, decided to wear ten of them at once and take them off one at a time to lucky winners. He feared for his life when several middle-aged women mauled him.

Cat leaned over and whispered, "Wacko at three o'clock."

Krazy Karl marched toward us waving one hand in the air. I could always count on him.

He had on rumpled casual clothes, his hair was its typical mess, and there was a lot more of his forehead showing than when we first met in Richmond a decade before. He did have a great smile. Plus, he was in terrific shape from climbing radio and TV towers for a living. A not-so-faint musty odor filled our air space when he came close.

"It's Wiiiiild Wendy!" My first air name.

"Hi, Karl!"

Cat kicked me under the table. I kicked her back. When radio weirdoes show up at station events they rarely leave. He gave Cat an evil stare. She stood and walked away.

"I just climbed a tower a thousand feet tall!" he told me. "Wanna see?"

He flipped open the cover of his iPad, swiped a few times, and treated me and Donna to dizzying views from atop dozens of towers. It looked like he'd taken them from an airplane, but he hadn't. He climbed towers without one thing connecting him to a ramrod-straight ladder.

If that's not crazy, I don't know what is.

"What does a tower climber do?" Donna asked.

His eyes danced between the two of us as he launched into a description of fixing damage after lightning strikes (a common occurrence), replacing old antennas, using thick winch cables to hoist buckets filled with tools and parts.

He also did things on the ground, "Like blow up rocks with liquid dynamite to make holes to pour concrete in to support new towers."

He lost us in a rush of techno-babble after that. No doubt Mensa material, but a wire had crossed somewhere. All the therapy and medication in the world couldn't uncross it.

"I have tiny holes in my organs from the high RF output."

I'd heard this before. Donna's eyes popped more than was normal for her.

"Stations are supposed to reduce power when I go up, but sometimes they don't if it's during a rating book because they don't want to lose listeners, but now they have meters we wear that sound an alarm if they're too high, but after all that climbing, you think I'm going to back down? I get the job done no matter what. That's why I'm the *best*. One day you'll realize and marry me, Wild Wendy. I mean, Jazmyn. Ha-ha-ha-ha-ha!"

A listener who had just appeared quickly left.

"How can you have holes in your organs and still be alive?" Donna asked.

"Because I'm super-human!"

Freddy asked Karl if he was in the market for a new car. His polite, "No sir, I'm not, thank you," coupled with my "He's okay" look, caused Freddy to shrug and back off. Cat returned and did not make eye contact with Karl.

Luckily, more fans showed up.

Karl lurked in the background. When he saw that Cat was getting most of the attention, he announced, "I'm calling your boss and telling him he needs to get rid of her. You're better." Right in front of Cat and the crowd of gathered customers. "And why don't you have photos out? You're prettier."

Cat acted as though he didn't exist.

"Karl, I'm new at the station. A lot more people know Cat."

"It's not right," he said.

Growing uncomfortable, the people standing around moved away. I rearranged the bumper stickers, getting every corner lined up just so.

"Excuse me," said a deep voice. "Perhaps you'll let the ladies' other listeners have some time with them."

"Shane Riley, man! I'd know your voice anywhere! I've worked on the towers of forty- seven stations where you were the voice!"

Just as he had done when we'd first met, Karl won Shane over with his enthusiasm and admiration for his work. He began ticking off each of the station's call letters.

"Hey man, thanks," Shane broke in. "I appreciate that you appreciate what I do."

"Shane, this is Karl Geinsler, the world-famous tower climber."

Shane smiled. "I've heard of you. You're a legend."

Bursting with pride, Karl took out his iPad again. Shane gently pulled him away. "Too much glare on the screen here. Let's go in the corner over there."

"He was gross," Donna said when Karl was gone. "But he did have a hot bod."

"Ignore him, Jazmyn," Cat said. "I've dealt with far more weirdos than you."

"He's harmless."

"Just wait."

After we'd chatted with more fans, Shane returned, this time without Karl.

"He had an emergency call."

"Thank you for taking care of him, Shane," Cat said in her best vixen voice. "What brings you all the way out here?"

"Ikea. A man can never have too many things to fix and build. Of course, by the time I look at five hundred things, figure out what to buy, get it home, unpack it, spread out the instructions and pop a beer ... we'll see how far I get."

"A man who can fix and build things," Cat said. "You have *so* many talents."

He smiled sheepishly. "I also thought I'd stop by to see if any of you would like these." He held up two movie passes to the station screening of a sci-fi movie later in the week. "Or you can give them away."

"Thank you, Shane," said Cat. "That's so nice of you."

"You don't go to station events?" I asked him.

"Not much of a social life these days." He was suddenly uncomfortable. "Have to run, ladies. Nice to see you."

I watched him walk out to his black Prius. He was wearing shorts with his Hawaiian shirt. I couldn't help but notice his great muscular legs. I hadn't pegged him as athletic. I turned back to Cat. She was watching him, too, but looked sad.

She shook her head. "Poor guy."

"Why?" I asked.

"His little boy has brain cancer."

I gasped. "I had no idea." I watched Shane drive away.

"If something like that happened to Marley I wouldn't be able to function," Cat said.

"His poor wife," Donna said. "I can't imagine."

"I have a feeling he'll be back on the market in the not too distant future," Cat said.

"I don't date people I work with," was my response.

"I was talking about him for myself, darling. He obviously drove out here to see *me*."

Oh my Lord, was she a piece of work.

"Why *not* date someone you work with?" asked Donna.

"The odds are it'll work out a lot better for the man than the woman," I said.

"Is that so?" Cat's grin confirmed what I suspected. She had to be boinking somebody high up. Probably Ken Crewett, the general manager.

Karl reappeared a few minutes later.

"I thought you had an emergency," I said.

"I was able to fix it remotely. There are a lot of cool toys now to make my job easier. But no one can climb a tower like me."

How soon would robots start doing his work? I wondered.

He reached for his back jeans pocket, pulling out a dirty sweat-stained WILD 96 baseball cap from the first station I'd worked for. When he showed me my signature, I had to smile. It had been the first time anyone had asked me for my autograph.

"It's a collector's item!" he cried. "But you need to hire a publicist. Nobody knows who you are here."

"Thanks for the heads-up."

Cat grabbed my arm. "Time for a break."

She pulled me to the ladies' room and lashed into me. "Don't acknowledge him!"

"You're overreacting. I've known Karl for years."

"And the station has a promotion department. Don't waste your money."

I made a mental note to hire a publicist immediately.

I locked myself in a stall after she left and did deep breathing exercises to calm myself. Karl did seem to be getting weirder over the years. Maybe I couldn't see him as clearly as she did. Was he a threat? Or was she threatened by his remarks?

He was gone when I returned to our table. So was Cat. Donna was very glad to see me.

"Cat just left. Said she'd be back to get us."

"She split? This is a paid appearance!"

"It's her limo. She can do whatever she wants."

"Hers?"

"You didn't hear that from me. Guess she wants people to think she gets special treatment."

Freddy was not pleased either.

"It's her time of the month," I said.

"Hmpf. I have three daughters and a wife. I get that all the time. How do women keep jobs is what I wanna know."

"What on earth is her problem?" I asked once he was out of earshot.

Donna nodded at a pretty black woman, hair and makeup done perfectly, who was pretending to study a car.

"She's a newspaper journalist. She'd like to interview you, not Cat."

Seeing her opening, the reporter came over to me. "I'm Tiana Daniels from *The Star-Ledger* and a big fan of yours. May I ask a few questions?"

You had to be careful what you said to a reporter, I knew, especially one who dressed like she wanted to move into TV.

"Sure."

She pointed a small recording device toward me. "How's it going with Cat Cruz?"

"I'm thrilled to be working with her."

I'd be thrilled to be working with anyone in New York.

"What do you make of the rumors WBRR will change formats?"

"I hope they're not true."

"Because you could be out of a job?"

"Could be out of one, could be in a better one. You never know in radio." Did I sound too flippant? "I'd be very sad if WBRR left the airwaves. It would be like Manhattan without Central Park."

She smiled. "What about the rumors it's going Urban Jack?"

Urban meant a station geared to an African-American audience. Jack was a mostly oldies format that used names like Fred, Bob, Simon to make the station sound hipper.

"Hadn't heard that one. Sounds pretty cool, but I'm afraid I'm the wrong race."

"Even given your relationship with Mr. Ree?"

I didn't flinch. "Past relationship. We're just friends now."

"Right, you're dating the VP of Pop Promotion for MGX, Nigel Hamilton-Jones."

I couldn't hide my surprise.

"I was at the Stones party sporting my club look. So how long were you with Mr. Ree?"

She was being so nice it was hard to be mean to her. "I'd rather not talk about him. I do love his new song and wish I could play it on the radio, but it'll never happen at The Bear and I'm fine with that. I love the music we play."

"And what do you think of *The Bear?*" she asked sarcastically.

I didn't take the bait. "It's visual, which is great for radio. People won't forget it. That's what matters."

More customers and fans had gathered. We wrapped it up.

"I'll be in touch if I have more questions," Tiana said, leaving.

I noticed the time. We were supposed to be on our way back to New York soon. I had to make Ree's photo shoot.

The station's account executive who was handling Bayonne BMW showed up. Barry was still young enough not to be bloated from too much drinking or beaten down from trying to sell something intangible. Radio was invisible, something you couldn't see, touch, or eat.

"Cat *left*? No way." He handed me an envelope with a $300 check in it, shaking his head.

I gave Donna fifty dollars from my wallet.

"No one's ever done that before," she said. "I log hours for this, you know."

"You deserve more."

Thirty minutes later I was fuming. We were about to call a car service when Cat's long white limo approached.

She strutted straight over to Freddy. "I'm sorry, but that crazy fan unnerved me. I've had too many bad experiences."

Blinded by Cat Cruz's seductiveness, he replied, "No problem. He gave me the creeps, too."

Barry handed her an envelope. If he was angry, he didn't show it. She was Cat freakin' Cruz. I had to put it out of my mind that he'd probably paid her more.

We climbed into the limo. Inside, I noticed several shopping bags. Cat was wearing new shoes and carrying a different purse.

"I went to the closest mall," she said without a trace of remorse.

My mouth dropped. "You not only left a paid appearance with a sponsor but went shopping in a state with no tax on clothes *and didn't bring us?*"

"I got you something," she said in a fake sweet voice.

She presented us each with a silver pen inscribed: *The Barenaked Radio Ladies*. They were from a store called Her Highness Fine Jewelry.

"Wow!" said Donna. "This is so cool!"

I tossed mine in my bag. "Yeah, thanks."

"What's wrong?"

"You left a gig! Just left! It reflects on the entire station, which reflects on *me*."

Cat studied her French manicure. "Freddy wasn't upset."

"Yes, he was. *I* had to smooth his ruffled feathers."

"If that disgusting fan of *yours* hadn't shown up ..."

"You're just upset because that reporter wanted to talk to me, not you."

She sniffed. "No one reads that paper."

"You don't need the money, Cat," my voice steely now. "Just *leave* and let people who really want to be on the radio—"

"I've been on 'BRR for *twenty years*," she snarled, her talons clutching the edge of her seat, her tiny body stiffening. "I'm a *legend*. I'm not trying to *prove* myself to the world. If anyone should leave, it should be *you*."

Instead of raising my voice even more, I lowered it to a near whisper. "Fuck. You."

In unison, we reached for our cells, checking them. No one spoke for a while. Cat broke the silence.

"I'm sorry, Jazmyn. I didn't know it would upset you that much if I snuck away and let you get all the attention."

What bullshit.

"Hey look!" Donna was pointing to a giant billboard.

I MARRIED THE STRIPPER. NEW FROM MR. REE.

There he was, wearing an apron around his waist, a long-sleeved white shirt and dress pants. On one hip was a small child. A slightly older kid stood looking up at him, tugging on Ree's pants. Ree held a skillet with bacon and three eggs sunny-side-up, his expression bewildered.

I'd seen that look many times. It still made me laugh. Until I saw in the background a white woman I swear looked like me doing a lap dance on an ugly dude.

"Is that him?" asked Cat with mild interest. "He *is* far from scrawny."

"You were really engaged?" Donna said.

"Yes."

"They shacked up for three years," Cat said.

"Audited marriage," I corrected her.

"*Wooooow*. How'd you meet him?"

Donna's genuine interest lightened my mood.

"I started out at WILD ninety-six in Richmond, Virginia, answering the request lines for minimum wage. They sent me out to spot bumper stickers and give away prizes as Wild Wendy. I was pretty withdrawn at school. But with a mike in my hand I could talk to anyone."

"It's phallic," Cat said.

Donna giggled. I didn't disagree.

"My first station appearance was at a place called Media Mart that sold TVs, stereos, computers. I was really anxious. Ree was an employee. He immediately put me at ease by giving me pointers on how to work the crowd. When I was done, he gave me a link to his music. I heard 'The Stripper,' flipped over it, passed it on to the program director. He put it on the night jock's 'Smash or Trash' feature. Listeners voted on whether to keep playing it or throw it out."

"You're getting goose bumps," Donna said, pointing to my arms.

I smiled broadly, remembering. "It won every night for three weeks straight. Ree had a record deal before he turned eighteen. I was promoted to full time, he became a superstar, and we were in love. It was amazing. For about a year."

"Must have been great to be living a cliché," Cat said.

"We were living a *dream*."

I asked the driver to tune in Z100 on the chance they might play Ree's new song. Nigel had told me it was under consideration there.

"That is, if no one minds," I said.

Cat took off one shoe, loosened its strap. "Go ahead. That's my *son's* favorite station."

"I love it, too," Donna said, then added, "So do you think I have a shot at being on the radio with my voice?"

"Hardly," said Cat. "You should try getting a job in the promotion department."

"I disagree," I said. "It's what you say, not how you say it that matters. You'd be great on a morning show."

"Ya think?"

"Anything's possible in radio. Look at Dork. Ohmygod!"

The opening to Ree's song had come on the radio. I yelled at the driver to turn it up as loud as he could. I started to text Ree but saw he hadn't answered my last text. And there was the serious lovemaking Nigel and I had been doing.

I wrote Nigel instead. Let him tell Ree.

Z100! Ree always said there was nothing like hearing his song coming out of a radio, and Z100 was as big as it gets.

Nigel instantly wrote back: *Where do you want to go on holiday? You name it!*

Me: *The Fat Duck.*

Nigel: *I can't wait to feed you snail porridge.*

Donna loved "I Married the Stripper." Our driver couldn't stop laughing.

Cat begrudgingly admitted it was catchy. She curled her lip in what I guess she thought was a sexy smile. "You're so ambitious, Jazmyn. I bet Ree had you in mind when he wrote that."

"Yeah, I'm ambitious. Am I supposed to feel guilty about it?"

"You did leave him for a better gig."

"There's a lot more to the story."

Donna stepped in. "Speaking of stripping, I'd do the *Penthouse* pictorial in a heartbeat." We entered the Holland Tunnel, a long underground lit-up tube that took us under the Hudson River and into Manhattan. I had been afraid it would freak me out because of the tunnel tragedy in Richmond. It did. I had to close my eyes. But was it the tunnel or Donna's comment that had unnerved me? Maybe I shouldn't be giving her so much encouragement.

She could take my place as co-host at the drop of a hat. Or rather, her drawers.

12

UNFINISHED BUSINESS

Ree's photo shoot was taking place in the legendary Flatiron Building, one of my favorite buildings in New York. I savored the lobby for a moment before rushing into the elevator.

It was lined with framed vintage photos and historical information. I read that it was built at the turn of the 20th century on a plot of land that had endured snide names like the Stingy Piece of Pie, and finally the Flatiron. When construction began, people were convinced the 21- story structure would fall over, and dubbed it Burnham's Folly after the man who designed it.

I thought of the names I'd endured over the years, on and off the air. All the people who'd said I'd fail.

Arriving at the photography studio, I heard Ree's music from the other side of the door. The song playing was "Don't Go," where you think he's pleading with a woman to stay. It turns out it's his dog that doesn't want her to go.

> *I'll miss our walks, the way men look at you*
> *Made me proud and jealous, too.*
> *I'll defend you, never offend you*
> *Can't you see? He's the dawg not me*

I walked in to find several stunning women of various races draped over leather couches, some holding flutes of champagne, most of them wearing next to nothing and heels so high they could qualify as stilts. They each gave me the down-up-down checkout.

Dressed in a dark suit and tie, Ree looked like the CEO of a Fortune 500 company. About as sexy as sexy gets, next to being naked.

Nigel rushed over. "How'd your appearance go?"

"A real bonding experience."

Ree nodded at me. "Did you see the cover for the album?"

"I just saw the billboard. Great placement."

"*That's* the cover. I look like an ass."

I sighed. "It's funny. Definitely catches the eye. Did you know Z100 played it?"

He burst into a big smile. "Yeah, I heard. What did the DJ say? How did it sound?"

"I didn't catch the intro but it sounded awesome!"

That put him in a good mood until the photographer, a gray-haired veteran shooter introduced as Carmine, said, "Perhaps you'd like to take your shirt off now? Why go to the trouble to be in shape and not show it off?"

"I'm trying to project a different image."

I moved closer. "Save the suit for a TV appearance or magazine article. You have to get people's attention. You know, *work it*, like you always say."

"Sexism applies to men, too," he said.

I looked over at the nearly naked harem. "Here's what's sexist. They're hardly wearing anything and you're fully dressed."

"You're right." Calling to Nigel, Ree said, "Can you put more clothes on them?"

"Think of all the other acts you're up against," I said. "You've got an incredible body, Ree. Men show theirs off just as much as women in this business. Hell, I may do it myself."

"What are you talking about?"

I told him about the *Penthouse* offer. He looked resigned. What happened to the Ree who wouldn't let me be covered in honey and hundred-dollar bills that listeners could grab?

These were different times, that's what.

"Can I get you anything, baby?"

One of the harem women (the best-looking one) was suddenly stroking Ree's lapel. Tall and spindly as a giraffe, she had high cheekbones, full glistening lips, and almond-shaped eyes the color of gold. I'd never seen anything like them. I couldn't tell what race she was. A little black, a little Asian, and a whole lot of sexy.

She gave me a look that meant *Take off, bitch.*

"No, I'm fine." He smiled, world-class flirt.

"I'm Cheetaya. You can call me Chee. Ree and Chee has a nice ring to it."

His face was unreadable. "This is Jazmyn, an old friend of mine."

Hers wasn't. "And I'm a *new* friend."

"Nice to meet you, Cheese."

He kept smiling. "We're having an important business discussion, Chee."

"Well, excuse *me.*" She strutted back to her seat, swaying her ass to the music.

"Nothing's changed, has it?" I said.

"Comes with the territory."

Too bad the things you want to change don't and the things you don't want to change do.

"Sure nothing's going on with her?" I asked. "You're wearing cologne."

Turning on his bedroom eyes, he said softly, "I knew you were coming."

"So!" Nigel's appearance made me jump. "How are you feeling about the shoot, Ree?"

He made a face of surrender. "All right. Let's try it without the shirt. If Jazmyn can take off hers, I can too."

"Bang on, Jaz. You agreed!"

"No!" I shouted into sudden silence. "He misunderstood."

"That's the deal, Jaz," Ree said. "If I strip, you strip."

My mouth went bone dry. Then my temper kicked in.

"A topless woman is totally different from a topless man."

Ree went into a girly voice while covering his chest with his hands. "I feel so *violated*."

"You're comparing apples and oranges. You need to sell your music."

"No more than you need ratings." He started to take off his coat. "Nigel, ask these ladies to leave, please."

"They're paid by the day. May as well keep them around. Don't they help you get in the mood?"

He shot me an intense look. Nigel had to have seen it. I ran my hand over my sweaty neck.

"What's he see in *her?*" Cheetaya grumbled as Nigel ushered the disappointed ladies out, answering yet another call on his cell.

The pretty-boy assistant to the photographer patted down Ree's face with powder.

"What shall we try now?" asked Carmine.

Ree handed the assistant his jacket, shirt, tie, and designer suspenders.

"Just for the record," I said to Ree, "this does not mean I'm posing for *Penthouse*."

He threw his head back, letting out a laugh I hadn't heard in years. The combination of his gorgeous smile, face, and body exuding pure joy sent another wave of warmth through me.

He took me by the arm. I hated how good his touch felt.

"Stick to your guns, baby," he said, now that Nigel had left the room. "I'm just giving you a hard time. How could he let you do that? Where's his respect?" He undid his belt. "I know you two are in the zone. I can feel it. But he's not right for you."

Ree's pants were now history. The assistant sucked in a gasp. Ree's look said: *Let's see Nigel top this.*

Few men could.

"Damn!" cried Carmine. He walked around Ree, scoping out every angle.

"Gorgeous," the assistant whispered.

"Love the unfinished tat. Unusual."

Looking to see that Nigel was still gone, Ree pulled me to his side.

"Quick, before he gets back," he said to Carmine. "Take a few shots of us."

After three clicks I pushed him away, still smiling.

"Listen Up" came on. Its slow, slinky beat had me moving in a seductive way.

Listen up, brother, I got a story to tell
Listen up, sister, I see your livin' hell
The man that you love, he just can't compete
With your power, your money, your better-than-him peeps

I blocked out the words that I knew were about me, feeling the groove. The more I got into the song, the more Ree got into looking good for the camera. The Faithful Girlfriend to Nigel knew I shouldn't be moving like that, but the Dancing Queen couldn't stop.

I turned to find Nigel looking none too pleased.

I pulled him aside. "Ree guessed we were together. He's cool with it. I was just getting into the song."

"Good, because it's time I stopped kissing his ass and he started kissing mine." He walked over to Ree, eyed his tattoo and turned to me. "Where have I seen that before?"

Mine was covered by my shirt. Carmine and his assistant were confused. I stepped in.

"We were going to finish them when we got married, okay?"

The photographer nodded to his assistant. "We'll be in the other room if you need us."

Nigel came closer to Ree. "If you make one move, *one*, I'll make certain your song disappears off the charts. Got that, mate?"

Ree stood to his full height, a few inches taller than Nigel. "I am not your mate."

"Jaz, you can't be serious about this guy?"

When I didn't answer, Nigel stormed out of the room.

I followed him into the elevator. "It's not like you and I have been going out for months," I said. Right in front of strangers. I was a New Yorker now.

"We have enough history for you to know if this is *serious* or not."

"Of course we're serious. I'm mad because *you* asked me to come to this shoot, I love to dance, and I got him to take his shirt *and pants* off like everyone wanted."

"You have matching *tattoos*."

"From *years* ago. Before I met you."

A woman standing nearby said, "You tell him, sister."

"And what about you and Olivia? How long did you date and were you ever going to tell me?"

"Olivia? We never dated! I met her when she was an intern at WPLJ. She asked me out but I wasn't interested. I have to be nice to her, though, with her position." He was smiling. "I'm sorry. I have no right to be possessive with you, love." He nuzzled my ear. "And thank you for getting him to undress."

"Who undressed?" the woman asked.

Nigel gave her a card that had a discount code for Ree's music. I was glad to see his fury subside quickly. And I liked seeing a bit of the caveman was in him after all.

In the lobby we stopped for a quick embrace. "Ree stopped being my problem a long time ago," I said. "Please don't ask me to do anything more where it concerns him."

"Done! It's too beautiful a day to argue or sit in a limo," he said. "Shall we walk a bit and talk?"

He gave his driver the rest of the day off. As we strolled, he said, "Let's talk about *Penthouse*. The promoter in me has an erection a mile long. The boyfriend in me—"

He *did* respect me.

"—has one that's two."

"Nigel!"

"Get down, Jazmyn Brown!"

We spun around to find Krazy Karl right behind us.

"Karl, what are you doing here?"

"So this is Nigel Hamilton-Jones." He thrust out his hand. "Hi, I'm Krazy Karl. I know that's what you call me. It's okay. I'd rather be crazy than boring. Ha-ha-ha-ha!"

Nigel reluctantly shook his hand, putting a protective arm around me. He was fully aware of Karl.

"Can we help you?"

"Get rid of Cat Cruz."

"Anything else?" Nigel said, not quite as nicely.

"Don't let her get mixed up with Ree again. He's all about himself."

That seemed to warm Nigel up to Karl. "That's the way all artists are. They have to be.It's a very competitive business."

"You're not right for her either, Mr. Phony."

"Karl, stop bothering me!" I said.

Nigel pulled me into the street to hail a cab.

"There are so many famous people in New York you can stalk," I called out. "Why me?"

He looked hurt. "Stalk? I'm your number one fan. Who's number two? Who's number two?"

He succeeded in making me feel bad. There was no number two.

"Now that I've met him, I'll get a restraining order," Nigel said once we were in a taxi. "I do it for artists all the time. How did he know where you were? Running into someone you know in Manhattan does happen, but the odds are pretty long."

"He must have followed me from the Bayonne event."

"My instincts are excellent with his type, Jaz. He's nuts."

"After all these years, if he was going to do something, he would have done it by now. Cat's the one who should be concerned. He really doesn't like her. There's no need for a restraining order on my behalf."

"I'll do whatever you like. Just say the word."

I loved that Nigel had the power to make things happen. When Karl first scared me in Richmond, I'd asked the station to do something. They said it was a free country. He could show up anywhere he wanted. They couldn't do anything until he did something illegal. When he did do something illegal, most likely, it would be too late.

"They can't get to a star, but they *can* get to you," a male DJ at WILD 96 had told me early on. "Be careful."

And yet, the whole point of being a DJ is to make the listener believe you were his or her best friend. It wasn't only men who were obsessive fans. I'd dealt with women, too.

That night as Nigel and I undressed for bed, my tattoo seemed to flash like a neon light. So did something else, to me.

Near my half grapevine was a tiny scar where my birth control implant rested. I couldn't put off motherhood that much longer.

13

CATFIGHT RADIO

Monday morning, thirty minutes before our show, Cat and I were seated in Rick Rivers' office. I wondered how he managed to get Cat in this early until it became clear she had called the meeting.

She was furious over an item in the Page Six column in the *New York Post.*

> *What new DJ in town was engaged to rapper Mr. Ree, has the matching tattoo to prove it, and is now dating Nigel Hamilton-Jones, the man at MGX Music promoting his new song? If rumors are true WBRR is flipping formats, will this DJ come up smelling like jasmine?*

Had to have come from the photographer or his assistant. At least *Penthouse* wasn't mentioned.

Rick jumped in. "I assure you WBRR is *not* changing formats."

"That's not what I'm upset about," said Cat. "I have it on good authority that our jocks are getting calls on the request lines saying Jazmyn is a nigger lover and has no business on WBRR."

I inhaled sharply. Did people still say things like that? In *New York?*

"This reflects poorly on the station *and* me," she had the nerve to say.

Rick pulled at his goatee. "I'm sure there was a tidal wave of racist calls. More concerning to me is you leaving the BMW appearance an hour early."

She shot me a nasty glance. Though I hadn't told him, she obviously thought I had.

There was a knock on the door. Our general manager, Ken Crewett, strode in. Tall, athletic, and model-handsome, he was a born salesman who knew how to make anyone feel great. I could have used his magic touch right then. If only I could be sure he was on my side. I watched the eye contact between him and Cat. She acted like she wanted him, but then she did that with almost every guy.

Ken seemed respectful and professional. He repeated what Rick had said about the station not switching formats.

"Ladies, we think your show has a lot of potential. We're bringing in Tommy Tucker, the best show coach in radio, to take you to the top of the ratings."

I looked at Cat. She was in shock as well. So much for getting me canned.

I was reeling for a different reason. Tommy Tucker had an amazing track record. We couldn't have done better. However, he was also known to be the asshole of assholes.

"He and his son, Titus, will be meeting with you Wednesday before you go on," Ken said. "Be here at eight sharp. And *Penthouse* called again. They want you both for an upcoming Women of Radio pictorial. Ten grand each."

Cat and I both said, "That's all?"

Rick nearly twisted off his goatee.

"Put us with *other* women in radio?" Cat huffed. "We deserve a spread all to ourselves and a lot more money. Right, Jazmyn?"

"I'm *not* posing nude."

"You don't want national attention?"

"Not that kind of attention."

Cat squeezed her eyes shut as she sharpened the tiny knives that were spring-loaded in them when they opened. "You are so unsophisticated. Nudity is beautiful."

Rick stood, looking at his watch. "Time to get ready for your show. Just think about it."

"Jazmyn, could you stay another minute?" Ken asked.

After Cat left, Rick brought up *The Star-Ledger's* website on his computer and showed me what Tiana Daniels had written.

> *One person who will be thrilled by WBRR's demise is its newest DJ, Jazmyn Brown, the former fiancée of rapper Mr. Ree who gave the world the skin-deep songs "The Stripper" and now "I Married The Stripper."*

"Thrilled if the station went under? *No way* I said that."
"Keep reading," said Rick.
I did, with several "shits" along the way.

> *Jazmyn expects the rumored change to Urban Jack to put her in "a better job" and can't wait to be able to play Mr. Ree's songs on the radio. How will Nigel Hamilton-Jones of MGX Music, her flame who also promotes Ree's records, feel about it? We can be sure he's not upset that WBRR, known for not playing new music, has added one of his artists. Since when is Streaming the Net classic rock?*

I felt like I'd been thrown off a cliff I thought was a ladder.

"I didn't know she was a gossip columnist." I studied Rick's large window. "Does that open up or should I just dive through it?"

"You're new in town and want to get press," Ken said, "but for the time being, no interviews unless someone from station management is there."

"She put a completely different spin on my answers! Ask Donna. She was there. I did not say I'd be thrilled about whatever she said I said."

"I'm sure you're right, but we're going to have to pull any new songs we're playing that are on the MGX label."

"I have nothing to do with picking the music!"

"It doesn't look good," said Ken. "Of course, if you stop seeing Nigel, do let us know."

I ducked into the ladies' room with exactly eight seconds to compose myself.

Cat gave me a curious look when I entered the air studio. "What did Ken have to say?"

"Oh, nothing. Just some formatics."

I scanned the log to see how many spots were in the first set. Noticeably more than last week. Excellent for the sales team and bottom line, but more clutter that listeners would want to tune out, making our job harder.

"Cat, how long has Howie been your agent?"

"Long. Why?"

"I have a meeting with him soon." Nigel had urged me to call him.

"I'm sure he'll tell you you're crazy not to do the *Penthouse* shoot."

We started taking calls from listeners. It didn't take long to hear an all-too-familiar voice.

"Cat, you're a bad DJ and you know it."

I jumped in. "Karl, that's not nice. Now be polite or I'll hang up."

Cat did it for me.

During a commercial break she told me, "John Lennon was shot by a guy whose album he'd just signed. This Karl nut will take a simple hello to mean you're best friends."

"And what about that liquid dynamite he uses?" Donna added.

I had a feeling they might be right, but Sheryl Crow was on the hot line and I had to tap into my inner Dork now. I cued up her duet with Kid Rock, "The Picture."

"Sheryl, you've dated Lance Armstrong, Owen Wilson, Clapton. But Kid Rock?"

"Jazmyn," Cat used my name for once to scold me, "what's wrong with him? I think he's hot. And Pamela Anderson married him."

"Exactly. They both enjoy being caught on tape having sex. Sheryl Crow wouldn't."

"What are you talking about? I know about Pam and Tommy Lee's tape, but—"

"Kid and the singer from Creed with their groupies. Cat, you didn't hear about that? You should stop reading so much *Town & Country*. Hey, we're ignoring our guest. So Sheryl, a great tune came out of your romance with Kid that we're about to play, so who cares, right?"

She was a class act and would only give us a "No comment." Cat talked about all the great causes Sheryl was involved in.

"Yes, she's an amazing woman, we know that," I butted in. "What I think is so awesome about you, Sheryl Crow, aside from being in fantastic shape, is that you were in your forties when you hooked up with Lance, who was as big as big gets then." No Lance doping questions allowed. "Doesn't that give you hope, Cat?"

"Who said I was in my forties?"

"Oh, then you look great for your fifties."

"I am not fifty!"

"Your show should be called the Barenaked Catfight," Sheryl commented.

Because I wasn't using my real name, it didn't bother me so much to be obnoxious, especially when Rick Rivers rushed in after Sheryl's call.

"Wait until Tommy Tucker arrives. You two are going to kill in the ratings. Kill!" He pretended to bare his claws, hissing and meowing angrily.

Cat said, "It's funny for two seconds. The listeners are revolting. They can't stand her!"

"Let's see." He pushed a request line button so we could listen on the speakerphone.

"Uh, man, play some Bruuuuuce. Are you really naked?"

Suddenly the room was filled with static.

I spun around, trying to figure out which button I should push, or what fader wasn't up, cursing until the music was going again.

"Now calm down," said Rick. "You're still not used to this board."

"I told you I should run it," Cat said.

"I'll never be used to it! It's so old and backward, I feel *young* and in the way."

He rushed to the wall of CDs and handed me one.

"Cue up 'Layla.' It'll give you time to regroup. It's seven-ten with a cold fade but jump in before the final tweets. Only the hard-core purists get pissed if you talk over it and there are only two of them left."

We received no fewer than ten irate calls from listeners complaining "You cut off the tweets!"

When the end of our show approached, Cat dashed over to the aircheck deck when my back was turned and pulled out the tape, infuriating me. Listening to my show was a ritual.

"That's mine," I said.

"I'll give it back to you," she lied. "How am I supposed to critique myself?"

"Obviously you haven't done that in years."

I lunged for the hand that was holding it. She was so tiny, I easily knocked her to the floor with me falling alongside her.

We were writhing around when Maxx barged in, bellowing, "My E-ZPass account was hacked. Two hundred dollars crossing the Verrazano in a week? Like I go to Staten Island. Had to—what the hell?"

All he saw were bare legs thrashing about.

"Gimme that!"

"It's mine!"

"No one's going to have it on tape that I'm fifty!"

I stopped struggling. "You are?"

"No! But they'll think it after that remark of yours."

Madd Maxx howled with laughter. His producer, Charlie Chaplin (real name Charlie Kaplan) walked in, looking his nervous self.

"Get a load of this, Charlie! We'll open with it and save E-ZPass for next hour."

Without any mention of his never going to Staten Island so as not to piss off listeners there.

Bowing slightly, Charlie handed him a pair of gold-accented headphones that fit his ears like a stethoscope (so they wouldn't mess up his fake hair, rumor had it). The gesture reminded me of James Brown's sidekick handing him his cape back in the day. Scurrying over to the microphone Cat had been using, Charlie unscrewed it, replacing it with Maxx's own microphone — a Neumann with gold accents that matched his headphones. The mike cost around $10,000. It was rock radio, I thought, not the damn Metropolitan Opera simulcast.

"With all the compression on the radio signal," Shane had told me, "It doesn't make one bit of difference what mike he uses. But it sounds good in *his* ears."

His Majesty did shoulder and neck rolls, loosening up for his "performance."

Trying to get through the door at the same time, Cat and I bumped into each other, falling back on our asses again. After she ran out, I started laughing so hard I almost peed. Charlie picked me up and pushed me out the door.

"Get out before Maxx does his break," he hissed. "He hates having people in here."

As I walked down the hallway toward the ladies' room, I heard Maxx's opening salvo.

"Anyone watching our webcam out there?" he said. "Hope you caught the end of the Barenaked Radio Ladies." He let out a practiced laugh. "And they pay me to do this?"

I raced to Rick's office. "The webcam was off, right?"

He tapped his goatee. "Hmmm. I think I turned it back on during your last song."

"You *think*."

One thing was clear. There was no one at this station I could trust. Maybe Shane. But that was it.

14

THE UGLY TRUTH

The Barenaked Radio Ladies did indeed generate media buzz. Negative buzz.

HOW LOW WILL RADIO GO? was one example. The newspaper critic thought it was blasphemous to trash up a legendary station like WBRR. Readers agreed, saying they tolerated Dick and Dork's juvenile antics because that was what a lot of morning radio shows were like now. To have that kind of bad taste spread to the rest of the day was intolerable, they wrote. Sprinkled among the vitriol were "Cat's still smokin' hot" type comments and "Jasmine's bloom has died, rotted, and needs to be thrown out now."

Could this be one of those really, really bad radio "fixes" that made the problem worse? Would my career go down in flames with it?

Rick popped into the studio before we went on the air and said, "The local Fox station will be here soon to do a piece." To me he added, "All press is good, Jazmyn. It'll blow over."

"Oh, crap," I said. "I don't have enough make-up on for TV."

"You look beautiful." Cat was gloating. She added after he left, "I'm always prepared for cameras. If it's not a TV crew, then it's someone snapping a photo or wanting a selfie with me."

"So *that's* why you wear more make-up than a clerk at Sephora."

I'd have to start doing the same.

Pablo Delgado from Fox was a longtime Cat fan and friend. Though he was warm to me, I caught a trace of pity in his eyes when he said, "It's not easy being new in New York. This is a tenure town. Refusing to go away counts for a lot."

For the good hour that he stayed, my answers were pretty lame. I was paranoid about saying anything that might be taken out of context. But if I played it too safe, I'd be edited out — even if we were only wearing big bath towels wrapped around our middles. Yes. I swear.

"Do you really not get along with Cat or is it an act?"

How was I to answer that? If I said it was an act, then I was a fake. If I said it wasn't, I came off as a bitch. And why didn't he ask her the question, too?

Because she had seniority in tenure town.

"Who says we don't get along?" I laughed. "Okay, there might be a little friction, but it's like sibling rivalry. There's a lot of mutual respect here."

Cat added, "People can't keep living in the past. This is a fresh approach."

"The show is all in fun," I said, "and a lot more interesting than saying, 'And here's another forty-minute rock block.'"

What ended up in the *twenty-second* clip? Cat showing plenty of cleavage, cooing, "People can't keep living in the past. This is a fresh approach." And a split second of my face, so pale it looked like flour had been thrown on it.

Plus the video of us wrestling on the floor during the Maxx changeover, which also made it clear we didn't do the show naked. If only talk of a *Penthouse* shoot would disappear with this bad press I was getting.

I was ushered into a spacious office overlooking lower Fifth Avenue. Super-agent Howie Kamen came out from behind a large antique desk and shook my hand. He was instantly likeable and dapper, as I expected. We settled on a dark-brown leather couch dotted with gold pyramid-shaped metal studs all over it.

"Let me give you the Big Picture," Howie said. "I can see you hosting TV shows and recording lucrative national voice-overs. Only a handful of radio personalities take home big paychecks. You're at the perfect age to take it to the next level."

He talked about opportunities: entertainment reporter for a local TV station, TV shows that needed hosts, radio co-host in Boston.

"Leave New York? I just got here. I've been dreaming of this since I was sixteen."

"Full-time radio openings don't come up here that often."

"But I have a radio job."

"What if 'BRR flips?" he asked. "The predictions are it'll go Young Talk or Urban Jack."

"The Young Talk audience is what? Twenty to forty. That's me."

"It's not easy for talent to switch formats in New York with so much money on the line."

The main ingredient in talk radio was controversy, he said, which meant being ticked off three to four hours straight every day. Not many women could do that, or rather, *wanted* to do that. Most successful ones were advice-givers.

"You're too late to the party. The major talk platforms already have all the women they're going to hire."

"What about Wendy Williams and Angie Martinez?" I countered.

Before she made it big in TV, Wendy had been dubbed the female Howard Stern of urban radio. Angie was the Queen of Hip Hop radio and had recorded her own albums.

"Why can't I do what they've done, a music show with personality but at a rock station and afternoon drive?"

He repositioned himself on the sofa. "I believe the last time that happened in New York City on a commercial rock radio station was when Meg Griffin was at K-ROCK." He squinted as he searched his memory bank. "That was the mid-1980s."

No way. Before I was *born*?

"It's time for a change then."

"I wish it was that simple. Delilah's the pinnacle for a white woman playing music. Nurturing and not a wise-ass."

He was referring to the nighttime smooth-talking syndicated host known for dedicating love songs to her listeners and promoting the adoption of children.

"Jazmyn, this isn't *my* view," he said, "but the attitude prevails that minority men are used to sassy women. Only white men who are gay can handle them."

I missed his next few sentences as I mentally dislodged the pickaxe that had landed between my shoulder blades.

When I tuned back in he was saying, "Ariella was one of my first clients. What a career she had. Stunningly beautiful. Interviewed everyone. Dated plenty of famous men. Didn't make the kind of money the guys made because she wasn't given the prime slots. Lower ad revenues, lower salary." He shook his head. "Now she's doing the graveyard shift for scale. Is that what they're paying you?"

Scale? *Ariella?*

"A hundred grand, with bonuses."

"Bonuses you'll probably never see. I'll push you into a higher salary but you need to think about where you're going beyond WBRR." He started pacing the room, like a lawyer trying a case. "The odds are very long you'll ever host an afternoon drive show in this market. If you want to increase them, get TV exposure. You'd probably do well. You have a big head."

I searched for a snappy comeback. "If I don't believe in myself, who will?"

"I meant the actual size of your head. Larger heads look better on TV. Though a strong ego doesn't hurt if you keep it in check."

To think all this time I'd been focused on my big ass and thighs.

He stopped pacing, eyeing me. "Are you sure you don't really want to do TV? I see it often with radio people. They like being a star and still having their privacy."

"Am I pretty enough to be on TV? All the women are knock-outs. You don't think I need chin and cheek implants?" To balance out my big damn skull.

"I have to see you on camera. Some of the most ordinary people look fabulous."

Was he saying I was ordinary?

"I can recommend a coach who will tell you flat out if you have potential."

Trying to sound upbeat, "No point in working all my life to get to New York if I'm not going to make the most of it." He liked that. "But I draw the line at posing for *Penthouse*." I pounded my fist on the arm of the leather sofa and hurt myself on a metal stud, pretending not to notice.

He sat beside me. "If you did it, no one could say you're not a knockout. You would end up feeling better about your appearance. Most women who have posed nude say it helped their career, not hurt it."

He told me to talk it over with my parents and friends. What they thought was often what worried women the most in these situations.

"I think you're very attractive, Jazmyn. *You* had doubts you were pretty enough for TV. But if I may be blunt, you're a nobody. The ink your show got is old news. National exposure would help considerably in renegotiating with 'BRR. And let's not ignore the fact that radio as we know it with a transmitter and an AM/FM dial may not even exist in another ten years."

I'd heard that dire prediction for years.

"Whatever form it takes it will still need talent to play music," I countered. "It can't all be digital readouts and voice sweepers."

"The number of positions for DJs is rapidly disappearing."

"All the more reason to make a name for myself now."

He smiled. "Okay, you've convinced me you're in it to win it." He said he could get me at least fifty grand for *Penthouse*. "Save it for lean times. And there will be lean times." He straightened his Hermès tie. "Unless you marry well, like Cat did."

He walked to his desk, punched a button on a device, and asked his assistant to summon Josh, the head of the voice-over department.

"Working with Tommy Tucker is a golden opportunity," Howie said as we waited for Josh to appear. "You have spunk. Maybe you *could* swing middays in a talk format."

"Why is it always middays? I want afternoons! Bigger audience. Bigger paycheck."

"Why not mornings? That's the biggest."

"For the main star, but I'd be the co-host or side chick."

A rare exception to that on-air formula was the caustic Darian O'Toole. She had been hired to do mornings in New York City in the late 1990s as that station's answer to being trampled in the ratings by Howard Stern. She didn't last long in the Big Apple. She wound up in San Francisco and an alcoholic. She was dead by forty.

Josh Osterbach swept into the office and sat in a chair across from us. A Truman Capote look-alike (but taller), he seemed thrilled to meet me.

"You have a fantastic voice," he said. "I had three auditions today I could have sent you on." Then came the reality check. "It takes a while for radio people to break into the VO biz. Casting agents are looking for actors. You have to prove you have versatility and a well-honed inner clock. If they say trim off half a second, you do it. That's where DJs have an advantage."

I needed separate demos, he told me, for commercials, promos (for upcoming TV shows), narrations, radio imaging (with a different demo for each format), and character voices, if I did them.

"Each one should be under a minute," he said. "And get your own website."

I promised to give them an answer soon and left Top Talent in a daze. I had a bad feeling.I wasn't sure why. Something told me I had to talk to Ree.

"Have you made my single your ringtone?" were Ree's first words.

I trilled "Me-me-me-meeeeee!" like an opera singer warming up.

He laughed good-naturedly. "I've waited ten years for my career to pop again, just like you've waited as long to get to New York. Download 'I Married the Stripper' as soon as you can. Record companies look at that chart as much as any other."

"I know, Ree. Who do you think you're talking to?"

"My first true love."

I got choked up, until I heard a woman's raucous laugh in the background.

"Sure, I'll download it," I said icily. "It'll help Nigel's bonus."

"You really know how to hurt a guy."

"From the sound of your company, you don't seem to be hurting."

"That's Tamara Slaughter, my publicist."

She was a legend in the music biz PR world. I could hear her talking to someone. Ree pulled her away. "Just for a second. Tell this person you're not my woman."

I heard her say, "No, I'm your servant."

She got on the phone. "I'm married with two kids. The last thing I want is a rapper boy toy." To him she said, "Who is this anyway?" Then, "Ohhhhh!" like she knew all about me.

Ree got back on the line. "I have to run. And thanks for talking me down from my high horse. You know it's my insecurities. From now on, I'm listening to whatever you say. If only I could get you to listen to what *I* say, like Nigel's not for you long term."

"Excuse me, but there's a reason I called you. I wanted your opinion on what this big agent says I should do."

"Ree. Hang up *now*," Tamara said. "Are you purposely trying to screw up your career?"

She was right. Ree needed Nigel one hundred percent on his side. Anything less, and what was surely his last chance to make it would vanish. If I really cared about Ree I had to stay away from him. And what advice could he give me that Nigel couldn't?

"I'll call you later, Jaz."

Before I could say "Please, don't" he had hung up.

Nigel's beautiful two-bedroom condo was on the 48th floor, not far from where Cat Cruz lived, with a spectacular view of Manhattan. Millions of lights twinkled as far as I could see. Warming my tummy was a fine cognac we sipped while cuddling on his comfy couch.

"What a vision," I said.

"In the daytime, when the fog rolls in, it's like being inside heaven."

"It's fascinating to see the change between the day and night views. It's like one city recedes and a completely different one emerges."

This was a long way from those awful apartments I'd lived in before the Westwoods'.

I had expected Nigel to have a high-tech, sleek, masculine place, filled with signs he was in the music business. It seemed more like what his parents' manor house in England must look like, with antiques, swag window treatments, and beautiful large plants.

I had also expected him to be furious over the WBRR ban on MGX adds. He laughed it off. "It was a knee-jerk response that will blow over in a day. I'll simply withhold something at another station that they want and all will be fine again."

Blow over it did. It had been an exceptional week for MGX Music chartwise. Nigel had taken me and his staff out earlier for a lavish dinner at a trendy restaurant where the food was piled into neat, layered towers. At another table had been Trudie Styler, Sting's wife. Nigel smoothly talked her into coming on my show.

It was moments like that, and this one with Manhattan glittering below us, when I felt I'd hit the love jackpot.

Okay, all those new mattresses I bought in each city I worked in? It wasn't just because they wouldn't fit in my Cruiser. The "clean slate" thing had to do with washing away the vibes of whatever guy I'd chosen as my bed partner for the duration of my stay. I was taking care of my needs. Physical therapy. Was Ree being celibate? Of course not. Without sex I would have been even more miserable. At least that was my thinking.

I never did find someone in Houston. There was something about the upscale environment I was living in that made me feel embarrassed to have a guy slithering in and out of there. The men post-Ree/pre-Nigel had ranged from a grease monkey to a doctor. Never a co-worker. Never. There was one thing they had in common, though. They thought what I did for a living wasn't real work. When I'd try to ease them out the door so I could sleep, they'd say things like "Yeah, must be exhausting to push buttons and listen to Mariah Carey."

Even when I was with Ree, our pillow talk was usually about him. Or us, but what we would do once this and that happened for *him*. Nigel was the first man who focused on me and my career as foreplay.

It was quite an aphrodisiac.

I put down my brandy snifter and gave him a sexy smile. "I've been meaning to tell you, your decorator has great taste."

"*I* did it." Nigel playfully pinned me to the sofa. "I'm the total package, love."

I toyed with the collar of his white button-down shirt no longer tucked into his jeans and studied his face. Man, was he easy on the eyes.

"You do have exceptional assets."

"Did you say I have an exceptional ass?"

"That too." His hands slid down to rest on mine. I felt a jolt between my legs.

"Yours isn't too shabby either."

"Mmmmm, thanks for the Trudie intervention," I said. "I never would have done that."

"Helping you in any way is a pleasure. Tell me about your meeting with Howie."

I spoke more to the ceiling than to him, but we never stopped touching each other in some way. "Nigel, I've spent a long time focused on being on the radio in New York. Now I'm here and Howie thinks I should do other things. I don't see myself as a TV host or pitching products. And I surely never wanted to pose for *Penthouse*."

"You know what Howie's job is, don't you? To make you feel a little insecure."

"That makes no sense."

"It's true in any business. It makes you more open to negotiation. However, Howie *will* get you a better deal at 'BRR than the one you have."

I was learning a lot from Nigel. "I'm so lucky to have you."

We kissed. And kissed. I loved kissing him. He was a friend, lover, advisor, and would also be a good provider during those "lean times."

"I'll support you in whatever you decide," he said.

My hand wandered south.

"Howie suggested I talk to my parents about the nude photo shoot. I'm nervous, Nigel. That tells me it's not a good idea."

"Whether you do it or not, WBRR isn't forever. You do need to stand out," he said as he moved my hand to where he needed it most. "Look at it as building infrastructure. Laying the wiring, so to speak."

"I need to lay something else right now."

He pulled me up and toward his bedroom. The Grand Coulee Dam was about to burst.

I had expected him to be a neat freak, but again he ripped off the covers and threw me on the thick mattress. We couldn't get naked fast enough.

"You're so sexy," he said. "I've wanted you from almost the moment we met."

"Almost?"

"It was those exotic Eskimo sounds you made with Pink that hooked me. Do some."

"Urrrreeeeaaaah. Urrrrrrrr. Ahahahahah. Urrrrrr."

We broke into raucous laughter, which brought us closer. Soon I was at the brink of ecstasy. He made sure I was satisfied first, then topped off his performance with a lighthearted "Jolly good!"

The first time he'd said it I thought it was funny. Now I tried to make a joke, hoping he wouldn't say it every time. "I bet the neighbors will be saying the same thing, Nigel."

"Yes, you do know how to show your appreciation."

"Am I too loud?"

"A woman can never be too loud."

I snuggled close, about to say, "That was incredible," when he said, "You're incredible." It struck me as far more romantic.

He draped his arm over me, his warm breath on the back of my neck as we spooned. I couldn't help thinking how it used to feel with Ree.

Shit!

Neither one of us could get back to sleep. Was his insomnia catching or was it the dull city roar outside that I still couldn't tune out? At two a.m. I announced I was heading to the station to work on new VO demos. It was the only time the studio would be available.

"Also, there's one other person I want to consult regarding Howie," I told Nigel. "Ariella. He used to be her agent."

He sat up. "I hear she was as bad as Cat in the bitch department."

I slid my feet into new $400 sandals, courtesy of Nigel.

"If she's really seventy, surely she's beyond that."

"Maybe she's worse."

15

White Bird in a Golden Cage

Walking around a radio station in the middle of the night is eerie. You hear the show on the air playing in every hallway, the lights are on, but the place is empty, as though evacuated. Occasionally you'll see a janitor.

I walked by Rick Rivers' office door, which was closed. Stopped. Backtracked.

On Olivia's desk, just outside Rick's office, was a framed photo of her, Rick, Nigel, and Streaming the Net. Just how deep did her feelings for Nigel go? Why didn't it concern me the way it would have with Ree?

Because I felt secure with him, the way it should be.

My heart fluttered as I approached the jock studio in anticipation of meeting my idol. I peeked through the small window on the door. Ariella was sitting in semi-darkness, her eyes closed, blasting Pink Floyd's "Wish You Were Here." She looked too serene to interrupt. No way was she in her seventies. Sixties, *maybe*.

I wondered what memories she was reliving. Hanging out with the band? I'd lost a lot of respect for Floyd after hearing about the lawsuit that raged between Roger Waters and the other members over who could use the giant flying pig at concerts.

Ariella segued into Cream's "Strange Brew." She saw me, motioning for me to enter.

Toned and vibrant, she wore jeans and a colorful long-sleeve open shirt over a black tank that showed she still had all the right curves. Layers of turquoise necklaces almost camouflaged the thin silver cord attached to her reading glasses. She had several rings on both hands.

She extended one toward me. "Hi, Jazmyn, I'm Ariella. Saw your photo on the website." She eyed me. "I like the Jean Harlow hair. I had it once when I was young enough to pull it off."

There wasn't a trace of a bitch in her, I thought. I took in her beautiful, full, strawberry blond locks. "Thanks. Your hair looks great."

I'd later find out it was a wig. One of dozens that she owned.

She slipped on her half-moon reading glasses to check the time left on Cream. As she did her next break, she pick up a piece of paper with notes scribbled on it and said hello to the night crew at a Brooklyn diner, a guy up late writing a screenplay, and a couple in Connecticut awaiting the birth of their first child.

"Did you know someone in Queens yesterday tried to prove it was so hot you could fry an egg on the sidewalk?" she said to her invisible audience. "It took awhile, but it did indeed cook. What happened to it then?" Her voice turned mysterious. "We can only imagine. Look for another sweltering repeat performance today ..."

I considered how many thousands of times she'd talked about the weather on the radio and still managed to make it sound fresh and visual. The incurable radio geek in me was blown away.

A promo for the Barenaked Radio Ladies started her next set of commercials.

Peering over her glasses, "What happened to women's lib? One minute we were burning bras, the next we were having wet T-shirt contests."

"You have no idea how much I wish I'd been on the radio in the past when there was still such a thing as class," I said.

"Class on the air, perhaps. You have no idea how much harassment went on. And how little women were paid." She banged closed a CD case. "Some still are."

I kept my mouth shut.

"Welcome to The Bear, Jazmyn." She made a comical face. "Judging from what I heard with Cat, you're not only a great DJ but a tough broad. That's a compliment coming from me."

She had no phone op or producer, so I pulled her CDs and put them away for her. She still cued them up in the players. How many thousands of CDs had she retrieved and put back, and albums before them? I could tell she had a hard time making out the tiny print on the covers.

Every time she had to read one, she touched a remote button that raised the lighting in the studio. When she was done, she lowered it to restore the hip mood. There was a slight tremor in her hands.

I was hit by two thoughts. It was so cool she was still doing this, but I wasn't sure I would still want to be doing it at her age.

What else could I do?

I banished that thought as she cued up the "Rain Chant" from the 1970 *Woodstock* soundtrack.

"Were you at the festival?" I asked.

"Oh, sure. I was barely out of high school. What I remember most about that crazy weekend, besides our chief engineer Victor going from a Nixon-loving nerd to a flower child, was the absence of sponsors. They didn't even sell T-shirts, much less ones for fifty bucks."

In no time she was dishing out career advice as the songs played.

"Go with Howie," she told me. "Make as much as you can for as long as you can and *save* it. New York can suck a bank account dry like that." She snapped her fingers. "He was a great agent for me until I was too old."

There was that warning light flashing again.

"Did you ever think about doing something completely different?" I asked. "I do, every time I've been fired."

"I thought about being a psychotherapist a long time ago. You should hear listeners spilling their guts to me in the middle of the night."

"I think about doing something with animals. I like pets more than people sometimes."

"How about becoming a veterinarian?"

"Me? I wish. I don't have the grades or the money for school."

"Me neither," she said. "I opened a boutique in Chelsea, figuring no one could take it from me and I needed extra income. They tripled the rent right as I found out I had breast cancer. Had to close the store. The medical bills nearly bankrupted me, but I beat the Big C. Well, there's always a chance it can come back, or something else will try to take me down. So when 'BRR offered me overnights at scale, exactly what I'd earned thirty years before, adjusted for inflation but still scale, I took it for the medical benefits. Then something happened I never expected." She paused for effect. "I fell in love with being Ariella all over again."

The warning light vanished.

Wait. I was making more than the legendary Ariella. For how long?

Blink, blink, blink.

She eased up the fader for the rain chant, checked the time.

"My surgeon was a damn DaVinci." She pushed out her chest. "I feel sexy again, though the only guys who meet my standards aren't interested in someone my age." She looked at me with a happiness that surprised me, given what she'd said. "Doesn't matter. I had *plenty* of good lovin' in my time. Enjoy every minute of it while you can."

Bam. Ree's naked body popped into my head. Then Nigel's. I told her about the *Penthouse* offer. She shook her head.

"They asked me years ago. I had my lofty feminist ideals then. Today, the world can watch you screwing on the Internet and it boosts your career." She looked me over. "I'd find it hard to turn it down if I had the body, and you have the body. But if you're not comfortable, don't do it."

Her frankness was catching. "I don't understand why you're not set for life. You're *Ariella*. You had syndicated radio shows, a TV show, you wrote a column for a national magazine, did national voice-overs."

She adjusted the volume as the rhythmic chanting of the drenched Woodstock goers cross-faded into Santana's "Soul Sacrifice." Had I gone too far?

"It's simple," she said. "I spent more than I made, and lousy financial advisors lost the rest. I made one really good investment that my boyfriend at the time tried to talk me out of. I bought a little bungalow out on Montauk at the tip of Long Island for twenty-five grand in the seventies. It's worth a hell of a lot more now, though I hope I don't ever have to sell it."

"Surely you could have married well."

The comment hung in the cold studio air.

"Like Cat Cruz did? I came into this business when women wanted equality and independence, not marriage and kids. We had to work three times harder than a man and put up with four times more bullshit. But I have no regrets."

Even when her breaking down the door for other women to be on the radio then diminished her unique and powerful status? I couldn't ask.

"Nor did I sleep with anyone to get ahead."

I perked up. "Are you saying Cat did?"

"Oh yeah," Ariella said, "Cat's given it to every PD she's worked for, several rock stars, even Madd Maxx."

"No!"

She put her finger to her lips. "Shhhhhh."

"I knew it."

"And I made it with Dick and Dork at the same time. I just hope I was good."

So began my unforgettable friendship with Ariella.

"In other words," I said, "New York is no different from any other market. I wonder what's going around about me?"

"The worse, the better, I say."

I loved her attitude. "Speaking of Maxx, how much do you think he makes?"

"Three quarters of a mil, plus a lot of voice-over gigs."

"You're kidding."

She seamlessly segued into Zep's "Battle of Evermore" from their fourth album, one I couldn't recall ever hearing on the radio.

"What about Cat?"

"About a third of that. They justify Maxx's salary with a consultant title and expect him to draw stars to events," she said. "These days, he'd be lucky to get the bass player from a Zeppelin cover band to show up."

I was so caught up laughing I almost didn't catch her wince and tap her tummy.

"Anything wrong?"

"Just indigestion. Knew I shouldn't have eaten that Gray's Papaya hot dog with sauerkraut, but they're so damn good and the cheapest meal around. Never buy a hot dog from a street vendor that keeps them in water. Full of bacteria. You'll pay later."

"Thanks for telling me. There's mint tea in the kitchen here. Can I get you some?"

Now there was an edge in her voice. "I'm not helpless."

"I was just—"

"I'm only letting you pull the music and put it away because I've done it so many times I'd rather scrub grout. Now I know how Sisyphus felt. But I'd rather have it this way than on a computer.

If I can't touch the music with my hands, how can I connect with it?"

"Really? I'd much rather have the music on a computer."

She peered over her glasses again. "I just love feeling old."

Changing the subject, "What do you really think about The Bear idea?" I asked.

"We're on a sinking ship, I'm afraid. If I'm lucky, I'll end up on satellite radio, but they'll grab Maxx first. It'll be a sad day when this station goes under. Nothing lasts forever. The way you and Cat fight on the air, I have a feeling they're grooming you for Edgy Talk."

A tingly heat spread across my scalp. Part of it was the sadness over the station going bye-bye, but also why hadn't Howie said *that* instead of saying I was too late to the party and all that other negative stuff? Had he been trying to make me feel insecure, as Nigel said was his job, so I'd be thrilled to take any job?

I didn't want to do Edgy Talk. I wanted to be a female Madd Maxx, but not an asshole.

Ariella got on the subject of how sexist radio used to be.

"I remember when rock stations wouldn't hire a female announcer because a study showed that men didn't like the frequency range of the female voice over the air. How would they have known if they'd never heard one? What made that argument go away was when they realized women would work for a lot less. We've come a long way, but not long enough. It still applies to voice-overs. More men than women are hired, and often paid more. One producer told me, not that long ago, 'Men don't want to hear their wives tell them what to do, so why should I have a woman selling my product?'"

It couldn't be that bad. I had to play devil's advocate. "Radio is sexist for men, too. I know several who were passed over for a midday job because they didn't have a uterus."

She looked at me, bemused. "Think about what you just said. Middays. Less money. A woman's job."

"Okay, what about Rush Limbaugh? He made his mark in middays."

She smiled. "I happen to love Rush as a performer. Look, there are always exceptions and the world is always changing. Don't give up hope."

During The Animals' "House of the Rising Sun" I asked her opinion on what to do about Krazy Karl.

"There's no need to be mean. I say a silent prayer to guys like him. *I salute the light within you.* That, and a can of Mace, should do it."

I asked her about the key to the production studio. She said to talk to Shane.

"It's almost five. He's usually here by now. He gets in early to beat the traffic and leaves in the afternoon before Rick and the sales department pile more work on him."

"He seems like a really nice guy."

"The best. If only I was younger and he was single." She shook her head. "So sad about his son. But if I can beat cancer ... That little boy is getting the best possible care."

She wrote down her cell number, telling me to call, or come back, anytime. I left the studio beaming.

Until I heard her next song: "White Bird" by It's A Beautiful Day.

White bird must fly or she will die.

I stood there in the hallway listening as a funny feeling bumped around inside me. One I couldn't understand and didn't like. I decided it was just a growing pain, a part of life. It's not all hearts and kisses, honey. And it was just a song.

Shane was unlocking his studio door when I found him. "What time do you get up?" I asked.

"Three-thirty. It's the only way I can get everything done."

"I'm sorry about your boy. I'm sure he'll be fine. Children are incredibly resilient."

"Far more than any parent." He forced a smile. "What brings you in so early?"

"I need to use the other studio to make a laundry list of voice-over demos, according to the VO agent at Howie Kamen's."

"I have some scripts you can use."

He flipped through a stack of paper, picking out copy for me.

"Signing with Howie is a good idea. I had my agent listen to your show. She loves your voice, but right now she's repping several women she thinks sound like you." He paused. "I don't think anyone sounds like you."

"Aw, thanks."

"I'll put those demos together after you lay down dry tracks."

Ariella and Shane were two of the nicest people I'd ever met in this business. They made up for Cat Cruz.

I stopped by my mailbox (yes, an actual mailbox) to see what hate mail or invites to see an un-signed band play had come in. I saw an envelope with Krazy Karl's childish handwriting on it. No return address, as usual. Enclosed was a printed copy of an X-ray of his organs. The tiny holes in them were circled.

In the next moment my face was hot from embarrassment. His note that said *See? I'm not lying* was addressed to *Fatty Patty*. How did he know? She died the day I became Wild Wendy.

With Karl and his lack of filters, she was unlikely to stay that way.

16

TRUE CONFESSIONS

I'd sworn I wouldn't call Ree again, but I broke my vow before our meeting with the consulting guru Tommy Tucker. Nigel didn't know the reason for my alarm over Karl's note. Only Ree knew about Fatty Patty.

It sounded like he was in the middle of a party when he answered his cell.

"I'm at Mo's L.A. *chalet*. Shall I send him your sweet, everlasting love?"

"Ha."

Big Mo' Mack, a minuscule rapper who made Kanye West look pretty, had been living out of a beat-up Camry when Ree discovered him, back when we were together. His career quickly eclipsed Ree's. I loathed him almost as much as Ree did.

"How can you hang with him?"

"It's strictly business." His voice darkened. "The drugs are heavier than ever, Jaz. I had to come out by the pool."

I pictured hot women with practically no clothes on, or naked, surrounding Ree.

"You should hear him." He imitated his thug voice perfectly. "'We was tourin' Europe and went to CAP-ree. Dat's how ya says it, dawg. CAP-ree, not Ca-PREE. Know what I mean?' ... He can't even speak English and he's telling me how to pronounce Italian. But it's Hollywood, baby. Everyone loves everyone in public."

"What about in private?"

"Why does that concern you, Miz Brown? Did you dump the Brit?"

"No." I told him about Krazy Karl's letter. "He was outside the Flatiron after your photo shoot. He must have followed me from the Jersey event. How did he know about Fatty Patty?"

"I'd be more worried about him hurting you."

"He'd never hurt me physically, I don't *think*, but calling me Fatty Patty hurts me in other ways. It's just plain mean."

"Guys always tease girls they like."

"I can't let anybody know, especially Cat."

"You should be proud of who you are. People will look up to you, not down. And once it's out, you don't have to worry about it anymore."

"That's easy for you to say. You were always good-looking."

He let out a groan. "Baby, please don't go down this road again. I know I was a jerk in the past, but listening to you be insecure wasn't such a picnic either."

"With women hitting on you all the time and you flirting back? Who wouldn't be insecure? I put up with a lot more than most women—"

"Hey, look who's here. Cheetaya. Should I call her cheese?"

Was she really there?

When we hung up, I still had no idea what to do about Krazy Karl.

Or Mr. Ree.

To my surprise, Cat was on time for our meeting with Tommy Tucker. However, he and his vertically challenged son Titus, heir to the Tucker Transformational Talk empire, were running late. The slogan in their trade ads said *Our personalities don't beat the competition. They demolish them.* Tommy was pictured blowing up a radio tower with TNT. His tiny son was next to him, holding his hands over his ears, pain on his scrunched-up face.

Cat and I sat before microphones at a table in the extra production studio, sipping water with Rick and Donna as well, trying not to look nervous.

"The conference room is in use," Rick said, "and we'll have total privacy here ."

"I'm so excited!" Donna chirped. "I mean, I'm pinching myself night and day!"

Tommy Tucker had heard her girlish voice, loved her on the spot, and christened her Donna D. She was now wearing way more revealing clothes and heavier makeup. If she kept twirling her new hair extensions nonstop, I was going to pull them out one by one.

Okay, I was just jealous. She was officially an AFTRA union member repped by Howie Kamen, this girl with hardly any on-air experience, and making at least what Ariella was making. Maybe even what I was making (now at 125K, half of Cat Cruz's salary).

The heavy door swung open.

"Why shouldn't I increase my fee?" Tommy boomed into his cell phone. "I increased your ratings fifty-two percent and saved your ass. Goodbye."

What an entrance. Was there really someone on the other end of the line?

Tommy was so tall he could have played pro basketball. He came closer, arms spread wide. "My latest challenge! Three *beautiful* women!" He looked at the ceiling. "As if God hasn't blessed me enough."

Titus Tucker followed him. He appeared even shorter next to his dad. They were both sporting gray suits, skinny black ties, white shirts, and vintage Ray-Ban sunglasses. Between their matching outfits and slicked-back hair, they could have been members of a 1950s doo-wop group.

I could feel Tommy eyeing me lecherously behind his shades. "Know what we have in store for you ladies?"

We looked at each other, shook our heads.

"Afternoon drive on the Beeeeeeeear."

Rick stood up. "Uh, Tommy, it's not a good idea to say that just yet."

Tommy leaned on the table, his arms so long he would only have to move a few inches to be right in our faces. I got a whiff of a pungent odor, like he'd just eaten a pastrami sandwich or been hitting the bottle.

"Let's not pussyfoot around," he said. "It's *personality* that counts, not how well you can segue two songs in the same key." He stood up and thundered, "Rule Number One! Never learn the music! People tune in for what you have to *say*, not what you have to *play*. Titus. Number Two."

Titus sounded like his dad, deep and loud. It was strange coming out of someone so tiny. "If something's questionable, run it by me. I'll make the call."

"Like broadcasting two listeners screwing at St. Patrick's Cathedral," Tommy said, referring to the stunt that had led to Opie & Anthony being removed from the airwaves for quite some time. When you had to fill up almost 1,000 hours of shock radio every year, something was bound to go over the line.

I looked at Cat and Donna. They were both pushing their upper arms together so their breasts popped out. I rigidly leaned against my chair, arching my back to make my own more well-defined through my tight tank top. I was also wearing my short animal print skirt I was convinced had magical powers.

"This is my favorite part of a new working relationship." Tommy strode around the small room, oily radio voice booming. "It's like being given a mound of fresh, wet clay." He looked at Rick, not us. "Or in this case, a hunk of the highest-quality marble. All it takes is the right chisel and *Venus de Milo* will appear in *triplicate*."

It was hard not to laugh. He was a freakin' cartoon, and all too real.

After Tommy asked Rick to leave, Rick nodded at the phone. "I'll be in my office."

Alone, Tommy asked us to write down a question for each other, no holds barred.

"Before we start," I asked, "What about the flip rumors?"

He took off his sunglasses. His eyes were a muddy brown; the whites bloodshot. Unsettling as it was to talk to him with shades on, this was worse.

"Urban Jack ain't happening. Sonic doesn't have one urban in its cluster here. Where's the core alliance with advertising? All it has are stations for whites and Hispanics, and there are plenty of Latin stations already. Talk is the only possibility. All the more reason for you to focus on your content and not the music. The better it is, the better the chances you'll survive."

Ariella was right in her Edgy Talk prediction.

I wrote down my question to Cat: *Tell us about the love of your life.*

Tommy read what each of us had written, replacing his sunglasses. "Okay, Jazmyn. You ask first."

Cat took a moment to compose herself after I'd spoken.

"My sweet, wonderful Vee," she said. "Short for Viorel. He was a successful Romanian businessman. My parents worked for him, as servants, really. When they fled Cuba and came to America, no one would hire them. My father had been studying to be a lawyer and my mother was a nurse. They didn't speak English, but Vee had Gypsy blood and spoke Spanish. He always treated them well. He watched me grow up and fell in love with me. I loved him too but not in that way. Or so I thought."

She looked down, sniffling, and reached for her purse, pulling out a tissue. What a performance.

"He was diagnosed with lung cancer and given six months to live. He begged me to marry him and have his child." When she looked up, her eyes were rimmed with tears. "Then I fell in love with him the same way."

"What's going through your mind now, Jazmyn?" asked Tommy.

I wanted to say *Go back to acting*. "How long did he live after you married?"

"Eight years. He said my love cured him. He died of something else. Kidney disease."

Tommy said to his son, "You take over, Titus."

"Very moving story, Cat, but this is the moment when you have to bring levity to the situation. Figure out a way to get a laugh, then go to commercials or a song."

What could possibly be funny about this?

Cat stiffened. "Ask me to take my clothes off, fine. Make fun of my late husband, no."

Tommy slid into the seat next to his son. "Stay away from the deep questions, Jaz." Asking someone about the love of their life was too deep? "But as long as getting naked was brought up," he looked at me, "what's holding you back?"

"I have enough wackos to deal with. And it doesn't feel right."

"If you want to be a real star," he said, "you'll have a thousand more freaks bothering you. You need to decide how seriously you take your career."

I'd never been accused of having that problem before.

"Real stars can afford bodyguards," I said.

"When you're a *real star* you'll have the means, but first you have to become one."

The Cheshire Cat Woman couldn't suppress a grin.

I forced one of my own. "What's your question for me, Cat?"

Tommy handed it to Titus. "Hmmm," he said, intrigued. "She'd like to know why you were so lonely growing up."

I pretended not to know what she was talking about.

"You said the radio was your best friend and you were withdrawn."

My conversation with Ree came back to me. I was surprised to hear myself blurt out, "Because I was fat."

There. It was done.

"How fat is fat?" she asked.

"Fat enough to be teased about it."

Tommy jumped up. "Think of how great it'll feel to stick it to those assholes when they see you in *Penthouse!* Finally, you can say *nah*-nah-nah-*nah*-nah."

His son added, "You'll be a *role model*, Jazmyn!"

Ree's exact words.

"And men will desire you more than ever," Cat purred. "After I posed nude, the quality of men I attracted went up a hundred points. Rich, fabulous, educated men."

Was there something wrong with me? If that was what made a guy want to know me better, I wouldn't give him the time of day.

I looked at Donna. "What about you?"

"If they paid me, sure. I took my shirt off for a spring break video and didn't get a dime."

The Tuckers turned toward each other, pupils turning into dollar signs as they asked Donna what other adventures she'd had.

She'd bungee-jumped, sky dived, and wanted to join the circus when she was a kid.

"Radio's pretty close," Tommy said.

"What's Donna's question?" I asked.

"It's not that interesting," she said in her childish voice. "What's a radio *cume*?"

Titus rested small arms on the table in front of her. "There are two factors that make up radio ratings. Cume is how big the audience is, the cumulative number. TSL is time spent listening. Think of a cock, Donna. Cume is how big it is, TSL is how long it stays up."

"This is it!" cried Tommy Tucker. "Cat's the sexpot. Donna's the wild girl who's innocent, but not too innocent. Jazmyn's the Extreme Makeover nerd and voice of reason."

"What?! I thought I was the bad girl who asked the questions no one else would."

"No, Donna D. will be the Dork. By the fall rating book all the kinks will be worked out. Titus, show Donna how to edit this all up."

They were recording us the whole time. Conference room was in use, my ass.

17

GETTING PAST THE PAST

Before I followed Howie's advice and called my parents about the *Penthouse* spread, I searched the net for stories of women who had posed nude and how they felt about it later, particularly famous women. I knew the only opinion that mattered was how *I'd* feel about it, but *they'd* gone through it.

Jenny McCarthy posed for *Playboy* when she was twenty "to pay off my college debt," she told Wendy Williams. Again to buy her parents a new home, and a third time, at age 39, to pay for her autistic son's tuition. In a *Huffington Post* piece, she described the last shoot as gorgeous, classy, elegant.

Why would Cat want to do it again? She didn't need the money. Had to be the ego trip of it; needing to know she was still hot at her age.

I searched for "nobodies" like me who had posed nude. The ones saying they felt empowered far outnumbered the ones who regretted doing it. Most of those said they couldn't handle all the fame it brought them. In my case, that was the point, wasn't it?

I easily conjured up sad, lonely Fatty Patty. She was always lurking in the shadows. I *did* want to purge her from my system forever. I *did* want to stick it to all those jerks who'd picked on me at school, the boys who sent ten pizzas to my house.

I called my parents in Richmond at 5:30 sharp, before Daddy had his after-work drink. He'd still be in his stubborn work head. It would increase the odds he wouldn't approve.

Mom answered. I told her my dilemma.

"Oh, my word," she said. "Well, I still look at photos from when I modeled. I know I'll never have that body again, but at least I did once."

When she'd met my dad she'd been a department store model. Their wedding photos showed them at a normal weight. But once I was born, my mother ballooned from a size eight to a fourteen and kept on going. Dad had followed suit and so had I.

"Mom, you had clothes on then. Big difference."

"Patty, please."

" It's Jazmyn."

"Oh, you and your names. I can't keep track."

"You wouldn't mind if the whole world saw me naked?"

"It's not the whole world. I don't read *Penthouse*. Nowadays girls walk around shopping malls wearing practically nothing. Pretty soon you'll be able to Google someone and read their entire medical history and tax returns. That's worse than being seen naked."

"Not to me."

"That reminds me," she said, "someone from your high school alumni club called. They're doing a story on you with then-and-now photos. Don't worry, I sent him one from ninth grade when you were at your thinnest."

I hadn't been thin since I was three.

"He talked so fast, this young man. I could barely understand him."

A bad feeling spun in my stomach. "Was this guy's name Karl?"

"I don't remember."

I imitated his run-on way of talking with deep breaths every few sentences.

"Yes, that's exactly how he spoke."

"Mom, that was Krazy Karl!"

"Oh, sugar. I'm so sorry!"

That's how he'd found out about Fatty Patty. "Did you save his address?"

In all his letters to me there was no return one, and that made me uneasy. I'd told myself he'd be easy to track down through his employer and not to worry.

"I scanned the photo and emailed it to him," Mom said. "I have his email address. Oh, darn. I should have known better. He did sound overly exuberant."

"Don't give *anyone* any information about me unless you ask me first! And let me decide what photos I want out there of me, okay?"

"You have my word, Patty. I mean, what was it?"

"*Jazmyn.* With a Z."

"A what?"

"Please put Daddy on the phone."

My last hope of backing out of the photo shoot was hearing him say no.

"So how's your fifteen seconds of fame going?"

"It's fifteen minutes. Going great."

"Yeah, I never thought you were a showbiz type. Sure proved me wrong. You're making more than I am."

"For the moment. It could all go away tomorrow. So, what type did you think I was?"

He pondered that. "I saw you as more like me. A corporate type."

"You mean a frustrated corporate type."

"A realistic corporate type. I knew I couldn't make a decent living as a trombone player." I heard him crack a smile. "I was good enough to impress your mom, though. That's what mattered. She said you wanted to ask me something."

I took a deep breath and told him.

"*Penthouse?* Why not *Playboy?* More tasteful."

"I don't have a say in who does it."

"Get at least a hundred grand."

"The idea itself doesn't bother you?"

"Of course it does, but I understand your business—and you—better now. It's all about being *cool* and looking good."

"You're being a fuddy-duddy!" Mom called out in the background.

"I'm being her father!" he yelled back. "So you'll never be able to run on a political ticket," he said to me. "Hell, I wouldn't be surprised if it didn't matter now anyway."

"Daddy, I can't believe I'm hearing you say this."

"The president of my company is black. I had to get with the times or be out of a job."

I felt my heart race. "How would you feel if I was dating someone black now?"

After a long pause, "If you love him and he loves you *and* treats you like a queen *and* has a good head on his shoulders *and* is a good provider and generous, you have my blessing."

He took a sip of his happy hour whiskey as I opened the refrigerator to find a cold beer. This deserved a toast.

"I saw an article in the paper about Ree's new song," he said. "From 'The Stripper' to 'I Married the Stripper.' What range."

"Oh, Daddy."

"I'm saying this because I love you and it kills me to see you hurt in any way. Please don't jump into getting married right away. Everything's great now. Wait at least a year until the hoopla around this song dies down."

"I'm not seeing *Ree*. I'm dating someone else. I think you and mom will really like him. But I did run into him recently and he's completely changed."

My father's answer took me by surprise. "My worry is, have you?"

I thought about that after we hung up. Did he think I was still obsessed with being *cool?* That was part of the DJ job description. Fuddy-duddies need not apply. As for looking good, everyone wants to look good!

"The world is still a racist place, no matter what you think," he'd said when I was with Ree. "You're making life harder than it already is if you stay with him."

"*You're* a racist," I'd said.

Now we'd seen a black man become president of the United States. If someone had a problem with Ree being black, that was their issue. Not mine. My father was probably mad at himself for not fulfilling his trombone playing dreams.

Another exchange from long ago came back to me. When Ree and I were dating and my dad had heard how rough Ree's childhood had been with a Welfare mom, her abusive boyfriends, deadbeat dad, constant evictions, he issued another warning.

"You're dealing with a man with serious issues you can't fix, Patty. Very few people can get past their past."

That was what bothered me the most. Could we *both* get past our pasts?

18

THE MYSTERIOUS SPARK

Nigel and I were officially a couple. No more hiding. No more nights sleeping alone, except when he was away on business. When he was, it felt strange to have a bed all to myself.

His parents were coming over from England soon. He couldn't wait for me to meet them. He even suggested my parents come up for a visit, offering to fly them in. I didn't tell him they could barely fit in an airplane seat.

"Let me treat them to a show. Whatever they want to see."

Those seats weren't comfortable either.

"Let me check with them," I said.

A part of me hoped my parents wouldn't be able to make it. I was sure their obesity and lack of highbrow culture (something I was sure the Hamilton-Joneses possessed) would mute any wedding bells. Not that it should matter. He was marrying me, not them. On the other hand, if I didn't meet their expectations for a daughter-in-law, it was better to know sooner than later. Oh hell, if that was the case, I didn't want to know ever.

Did I love Nigel or did I just love being his girlfriend and all the wonderful window dressing that went with it? Did I truly need him or did I just need him the way someone tossed into a shark-infested ocean needs a lifeboat? Was I merely starved for someone who made it all about me because I was still deeply insecure?

There was another way of looking at it, I told myself. The way successful women like Cat view life. *I deserve this kind of treatment because I am a goddess. Damn straight it's all about me.*

How Nigel responded to my parents would clarify a lot.

Cat's assessment of Nigel? "You could do better."

"At least he's not older than my father."

That exchange wouldn't make it on the air. Putting Nigel in a bad light to the world would surely come back and bite her in the ass. A prized interview would go to someone else, an all- access pass would be denied.

Despite the media flogging, our show was gaining steam with the general public. We weren't always taking swipes at each other. One popular feature on our show (that Cat took credit for) was He's Got Legs, where men sent in photos of their legs, and sometimes more. We critiqued them while talking over the instrumental part of "She's Got Legs" by ZZ Top. Another was Collectomaniacs where we unearthed weird rock memorabilia being sold online. How about $7,000 for David Bowie's "Rebel Rebel" Mexican 45 with the orange label. Or someone asking a million dollars for the Partridge Family's Screen Gems records.

"Hey, Cat," I said on the air, "I bet you've got a stash of cool vintage stuff. Why don't we auction off some of it and give it to charity?"

I detected a moment's hesitancy as she crafted her response. A zinger had to be coming.

"That's a great idea, Jaz. What about you? Oh, sorry. Our audience wouldn't be interested in a Justin Beiber T-shirt."

The phones lit up with parents wanting just such a T-shirt for their daughters, and older women wanting it for themselves.

To my delight, Nigel had been listening. He came through with a Justin tee. Then listeners started sending us items we could give away for charity. Yes! We had lift-off.

As the talk and commercials increased, the number of songs we played each hour decreased. Edgy Talk was coming. Between celebrity news and the endless stupidity and greed in the world, we never ran out of topics.

Donna D. rarely took Cat's side or mine. Not having an opinion made her less interesting, and she knew it. To compensate she attended the Coney Island Sideshow School and learned how to swallow swords, eat fire, and walk on broken glass. She also stood by the entrance to the Holland Tunnel at rush hour in a bathing suit to see how much men offered her for sex, their crude comments all caught on tape.

"How else am I going to make a name for myself and earn a decent living?" she told me. "I won't make side money announcing with my squeaky voice."

If I wanted to be a female Madd Maxx, she wanted to be a female Dork.

Would we ever see their paychecks? Probably not. Not only was Dork paid a seven-figure salary, he was off work by ten a.m. and spent the rest of the day playing the stock market. He had amassed a fortune that would last him several lifetimes. Dick, however, had a cocaine habit that had started when he was first switched to mornings. Afraid he'd sleep through his alarm, he'd snorted coke all night to stay up, certain he'd stop once he adjusted to the crazy hours.

That was eighteen years ago. No wonder he looked like death warmed over.

The moment our last on-air break ended, Cat vanished from the premises. I usually hung around a bit to schmooze with people at the station. Everyone but Maxx.

Shane and I had become good friends in the course of working on my voice-over demos. He was a true pro, pushing me like no one had before. We got on the subject of how we became radio geeks. Our stories were similar. Growing up, he considered the

DJs on the radio his real friends. Sometimes he talked into a hair-brush pretending he was on the air.

"With my *voice of God*, as I often heard I had, a lot of people told me I should be on the radio. I didn't think I was hip enough, nor godlike."

Instead, he had gone to college and majored in comparative religions.

"One day a professor asked me to narrate a short film he was making about St. Ignatius, founder of the Jesuits. He offered me extra credit. It ran on a local TV station in the wee hours as public service programming. Next thing I knew, the TV station was calling me to be their voice. I didn't even know what that meant!" He laughed at the memory. "That led to a local advertising agency throwing money at me. But it was too sporadic to consider as a living. A producer told me I should get a job on the radio and do voice-overs on the side. That was in St. Louis. Bounced around a lot before I landed here."

"What was your air name?" I asked, as I sat back on a small sofa that looked like it had been around since the 1970s. There were a few stains on its fabric I did not care to identify.

"The first was Shane Steele. Made me feel invincible. The last, Shagadelic Shane, made me feel like an ass."

"I can see why."

"I was replaced by a voice-tracker in Washington, D.C., and decided to take a chance growing my VO biz instead of looking for another on-air gig that would end the same way. I got lucky when this job opened up. The pay is fantastic, I can do freelance work, and I don't have U-Haul's toll-free number memorized."

I shared a few reasons I'd been axed or passed over for a job throughout the years.

"Not the right ethnicity. The general manager's wife didn't like me. I accidentally offended a sponsor. And, of course, the voice-tracking to save money line."

We indulged in more BTB (Bonding Through Bitching) and lamented that DJs all over America were losing their jobs to voice-trackers.

"Or worse," he said, "to no DJ at all. Just someone like me barking imaging statements. Don't tell anyone, but once in a while I crank up my pirate station, change my voice electronically, and have fun."

Anyone could podcast on the Internet, but to have a real radio frequency beaming out of your home? *That* was cool.

He handed me a flash drive with my demos. "Your down payment on a Manhattan apartment is in the hands of fate. Let me know what happens."

"With the flip rumors flying, I hope something does."

"I live by the Zen *koan* that every day is a good day."

When your child is fighting for his life, the drama of radio must seem obscenely petty, I thought, but didn't say. I was afraid we'd both start crying.

Mega Casting took up an entire floor of a high-ceilinged five-story building in Chelsea. There were people of all ages and types waiting outside various rooms. Stage moms hovered with their child actors.

I found the audition for Kwell and signed in. I had no idea what it was, nor did Josh's assistant, who had called me with basic info: where to go, when, that it was a national TV VO (which could mean tens of thousands of dollars in residuals), and that they were looking for "a young mom."

What could the product be? "*Kvell* means to burst with pride in Yiddish," Josh's assistant said. "Maybe Kwell makes you super proud of clean kitchen floors or something."

My guess was it got rid of bad smells or was a hair product that stopped the frizzies.

I looked at the talent I was up against. Most were women my age. The direction on the top of the script said: *Educated but not snobby. Caring but not smarmy. Distraught but not hysterical. Warm but no smile.*

Okaaaay.

The narrative was told from the perspective of a mother who never in a million years thought she'd need a product for killing a scabies infestation on her child.

"Scabies!" I cried out.

My gut reaction was to bolt. I could feel the other women eyeing me to see if I would. Was Josh testing me to see how picky I'd be?

I called Nigel for guidance.

"It'll be a funny bit when you're honored with an award some day, love." He took a beat. "But don't be surprised if listeners start sending you bottles of it."

I called Josh's assistant. "Kwell is a *scabies* ointment. I think I'll pass."

"Ewww. No problem," he said. "Thanks for calling. It gives us time to get someone else out there. Another one came up you'll love. They want a female DJ! How's that?"

"Perfect. What's the product?"

"MTV Video Music Awards."

"I'm there."

I saw Ariella as soon as I walked into Dawson Casting. Waving, I looked over the signup sheet. Already on its fourth page, it reflected a Who's Who of New York radio women, plus a lot of names I didn't recognize. The last name on the sign-in sheet with a check mark next to it was Cat Cruz. That meant she was inside auditioning.

The first line of the script read: *What nominee for best new artist has a collection of bellybutton lint?*

I sat next to Ariella. "Do you know what new artist has a collection of bellybutton lint?"

"Nope. Nor old artist," she said. "Could be made up. They don't want the real copy circulating." Impatiently she hit her rolled-up script against her palm. "This is a waste of time, you know. I only do these to let casting agents know I'm not dead. They want a *parody* of a DJ. The real scream is when they ask for 'an Ariella type' and I don't book it."

The woman sitting next to her overheard her comment. "I was in a print campaign once," she said in a weary voice. "They called me in for the TV audition. There I was, a life-size cardboard cutout. They said, 'We're looking for someone like her.' I said, 'I *am* her.' I didn't get the job."

And I thought being a DJ was a wacky way to make a buck.

"Want to grab a coffee after?" Ariella asked.

"I'd love to, but as soon as I'm through I have to see an on-camera coach to assess my potential."

I couldn't quite read her expression. Was it envy or pity? Or both. Her "good luck" was equally as cryptic.

"Has Cat been in there a long time?" I asked.

"Long enough." She lowered her voice. "When she first came on board at the station, I was very nice to her, refusing to encourage the catfight the guys at the station wanted to see. Then I started getting offensive mail and phone calls. Then the GM got them."

"How offensive?"

"Oh, her *Playboy* photos with comments like 'Move over you dried-up old hag.' If they were just to me, I could handle it. But to my boss?"

"You think Cat was behind it?"

"It doesn't matter. It's what got me thinking about opening my store."

The door to the casting room opened. Cat strutted out and gave us a big phony "Hi!"

The casting director was a hardened older woman with hip glasses and super-short hair. She softened when she called Ariella into the auditioning room. It was clear they went way back.

Cat was out of there in two seconds with a "Gotta run. My driver is double-parked."

After she was gone, I heard another woman say dramatically, "My driver is double- parked!" It was followed by laughter from the DJ clan. I could tell who they were from having seen them on the Internet or in *Billboard.* I moved in their direction and introduced myself.

It didn't take long before the BTB started. Snarky remarks ranged from how few VOs were for women and no one expected to get this gig, fewer paid appearances, the social media they were expected to do nonstop. One well-known DJ told me she'd been out of a full-time job for years after the station she'd been on for a decade disappeared into radio heaven. She was getting by on part-time work and voice-overs.

I was tempted to call my agent to get back into that scabies audition.

I also considered standing up, like I was at an A.A. meeting, and stating *I'm Jazmyn and I'm a disc jockey.*

Despite the bitching, there was a warmth, a camaraderie, I could only feel with other female DJs. I loved it.

One said to me, "Sorry to hear about the flip rumors, especially when you just got here."

Another added, "And having to work with Cat."

Forty-five minutes after my call time I had my shot. "Say your name and slate it 'Take ninety-three'," the casting director said, not at all interested in who I was or my attempt to chat her up. There were ninety-two reads before mine?

I read one line and she cut me off.

"Be *more* excited. *More* over the top. *More* DJ-like."

She wanted parody, as Ariella had predicted. I did what she asked, ridiculous as it was.

"Great. Thank you."

"That's it?" Other women had been in here a lot longer.

"You nailed it."

Her tone was clear. I'd blown it.

I was finding it hard to make appointments on time. It often took thirty minutes to go one mile in a cab, and any time I hopped a subway, the train would be pulling out of the station, making me wait, wait, wait for the next one. So when I triumphantly arrived at the Upper West Side brownstone of on-camera coach Darla Sharp with seven minutes to spare, I was surprised she was scowling at me.

"I'm here for the coaching consultation. Do I have the wrong address?"

"No, you have the wrong *time*."

"Oh, no. I thought—"

"You're *early*. Can you walk around the block and come back when you're supposed to?"

So I did, while feeling like a complete fuck-up.

I had been expecting a polished, cosmopolitan, well-dressed woman — the way she looked on her website that claimed she had coached some of the biggest names in the business. This Darla had a face that had never seen Botox, or not for some time (you could *hide* things in the two vertical lines between her eyebrows). An inch of gray roots framed her face. Faded blond hair was haphazardly pinned up and her plump body was stuffed into a tight gray sweatsuit.

She took me to a cramped, bare-bones studio in her basement: a video camera on a tripod, a teleprompter, a couple of lights, and an old desk.

"This is temporary," she said. "I'm in the process of merging with another company and moving. It's insane. Wait here."

While I did, I heard a screaming match go on above me between her and a young boy I assumed was her son.

She returned sipping a huge mug of coffee. There was a softer air about her. "Sorry I wasn't very cordial when you arrived. You'll understand if you ever have kids. That is, I assume you don't already. You wouldn't have arrived early." She briefly smiled.

I shook my head. "My career is all-consuming. The thought of trying to do both terrifies me."

"Your instincts are right. Even if you have a partner, they require time and effort, too. Especially a man."

She began reeling off her story while briskly positioning the monitor, clipping a mike on me, and adjusting the lights.

"I was a TV reporter. Did a story on foster kids. Sit over there. Decided to adopt one. Kid had major issues. You need to be higher. Put that telephone book under your butt. Couldn't do my demanding job anymore because I was single and had no support, so I started coaching for a big company. It folded and I had to strike out on my own. Not easy. Look at these scripts."

"What about makeup?"

"This is to see if you translate well on TV. Makeup can't manufacture that indefinable *it* quality. What's your name?"

She scribbled it down on something as a loud thumping started directly above us. Her annoyance returned. She flew up the stairs. Screamed at her problem kid, who gave it back in kind.

She raced back down to me. "I hate the summer now. No place for him to go." She stood by the camera. "Ready?"

"No. I was distracted by all the—"

"You think a newsroom isn't distracting? You think being out on the street isn't distracting?" A thought ricocheted through the pinball machine of her mind. "You brought cash, right?"

"You don't take credit cards? Pop money?"

She wasn't happy. "There's an ATM on the corner. I usually charge one-fifty but because of the circumstances I'll take twenty off."

I had just enough cash on me.

"Don't yell at the camera. Pretend it's right in front of your face. You seem nervous. The camera sees all, knows all. Chin down, chin down. You look like a horse neighing. Imagine you're on the *Today* show and no one messes with you, but don't lose your warmth. Strong and warm, that's the goal. Pretend you're being paid eight million dollars a year."

Trying to get the image of a horse neighing out of my head, I read a script about police thwarting a suicide bomber on a commuter train.

"You're not a hard news person," she cut me off. "Why are you here again?"

"I'm a radio DJ. Howie Kamen thought I should explore TV."

She nodded. "Entertainment fluff stuff." She took the scripts and rummaged through another pile. "Try this."

She handed me a story about Martin Scorsese's documentary on Bob Dylan.

"You lit up on that one," she said when I was done. "You're a Dylan fan, aren't you?"

"Major."

"Be that way with every script you read."

I tried.

"Come on, Jazmyn. You don't like every song you play on the radio, do you?"

"Mostly I do. If I don't, I say very little about it."

"You can't do that on TV."

She asked me to read a story on models and their fight against the fur trade. As I delivered the copy, her eyes were closed.

"Let's watch it back," she said. After we reviewed it, she shook her head. "How do you really feel about fur?"

"I don't own any because I can think of better ways to spend my money. I eat meat and wear leather so I can't justify having a problem with fur."

"Your conflicted feelings came through. You're not a good enough liar. Plus, you don't have that spark TV people have. Stick to voice-overs. That's why they sent you here. Agents want to know right away if there's potential. No sense in wasting every-one's time and your money."

I thought I was used to abrupt dismissals, but apparently not.

"I have no spark?"

"Not on camera."

I tried to get her to change her verdict. "What if I got chin and cheek implants?"

"If it made you feel a hundred percent better about yourself, maybe it would help, but again, I can't promise it would." She glanced at the last frozen image of me on the screen. "A camera is a funny thing. It either throws its mojo on you or it doesn't. If I were you, I'd count my blessings you're not right for TV. It's a cruel business."

I gathered my things, happily resigned to a life in radio. I didn't want to do TV anyway.

"You seem to know this business very well." I turned to her before I left. "There's something I'd like your opinion on."

I told her about the *Penthouse* offer. A big smile lit up her lined face, startling me.

"That's a whole other ball of wax! With Photoshop, makeup, lighting, and the fact that you're young and *naked* — it's impossi-ble to look bad."

"I was thinking more about how I'd feel in the future, like when I'm a mother."

"Wait here."

A few minutes and more screaming later, she returned with a large manila envelope. She ripped the staples out with her ragged fingernails. An issue of *Hot Young Babes* was inside. She flipped to a pictorial of a young woman in a cheerleading outfit doing dirty things with a baton.

"That's me."

I saw no resemblance whatsoever.

"Have to keep it hidden from my boy, but look at how gorgeous I was!"

Not to mention a natural blonde.

"It's depressing getting old." She slid the magazine back in the envelope as if it were a rare onionskin manuscript. "I keep telling myself to burn this, but there's something, I don't know, nostalgic about it. I felt so good about myself then. So sure. So powerful. I could seduce any man, any camera."

My mother had said something similar.

"You went into hard news after having done this?"

"Changed my name, hair color, hair style. Plucked my eyebrows differently." She put a finger to her lips.

At the door she said, "Despite how it may appear, I really do love my son. I wanted out of what I was doing. I love being a mother more than anything. I tried being the Yuppie mom, all nice and concerned. It's not his language." She shrugged. "We all make our choices. Good luck."

I wandered down the street in a haze, as though my youthful notions were sloughing off and I was molting into an older, tougher version of myself.

It was hard to get three things out of my mind for the rest of the day. What she said as we parted, the way she looked in her *Hot Young Babes* days, and the words *You have no spark.*

19

INDISPOSED

The New York Hilton teemed with the funky chic crowd that had gathered for a star- studded roast to benefit the T.J. Martell Foundation, a music business favorite that funded research to fight leukemia, cancer, and AIDS. The man being roasted was Mickey Green, chairman of MGX Entertainment, parent company of MGX Music. With his notoriously vindictive nature I wasn't expecting the insults to go very deep. After asking me to punch up his roast speech, Nigel watered down my changes to lame, safe remarks.

I couldn't put my finger on what was dampening my initial feelings for Nigel. His calling me "love" all the time, that I used to adore, was starting to bug me. And if he said "Jolly good" one more time after he we made love ...

Was it that I wasn't feeling for him what I'd felt for Ree? I was seventeen then. Ree was my first love. I'll never feel that kind of passion again. But I could be on a remote island selling coconuts with Ree and still have fun. If Nigel and I really did retire to a B&B in the English countryside, would we be happy?

Tonight I was wearing a Versace dress he'd given me that would have prompted my father to say if he'd seen it, "That's a pretty slip. What are you wearing over it?"

How was the impending meeting of our parents going to go?

Nigel was looking quite handsome in a tux. I felt the jazzed crowd stealing glances at us. Pointing out various members of the New York radio talent pool, Nigel squeezed my hand tightly. His was uncommonly damp.

"Don't let go of me, love."

Was he coming down with the flu?

He kept his right arm around my waist and a program in his free hand. When anyone said hello, he nodded and raised his program instead of extending his arm for a handshake.

"Have to use the loo," Nigel said.

I looked at his stricken face. "You're turning green."

Before I could check his forehead to see if he had a fever, he dashed off.

I couldn't worry about him for long. I was soon approached by people who knew who I was. "Welcome to New York, Jazmyn. You sound great!" More guests crowded around me echoing the thought.

Cat was probably above attending something like this. I shouldn't be surprised she hadn't shown up. Then I looked at the program. She was introducing Steven Tyler.

More time passed. I called Nigel. He sounded terrible. "Are you okay?"

"Positively breezy."

"Where are you?"

"Room 875. Couldn't use a public loo, if you know what I mean."

"Oh, no."

"Tell me how you got over your fear of public speaking."

He sounded desperate. Mr. Smooth afraid of speaking to a crowd? Tonight did promise a galaxy of stars. Set to perform, or roast Mickey Green, were Adam Levine, Cher, Steven Tyler, Lady Gaga, and the one who rattled Nigel's nerves the most: Sir Paul

McCartney. There were also a few up-and-coming acts, including Mr. Ree performing "I Married the Stripper."

"I can talk to anyone one-on-one," he said. "Put me in front of an audience? I turn to jelly. I worked with a coach. It all goes back to a traumatic moment in my childhood when I stood in front of my third-grade class to give a report on photosynthesis and couldn't pronounce the word or remember a thing I was going to say. Then … let's just say I didn't get to the bathroom in time. I was humiliated. Do the roast for me. It'll be a great break for you."

Nigel had never seemed vulnerable to me before now. I was touched, relieved even, that he wasn't perfect. Neither was I. But give his speech?

"I'll leave the script outside my door," he said. "Make sure you say I had *food poisoning*. But first tell the person in charge what's going on. Then come get the speech. Call me when you're on the way."

I spotted a woman wearing a nearly invisible headset and the look of a killer.

"Fuck!" she reacted to my news. "You're not doing it. Nobody knows who you are and we already have a 'BRR jock."

She stalked away. I ran after her.

"Mr. Ree would do a fantastic job."

"He can do a rap song, not roast *the* Mickey Green."

She disappeared, swearing at whoever was at the other end of the headset.

I spotted Ree in the crowd of poseurs. He was in a tan business suit, looking drop-dead. He stopped talking with a hot young woman the moment he saw me.

"Miz Brown!"

The woman glared at me as he gently maneuvered away from her.

"Food poisoning, right," he said, when I told him about Nigel.

"I swear, Ree."

"A little birdie told me Nigel has a world-class fear of public speaking."

I said nothing.

He whispered in my ear, "When you're ready to leave him, you know how to find me."

He started to walk away. I pulled him back.

"You could have a top model or famous actress on your arm right now. And they'd be better for your career. Why me?"

He turned on the look that always laid me flat.

"I don't want them. I want the woman who fell in love with me and believed in me when I had nothing. The woman who defied her father to be with me. The woman who has the other half of my tattoo on her arm. The woman I think about every single day. Got it?"

I watched him swiftly disappear into the crowd. I got it all right.

The woman Ree had been talking to gave me another hateful look. Could I put up with all that again, too?

I called Nigel to tell him there was no need for me to come get the speech. "I'm a *nobody*," I said.

He apologized for deserting me and said he'd see me tomorrow. The lights in the lobby flashed and we hung up. I did a double take. Was that Shane over by the bar in a tuxedo?

"Thought I'd support a good cause," he said.

I admired him from his polished leather dress shoes to his mother-of-pearl buttons to his clean-shaven face. He was quite pleased by my reaction.

"You look fantastic, Shane. And you have the cutest dimple in your chin."

"I wanted to make sure my razor still worked."

"Don't ever grow a beard again."

He was honestly embarrassed, which embarrassed me. He was married!

I looked around. "Where's your wife?"

"At the hospital with Charlie."

I smiled. "Charlie. What a cute name. Do you have a photo?"

He brought out his wallet and showed me one of the cutest little boys I'd ever seen; a Renaissance cherub with a head of golden curls and mischievous sapphire eyes. That this child should suffer for one second was shattering. My eyes flooded with tears.

"He's missing the hair now," Shane said. "He loves his 'chrome dome' so much he says he's going to shave his head when it grows back in."

I managed to say, "What a trouper."

"It's effortless for him. Or so it seems."

"How old?"

"Five."

The lights flicked on and off several times.

"This is great timing, Shane. My date is indisposed. Would you like to sit with me?"

"It would be my pleasure." He offered his arm.

We were seated at one of the best tables, right by Cher. Shane was respectful without being an embarrassing starfucker. She told him about a charity she was involved in called Get-A-Head that helped people who had diseases of the head and neck. He told her about Charlie and his brain cancer.

I nudged him. "Show her his photo."

"He's adorable," Cher said, getting as emotional as I did.

I scoped out the other tables nearby while they bonded. Cat was at the best possible table for a classic rock DJ, with Sir Paul, Mickey Green, and Steven Victor Tallarico, a.k.a. Steven Tyler. She and Steven kept leaning into each other, whispering and laughing. Sexy in a low-cut red dress, Cat kept touching his upper arm, which was soon resting on the back of her chair.

She came over to our table to introduce herself and say a brief hello. "You look fabulous, Cher," Cat said. "You're welcome to come on my show anytime."

I turned to Cher. "That would be *our* show." She raised an eyebrow.

"You're still new in town, Jazmyn," Cat said. "There's a six-month probation period in New York. Most don't make it." She shot Shane a sexy smile. "Nice to see you getting out."

"Do you want me on as a guest or a referee?" Cher asked after she walked away. She leaned over. "You have my sympathies. Working with a woman like that is—"

The room went dark and the crowd roared, cutting off our girl talk.

Mickey Green was a classic rags-to-riches-to-rags-to-riches story. He'd been married several times, sired children in and out of wedlock, had overcome a cocaine and gambling habit, gained a lot of weight and lost it, and had an unauthorized biography published that prompted him to write his own. Whatever was brought up tonight was sure to be public domain.

The applause was thunderous when Cat strutted out.

"Hi everyone. I'm Cat Cruz from the Barenaked Radio Lady show on WBRR."

Lady.

"It's an honor to be here tonight with my clothes on for a change." That got a big response from the men in the well-lubricated crowd. "Though I might make an exception for our next guest. Ladies and gentlemen, Steven Tyler."

He kissed her before taking over the mike, a full-on tongue tangler. Miz I-don't-sleep-with-rock-stars.

Nigel was meant to go on after Steven. Radio demigods Paul "Cubby" Bryant and Elvis Duran took to the podium. To my surprise, they introduced Ree as the next roaster! How had he won over the bitchy director?

With his usual dazzling charm, I supposed.

"Good evening," Ree said. "It's an honor to be asked to fill in for promo domo Nigel Hamilton-Jones who couldn't be here tonight. I'd like to thank him and everyone at MGX for the great job they're doing with my new single. It's not easy to bring a career back to life ten years after a hit was at the top of the charts. I appreciate the faith. But I wouldn't be standing here at all if it weren't for Jazmyn Brown, now star of the midday show on ninety-nine The Bear. Thank you, Jaz."

My face was red hot. What a wonderful thing for him to say.

Cher leaned in as the room filled with applause. "Touché. And if you don't want him, give him my number."

"Mickey Green," Ree looked at him in the audience and stretched out a hand, "you're like a father figure to me. You've taught me so much in the short time I've been with MGX. Like an artist should audit their record company's books every year, no matter what." Mickey violently shook his head. "Did I get that wrong? *Never* audit the books?"

I started breathing again when everyone laughed. After he served up a few more digs at corporate greed he moved on to artists.

"What's the difference between a coked-up one-hit wonder and roadkill?" Beat. "Nothing."

"What do you call an artist who parties all night and doesn't want to be bothered before noon?" Beat. "A future has-been."

If the best humor comes from recognizing the truth, Ree had hit a bull's-eye. The crowd loved him.

He saved the best for last.

"Ladies and gentlemen, I have a bet with Mickey that he doesn't have the *cojones* to strip for you tonight. Come on, he's makin' all this money off strippers, he should know what it feels like, right?" Stunned silence. "What? You think he's that ugly? Come on, clap if you want to see Mickey Green strip right here, right now!"

A woman stood up and screamed out, "We want YOU to strip, Mr. Ree!"

The applause turned into a standing ovation. Mickey worked his way to the front of the stage. "I Married the Stripper" began to thump. I couldn't believe what I was seeing. They dragged it out and eventually stripped to the waist, then turned and dropped their pants and drawers. Every cell phone in the house caught the moment.

Shane said, "Thanks for inviting me to sit with you. My original seat was way in the back. I would have missed seeing the hairy mole on Mickey's ass."

I invited Shane backstage after the show. I would say hi to Ree, tell him he was phenomenal, and leave.

Cat was whisked right through with her all-access pass. I soon discovered we didn't have the right credentials. Ree's publicist, Tamara, came to my rescue, though she did say, "Ree's going to be a very busy man with a European tour being squeezed in."

Was that a warning or a brush-off?

Back in his suit—no tie—Ree was reveling in all the attention he was getting from women, reporters, and other artists. I worked my way through the throng. Shane fell into conversation with someone he knew.

Just as I reached Ree, reporters cornered us, camera lights flashed. We were bombarded with questions. Ree had been right years ago when he'd said being in the spotlight felt like target practice — and you're the target.

"Show us your matching tattoos," yelled one reporter. Mine was in plain view.

Ree smiled. "I've done enough undressing for tonight."

"Jazmyn, is it true you and Cat are posing for *Penthouse*?" asked another.

Ree said, "Jaz is above that."

He drew me to him protectively. It was too powerful. I *could not* get sucked up in this life. It had no basis in reality.

Nor could I pull away.

"Are you two dating again?" a female reporter asked.

"We're just friends."

"After that performance, *why*?"

Cat added, "*I'll* be in *Penthouse*, but Jazmyn's too uptight. She's dating a guy who raps about stripping and she's worried?"

"We're not dating!"

Ree whispered in my ear, "It's just a matter of time, and you know it."

My heart hammering away, I found Shane and split.

20

A Million Pieces

Shane drove me back to the Gramercy Arms, the hotel I was temporarily staying in until life on and off the mike sorted itself out. He kept the talk to business, asking if I'd be interested in doing imaging for stations in other markets.

"As long as I don't have to say 'soft rock.' How can rock be soft?"

"That sounds like a *koan*," he said.

"What is that? I had no idea what you meant the first time you said it."

"An unanswerable question posed in Buddhism, like 'What's the sound of one hand clapping.' Meditating on it brings enlightenment."

I was intrigued. "Are you a Buddhist?"

"I see the good in all religions. If I *had* to choose, that would be my first choice."

At a traffic light a young couple almost walked into his silent Prius, oblivious to anything but each other.

"The power of attraction to blind you is something, isn't it?" Shane said.

"That's an understatement. You saw what went down backstage. Ree wants to get back together. Can I stomach his life again? It's too crazy. If you think it's hard getting to the top, try staying there."

"Aren't you dating Nigel?"

I watched the lovers round a corner and disappear. "Yes."

When I turned, Shane was gazing at me intensely, as if he were studying every pore on my face. And liking what he saw.

We both turned back toward the traffic light. "You look very pretty tonight, Jazmyn."

Flustered, I hugged my bare arms, looking out my window again. "Don't go there, Shane. You're married."

He pulled over. "Sorry. I didn't mean to make you uncomfortable. That slipped out. Yes, I'm married. But not in my heart."

I'd heard that line before and was sorry I'd believed it.

Truthfully, it had taken me all of two seconds to check if Shane was wearing a wedding band when I'd first met him. When I saw he was, that was the end of that idea.

"Given what we're going through now with Charlie," he said, "it's not a good time to make a change. I've taken up running to let off steam. I'm not cheating on her, or looking to. I'm pretty sure she's already found someone. We're just waiting for Charlie to recover or ..."

He pushed his glasses up, cleared his throat.

I touched his upper arm. "She's crazy to let you go."

At the same moment we both said, "Do you want to—" We laughed.

"You first," he said.

"I just wondered if you'd like to go somewhere to talk, like a Starbucks," I said. "What were you going to say?"

"The same thing. I know a quiet place where the coffee is fresh, and it's a part of New York you'll probably never see. At least, I hope you never have to."

I gave him a quizzical look. "Let's go."

We headed up the FDR, exited at East 61st Street, and made a right onto York Avenue. I saw a Sloan-Kettering Cancer Center sign as we pulled into a garage.

"He'll probably be asleep." He glanced at what little I was wearing. "Mind putting on my jacket?"

He parked the car and told me he often read to the terminally ill children. "I change my voice for the characters. It's a welcome break from what I do all day long."

Once we entered the Children's Cancer Center we spoke in hushed tones. It had a calm, almost churchlike quality. It was an impressive space with bright blue walls and bold paintings. A large area had a 20-foot ceiling and a vast skylight, with thousands of glass objects and kinetic sculptures on the wall that could be activated by standing on inlaid footprints.

"I can see how a child could become lost in that," I said. "I could."

He showed me the private treatment bays for outpatients, which were equipped with multimedia entertainment and Internet; how all the furniture in the Recreation Center was on wheels so they could reconfigure the room as needed. The patient rooms were big enough for an additional bed for an adult to sleep in.

How awful it must be to see your child dying, to feel so helpless.

The nurses weren't surprised to see Shane at this hour, though dressed to the nines was out of the norm.

"Lookin' mighty fine, Mr. Riley. You should wear a tuxedo more often."

"Thank you, Yvonne." He introduced us. "Jazmyn's the new DJ at the station. I wanted to show her something that isn't in a New York guidebook."

"You're the new Barenaked Radio Lady?"

"Afraid so."

"I'm an Angie Martinez fan."

"So am I, but don't tell anyone."

She smiled. "Okay, you can stay." She turned to Shane, "He fell asleep an hour ago."

"I won't disturb him."

I removed my high heels, tiptoeing into the room behind Shane. The way the moonlight hit his slumbering son was like watching a translucent angel. Charlie was so thin, so pale. He could have floated right out the window. I choked back tears as Shane gazed at him lovingly, resisting the urge to touch him.

Shane looked movie star handsome in his tux, as well as loving and kind. How could any woman want to divorce him?

I slipped out to the nurses' station. That little boy! That little boy.

Yvonne looked up from her computer. My expression could not be concealed. "He's beautiful, isn't he?" She handed me a tissue. "Both of them."

I squeaked, "It's so sad."

She motioned for me to lean in. "I've held this job a long time. I've seen a lot of marriages break. I've seen them grow stronger. I don't think Shane's will last. But his heart is in a million pieces right now. Will be for a long time."

I sniffled. "We just work together. We're just friends."

"You're the first woman who isn't family or his wife that's visited. Just giving you a heads-up."

I felt for Shane and liked him immensely. But I was ready to love someone *now*. Ree's backstage plea had changed the game.

I want the woman who fell in love with me and believed in me when I had nothing. The woman who defied her father to be with me. The woman who has the other half of my tattoo on her arm. The woman I think about every single day.

Could I resist that?

Shane dropped me off at my place, no awkwardness in sight.

Still, I couldn't sleep. I tuned in Ariella. After she kicked off a long set of music following commercials I called her for advice.

"Sleep with Ree but don't break up with Nigel. There's no ring on your finger, yet. Get Ree out of your system before there is one."

"What if it gets *Nigel* out of my system?"

"Oh, to be young again. Artists are great fun, Jazmyn, but they can be so fragile in every way."

"I just don't feel for Nigel what I feel for Ree."

"Then I would say you're screwed."

It took a moment to counter that.

"Maybe I should look at it this way," I said. "If Ree and I get back together and crash and burn, Manhattan is full of other men. My life here is just starting."

She said more thoughtfully, "I'm full of shit. Really, I am. I was only married for two seconds ages ago. What do I know? Maybe neither one of them are Mr. Right and you'll meet someone new." She paused. "Just don't stay single for too long."

21

THE URGE TO MERGE

I hadn't been this nervous before my first WBRR show.

I was in Nigel's kitchen preparing (and sampling) expensive cheese, crostini, and Mediterranean olives for the arrival of our parents. I popped two dark chocolate truffles laced with bourbon from the refrigerator. I could already feel my ankles swelling. I had to stop.

The plan was to have drinks and "nibbles," then walk to Gabriel's, one of the best restaurants on the Upper West Side. I hoped Mom and Dad could handle the six blocks.

Nigel came out of his bedroom wearing dress slacks, fixing his cuff links on a fine white shirt. His dread of public speaking aside, he exuded total confidence and class. I could have a fabulous life with him. Let his artists be the drama I needed.

"Is something wrong, love?"

"You look so good, Nigel."

"So do you, as always."

"Let me do that."

I worked the silver cuff links into each sleeve, imagining myself doing this ritual for decades.

Did I mention how good Nigel smelled?

I wanted to give him a kiss. Did I mention what a great kisser he was?

"Darling, you're shaking," he said, as he held out my trembling hand.

"I'm nervous about meeting your parents."

"At last, I see you have a weakness, too."

If only he knew. "Excuse me, Nigel. I need to finish getting ready."

I'd taken to carrying a big shoulder bag around during the day to house my phone, iPad, earbuds, chargers, bottled water, snacks, make-up, whatever. I had to find something more dainty for this dinner. I picked a small black purse that dated back to my time with Ree.

Then I saw it. On the bottom of the purse.

Oh, shit.

An old emergency Percocet wrapped in foil.

No way could I be shaking like a leaf and stuffing my face tonight. This would calm me and my appetite down better than any drink. The pill was really old. Would it work? Should I do half or all of it? I got my answer when I tried to break it and couldn't.

I shouldn't.

But I did. I was hoping it was so ancient I'd get a mild buzz at most.

The house phone rang and Nigel made his way to the front door. I grabbed the Pinot Noir breathing in the living room and took a quick sip straight from the bottle to help the Perc go down.

Rose's lilting voice filled up the foyer as she and Teddy arrived. I came out to greet them. They were trim and fit, and spoke so rapidly, with such a strong British accent, that I could hardly follow them.

"I said you are *the picture of good health*," Rose repeated as we settled on couches facing each other. "Good health is so important, isn't it, Teddy?"

"Harumphmagus."

Nigel poured the wine, I passed a plate of hors d'oeuvres.

"We walk two miles three times a week, don't we, Teddy?"

"Heyabushakum."

"And bicycle on the weekends. Of course there's tennis, croquet. Do you play?"

I held out my wine glass to Nigel, stopping myself from popping another nibble. "I'm waiting for Nigel to teach me."

"I'm sure she'll be a natural." Nigel poured a mere splash.

"You're so thin," Rose said. "Must be great metabolism. I bet it runs in your family."

I said nothing as I smiled.

The house phone rang again. That had to be my parents. I stood up with Nigel and followed him to the door.

I whispered, "I need to tell you something. My parents are ..." I held my arms out from either side of my body.

"Surely you jest."

I shook my head.

He chucked me under the chin. "Even if they are salad dodgers, so what? They made you."

When they came through the narrow door, turning slightly sideways to do so, Nigel momentarily froze. My parents bore equally astounded expressions. I was confused. Thankfully we were in the foyer, far from the living room and Nigel's parents.

Nigel politely offered his hand to my mother. "Charmed to meet you, Mrs. Brown."

"I *love* your accent." Turning to me, she said as Nigel shook hands with Dad, "He's adorable. And look at you. Thin as a whippet!" She turned to Nigel, "Not that it's anything unusual."

My father held me back as Nigel and mom went inside. "He's not black."

"Gee, Dad, I hadn't noticed."

"I take it he's not a rapper, either. Look at this place. It has furniture. Very swanky."

When Ree and I were together, a bed was about the only furniture we had.

Nigel's mother and father blinked at the sight of my parents. I felt a mix of embarrassment and pride as they lowered themselves onto the opposite couch with a soft grunt. Since I'd been a kid, picked on for being fat *and* having fat parents, I'd grown up wishing they were invisible. Why couldn't they move through life with the ease of a Rose and Teddy? Yet I was proud that they didn't care what others thought of them. If only I could be more like that.

They didn't touch a morsel as they talked about the trip up and how much nicer it was to drive than fly.

"Yes." Rose's good breeding kicking in. "It *is* far more civilized. We were practically strip-searched at Heathrow!"

His father said something indecipherable.

"Could you repeat that?" Mom asked.

Nigel glanced at his watch. "We should make a gentle move if we want to get there on time. Perhaps a cab would be a good idea?"

"Oh no," said my dad, "we need the exercise after sitting in the car all day."

Across the room my cell lit up, playing "I Married the Stripper." Nigel looked unpleasantly surprised. I got up and sent it to voicemail.

My heart flipped a few times when I saw it was Ree calling.

"Yes, about that gentle move," I said. "Shall we?"

We'd only walked two blocks, and quite slowly for the Hamilton-Joneses, when Mom and Dad had to stop, panting. Concerning me even more were the restaurant prices sure to give Daddy a heart attack.

"Why don't you go on?" I said to Nigel. "We'll catch up."

"Brilliant!"

I watched them charge off, looking behind to see where we were several times. I knew they were talking about us.

Mom said, "Should we have stayed in Virginia until he proposed?"

"So we're fat," said my dad. "What does that have to do with how he feels about our daughter? Afraid he'll think their kids will be butterballs?"

"Daddy, stop it. And no fussing over the menu prices tonight. This is Nigel's treat."

"He does seem like a nice fellow," Dad said. "I can tell he's smitten, Patty."

"It's *Jazmyn.*"

They both said, "You and your names."

I offered to hail a taxi. They refused. As we slowly made our way to the restaurant, we walked by a deli that was playing a familiar tune.

"That's Ree's new song!"

I stopped to listen but they pulled me on.

"Does Nigel know about Ree?" Mom asked.

"Of course. He's not only on his record label, Nigel's promoting him."

"How many kids does he have running around now?" huffed Dad.

"None," I snapped. That I knew of.

"Enough about your *old* boyfriend," Mom said. "Nigel's scrumptious." She linked her arm in mine. "I want to hear how you two met and how you knew he was the one."

"Did I say that?"

"You said it by the way you look at him."

I must have been gazing at him all lovey-dovey back at the apartment. Had it been because my parents loved him? How accepting Nigel had been of them? It was too soon to blame it on the Percocet.

How I wished they had looked at Ree the same way.

Gabriel's had warm golden walls, beautiful people, and heavenly aromas that could put anyone in a good mood. I excused myself to go to the ladies' room, checking my phone. The voicemail from Ree filled me with guilty excitement.

"My life is insane, Jaz. I have to hire someone to handle all the offers coming in, including one for my own TV show called—are you ready?—*Ree-ality TV*. You should be on it with me. It means nothing without you. Nothing."

I texted back: *A TV coach told me I have no spark.*

The next moment he called.

"You needed *me* to be in the room with you, that's all."

He had a point.

"Look, Nigel's a nice guy. Maybe I *should* step back. Maybe you two belong together."

My heart strained at the thought of parting ways with Ree. Every inch of me wanted him, except the part of my brain labeled Common Sense.

"The best marriages are based on friendship, not lust," I said.

"So you're saying you don't want him physically but you do want me?"

I scrutinized myself in the bathroom mirror, *zhush*ing my hair with my fingertips. "Nigel and I work in the same business. I don't want things to get messy."

"I got news for you, they always gets messy. I'll be in L.A. for ten days. When I get back, have it worked out."

"Is that an *order?*"

"Stop playing games with me, Jazmyn. You know you love me."

"I have to go. We're all having dinner right now. His parents and mine."

There was a pause. He put on a British accent. "Isn't that just tickety-boo."

It made me laugh in a way I rarely did with Nigel.

"Where are you?" he asked.

"I'm not telling." In one minute I'd become a five-year-old.

There shouldn't be this much confusion, I told myself, returning to the table. I should be alone right now.

Nigel pulled out my chair, which was between his and his mother's. He told me how stunning I was and that he had missed me.

Mom swooned. "He's so romantic, just like your father."

She and Daddy exchanged a look. Then rubbed noses, smiling.

"My, you certainly are an affectionate family." Rose's voice became even more lilting.

"Klooofmenemwa."

Teddy received a light slap on his hand.

Champagne had been poured. We politely raised our glasses.

"Here's to a night we'll always remember," Nigel said. "To my parents for coming all the way over to see me. To the parents of the woman I love and adore and whom I hope to know better." He turned to me, "And especially, to you, Jazmyn. I always had a feeling about us. I'm so glad I wasn't wrong."

I took a big gulp of the $250 Krug Grand Cuvee, the Percocet momentarily forgotten.

The choices on the menu should have been irresistible: marinated vine-ripened tomatoes with buffalo milk mozzarella, pappardelle with a duck and porcini ragù, wood-grilled meats, fish and vegetables, roasted quail, and positively sinful desserts.

I had zero appetite.

Nigel, Rose, and Teddy ate enthusiastically. I cut my artichoke lasagna into pieces and poked it repeatedly. And drank. That Perc *had* to be past its prime and I needed something to ward off this uneasy feeling I had.

Conversation was far from scintillating. My father was an accountant at a big corporation. Though my mother was no dummy, they weren't from the *upper-clahss* world of those with double-barreled names like the Hamilton-Joneses. As families go, we were worlds apart.

"India?" my father said, when Rose said they were planning a trip there. "I've never even eaten at an Indian restaurant."

"Really, Daddy? It's wonderful food, and healthy for you."

"That's probably why."

"You don't know what you're missing," Rose said politely.

I had to get this over with. I looked at Rose. "I used to weigh two hundred fifty pounds."

My mother let out an *Eep*.

Nigel coughed so hard I had to slap him on the back. "You're joking, love," he said.

"I'll show you our family photo albums some time. Mom couldn't get the weight off after having me. It's genetic."

Mom tried to save me. "Aunt Sue is quite thin."

"She's also a drunk who barely eats."

She mouthed: *T.M.I.*

"Do tell." Rose looked me over, as if making sure my weight wasn't an optical illusion.

Nigel wrapped his hand tightly around mine. "I'm glad you told me. It shows you have enormous discipline and that you take extraordinarily good care of yourself." Looking at my father, "No offense, sir."

"None taken. I know I'm fat and out of shape. And yes, Patty—I mean Jazmyn—has worked very hard to get healthy and stay that way. I wish some of her determination would transfer to me. I've given up."

Rose was smiling now at the sight of her son so in love, so grown up. "Yes, I think you are to be greatly admired, Jazmyn."

The champagne was long gone and I was on to a glass of wine. A familiar glow had kicked in. That stale Perc did have plenty of punch. No telling what was going to come out of my mouth now.

And I didn't care.

When Nigel went to pour water into my glass, I yanked it away, nodded at the wine bottle. He reluctantly obliged.

A few gulps later, I said to Rose and Teddy, "Did Nigel tell you I'm posing for *Penthouse* with two other women?"

Rose's eyebrows shot up so high I thought her scalp would lift off her head, but she flawlessly maintained her decorum.

"No, he didn't mention it."

"By jove," Teddy said. No problem understanding that.

Nigel said the British papers had topless women in them all the time. It was no big deal. "If it's done tastefully," he added.

"*Penthouse?*" Teddy and my dad said in disbelief.

"Have you considered what impact this will have on your children, Jazmyn?" Rose asked. "I assume you'll be having them at some point."

"Oh mumsy, it'll all have blown over by the time they come along." Nigel saw his chance to change the subject. "I've been thinking about names lately. If their grandmum is Rose and their mum Jazmyn, why not continue the flower theme if we have a girl?"

It was my turn to make an odd sound.

"It's a bit premature to be talking like that, Nigel!" his mother said.

"Not in this age."

"Yes," I gave Nigel a hard jab. "It's a bit prem-a-*toor*."

My phone started playing "I Married the Stripper."

I reached for my purse. "I'll put it on vibrate." Giggling, I said, "That sounds naughty, doesn't it?"

Nigel took my phone when he saw I was having difficulty working it.

"Allow me to download the Chloe Powers ringtone. That's what we need to promote now."

Was Ree already being pushed aside? Or was he golden now that his stripping duet with Mickey Green had gone viral.

I pulled my phone away from him. "I'm a rock DJ now. I'll put Streaming the Net on later."

He pulled it back. "I'll do it for you now. I know how busy you are, *darling*."

"Not nearly as busy as you, *darling*."

He handed me back the phone. "Whatever you wish." He leaned in and whispered, "I think you've had enough to drink, love."

"Love, love, schmuv."

"Isn't it wonderful you two communicate so well!" my mom rushed in.

Rose said, "I've never seen a woman have such starch with Nigel." She put on a flat American accent. "You go, girl."

"Tell me about Chloe Powers, Rose," I said. "I understand she's the daughter of a family friend."

"Yes. Very talented and very determined young girl from a royal line. We love her."

"Royal line? How about that! And quite beautiful."

Celine Dion was twelve years old when she met the man who would become her manager and later husband. He was thirty-eight then. Nigel with the fifteen-year-old Chloe? I could see it.

I planted my seed. "I'm sure you two will make a great team. No one can guide her career better than you, Nigel."

Rose leaned toward me. "Doesn't it make you jealous that he works intimately with so many beautiful young women?"

"Not at all."

Her eyes narrowed. *Yes! She thinks I don't love her son and she'll send me packing.*

She said to the table, "She's ideal!"

What?

"Every woman Nigel has gone out with has been too insecure to accept his close relationships with beautiful female stars. No wonder it never worked."

Everyone but me was grinning from ear to ear.

"Ms. Brown? You have a call."

In my hazy state it took me a moment to realize the waiter was handing me a cordless phone. Who would be calling me here?

"Just say the word, Jazmyn, and I'm there. To hell with L.A."

"How did you find me?"

"Asked Nigel's assistant."

Now Ree reminded me of Krazy Karl, and not just because I was high.

And why *didn't* I feel insecure with Nigel but did all the time with Ree? I didn't want to be like that anymore. The choice was mine.

"We have to give us one more try, Jaz. One more try."

Everyone at the table was staring at me. "I'm having dinner, Karl. Goodbye."

I clicked off the phone.

"Krazy Karl?" Nigel asked. "Jaz, that's going too far. I truly think a restraining order is needed. I'm very concerned now."

"Excuse me."

I raced to the bathroom, walking in circles until I could breathe normally.

A woman stood at the sink primping. From her hands I detected she was probably in her sixties or seventies, though it was hard to tell from her face. She was dressed in black from head to toe, a typical New Yorker.

"You don't look so great," she said.

New Yorkers often open up to strangers. After all, you were unlikely to see them again.

"I'm having dinner with my boyfriend's parents and *my* parents and my first true love keeps trying to get back with me, which I don't want, well, I do, but I'm sure it wouldn't work. I *think*. And my boyfriend is promoting his album, and it's just so complicated."

"Your first true love is a musician?" Her voice turned softer. "I dated a singer once. What a voice. Positively dreamy. And when he wrote songs about me? Oh! Couldn't get enough."

Her reverie stopped.

"Thank God I didn't marry him. Great in the sack but needed constant reinforcement from *other* women. And he was always broke." She paused. "Let me tell you, honey. Not having money can make you suicidal. Go with the guy who can take care of you." She was out the door in a blur of black.

I grabbed the ledge of the sink for balance. Holy fuck. What just happened?

I returned to the table, trying not to weave. "Sorry about that. I think I drank too much."

Nigel reached for my hand with a laugh. "You're cute when you're stinko."

The energy at the table had shifted. Everyone was quiet, grinning. Now what?

"Jazmyn, I've waited a long time for a woman like you." His grip tightened. "Someone with a great sense of humor, whom I can share everything with, who still loves me, even with my flaws. Who understands my business and who's so beautiful any man would be proud to be seen with her. I've already asked your father for his permission."

He got down on one knee.

A silence fell over the restaurant.

"I wanted this moment to be special, just like every moment is with you. What could be more special than to have our families with us when I ask you to marry me? For this is more than just a union of the two of us."

All I could think to say was, "What if I get fat?"

The woman from the restroom sat close by with two other women her age. She called out, "He'll be getting fat, too, sister!"

Laughter filled the restaurant.

"We'll work it through like everything else," Nigel said earnestly once the mirth had subsided. "No one knows what will happen in a marriage. All we know for sure is that it will never be perfect. Nor should it be."

Customers were saying, "*Awwww.*" The women at the other table gave me a thumbs-up.

I saw the Nigel I'd fallen for. The one who was stable, mature, husband-y, got me, my business, and was still a lot of fun to be with. So he didn't make me convulse with laughter; he always had my back. He was a fabulous catch. And our parents did seem to get along.

I was being an ass.

I could get Nigel to stop saying "Jolly good" in bed. I could help him overcome his fear of speaking in public. I would eventually understand what his father was saying.

Nigel lifted my left hand, slipping a huge princess-cut diamond on my ring finger. I heard applause, another bottle of champagne popping. Bubbling flutes were passed around our table.

"Oh look," said Rose, "she's crying. It's *such* an emotional moment, isn't it, love?"

22

Just Do It

The first hour of every radio show flew by as Donna and I scoured the net and social media for fresh news and information. Her Royal Highness would sit across from me flipping through newspapers. I was surprised the station still had physical papers delivered. When I mentioned it to Rick, he'd said, "Not for much longer."

Flip, flip, flip. I hated that sound! And I had a mind-crushing hangover.

"Cat, you read the paper the same way my dad does," I said on the air. "Loudly."

"Papers make noise, Jazmyn. I get more information reading them than from their websites. I see more. Look. There's an item about my good friend Steven Tyler in *Page Six*."

I'd seen it, but after that smooch of theirs at the roast I hated giving him any airtime.

"A porn star says she's having his baby," Cat said. "He's denying it."

That brought us to the topic of *Penthouse*.

We were definitely getting mileage out of just talking about all three of us doing the shoot. Ninety percent of our male callers were for it, and so were most of the women. Those against it mainly brought up Cat's ten-year-old son as the reason.

"We've discussed it," she said. "He's seen plenty on the Internet already. If I was with a man he'd have a problem. A woman doesn't bother him, not that he's planning on looking."

"Of course he's going to," I said, "and there's no un-seeing that."

"He'll recover."

We did a bit with my mother on the air as she and dad waited to get on the next Circle Line tour around Manhattan. She called me "Sweetie" so she wouldn't say the wrong name.

"Mom, I have to make this *Penthouse* decision today."

"Sweetie, just do it."

"Why?"

"So you can stop obsessing about it. Sometimes that's the best reason there is. And if that adorable fiancé of yours doesn't mind …"

"Fiancé?!" cried Cat and Donna.

"Where's the ring?" asked Cat.

It was in my purse. And now Nigel would hear I wasn't wearing it. I fished it out and Donna oohed. Cat issued a polite, "Nice."

Nigel had let me sleep in to the last possible minute that morning, so there'd been no time for me to say, "Look, I was really out of it last night. I'm not ready to be engaged." I figured we would talk about it that night.

Certainly not on the air.

"Nigel's so cute," Donna squeaked voice. "Let's see *your* ring, Cat. Oh, wow. It's huge."

"Is it?" she said as she admired it.

I was anxious to change the subject. "Tell us how Vee proposed."

"We were in a hot air balloon over the Belmont Stakes," Cat purred. "He said, 'Being with you makes me feel high as the sky and fast as a thoroughbred. What better place to ask you to marry me?'" She added a romantic sigh for effect. "How did Nigel pro—"

"From hot air balloons to Led Zeppelin, Chopper will be kicking off our Zep Fest tonight on ninety-nine The Bear – the best rock. Every time you hear a song from Zeppelin ..."

I gave an eye cue to Cat. She stared at me.

What were the details? I'd only had time to glance at the email from Rick Rivers. I looked at Donna. She frantically tried to bring it up on another computer. Oh, for the eco-unfriendly days of leaving written memos in a real mailbox. You could just grab the sheet of paper and read it.

Like a newspaper.

"You get something really cool if you're the ninety-ninth caller," I said. "Here's the new one from Coldplay."

Krazy Karl surprised me when he called, congratulated me on my engagement, and said about the nude pictorial, "You're not a whore. And you're engaged now. I wouldn't let the woman I was going to marry pose nude for anyone but me."

His maniacal high-pitched laugh filled the room. Who would marry Karl?

Donna said, "You do have a rockin' body, Karl. Your true love is out there somewhere."

The thought zipped through my mind *I wonder how many men Donna's slept with? Should I ask her?*

"You're a hive of hormones, aren't you, Donna."

She giggled. "That's the way God made me, I guess."

"God did a very good job," added Karl.

"Don't go there," warned Cat and cut off his call.

Suddenly static filled our headphones. Panic ensued. Being thrown off the air is what I imagine it feels like to fly an airplane and have the engines quit. No one would be killed, but sheer terror still rips through you.

"Check the meters!" commanded Cat.

"For what?" I screamed.

"I don't know! That's what the guys do."

Rivers barged in. "I texted the engineer. He'll talk you through getting us back on."

I couldn't resist. "Cat, if you hadn't hung up on Karl he could have—"

"He's probably the one who knocked us off."

"Bullshit. Stations go off the air all the time." Or was she right?

By the time that madness was over, we'd been off for twelve minutes. Long enough to not play a set of commercials, which led to Rivers wrangling over the log to figure out where to put them later.

It momentarily got my mind (and everyone else's) off my engagement to Nigel.

I called Ariella when I got back to my room at the Gramercy Arms. While we talked I doodled on a note pad.

"Forget what I said about Ree being a rock in your shoe that you should have sex with once in order to get it out," she said. "Once won't be enough and you'll end up staggering away from him like you just fell off a trampoline, plus lose your British Prince Charming."

"I *was* drunk when he proposed, but I'm pretty sure I didn't say yes. He put the ring on in front of our parents and an entire restaurant, and that was it. I didn't want to embarrass him."

She didn't say anything right away.

"You let him do it. There's a part of you that does want to marry him."

"There's another part that can't see *forever* with him."

"Very few people see that. Let me give you my therapist's number," she said. "You're not a true New Yorker until you have your own shrink."

I wrote her name and number on my doodle pad.

"Can I ask you something personal, Ariella?"

"Depends on what it is."

"Do you regret not having kids?"

"Sometimes, but I was having way too much fun and working day and night in my twenties and thirties. I couldn't see how to fit children in."

"That's how I feel."

"You still have a few more years to figure it out. That's one decision you do *not* want to rush into."

When we hung up I looked at my scribbles on the note pad.

I'd drawn a pacifier.

23

SHOOT ME

Rock music filtered through ceiling speakers in the WBRR hallways that were clogged with photography lights, thick cables, a stylist, an assistant, and a brawny guy who hauled the equipment and pretended he had no interest in seeing naked women.

And Rick Rivers. Having him at the *Penthouse* shoot creeped me out.

"Afternoon drive, Jazmyn. It could be yours."

"Did Madd Maxx have to do this?"

"Look at it as a competitive advantage you have over him."

Why was he even here? He should ogle the final product while behind a locked door, like everyone else.

The *Penthouse* photographer, an exotic Parisian named Flavie with a sensuous accent and long blond mane, asked me if I wanted an Ativan.

"It's for anxiety," she said.

"I know what it's for. No."

The session was taking place on a Saturday morning to ensure we had "privacy." Sure. I was showing my promised land to the universe. When the stylist started tweezing my pubes, it hit me how close the camera was going to get.

"Ow! Can't they get rid of these in Photoshop?"

Everyone but Flavie was banned from the soundproof production studio. The window on its door was covered with blackout paper. The room reeked of perfume. Trance music floated into our space only.

Under our decadently soft silk robes, Cat, Donna, and I were wearing only three things: garter belts, stockings, and super-high heels. The robe was mine to keep, along with fifty Gs (I lied and told my dad it was a hundred).

They took off their robes. I clutched the lapels of mine tightly to my neck.

"Ready, Jazmyn?" Flavie asked.

I didn't move.

"You're not the only one in these shots, you know," Cat said.

"It'll be fun!" squealed Donna. "And think about how famous you'll be."

I had been hiding in plain sight with different names and hair color so long, literally exposing myself was something I couldn't handle.

"I'll be right back."

I teetered to the ladies' room in those ridiculous heels, pulling out my cell.

"Ree." I was so choked up I could barely speak. "I need your help. I need *you*."

I told him what was going down.

"Baby, I told you how much I loved you and you got engaged to someone else!"

"I feel terrible about that. He just kept saying and doing all the right things. And I was afraid of being hurt again with you. But I don't love him. You're my true love. We have to give it one more try. Take me back, Ree." My voice cracked again as I repeated his lyrics. "Take me back. *Please*."

"You know I will. But you have to go through with the shoot. You made a commitment, it's all set up, and fifty grand is a lot of jack. Just don't do anything *nasty* nasty. Where are you?"

"The radio station. I'll break it off with Nigel after the shoot."

"Text me when it's over."

I had a pity-party cry, then headed to the studio.

Rick took me aside, pulling on his goatee. I was ready to yank it off with my bare hands.

"Jazmyn, I talked to Ken Crewett. No one's going to force you to do this."

He stared at my chest like he could see straight through the robe.

"Good. Then I won't."

"We'll let Cat and Donna be the Barenaked Radio Ladies and put you on at night, between Chopper and Ariella. I'll take two hours off each of their shifts and you'll do ten p.m. to two a.m."

If he had socked me in the gut it wouldn't have hurt as much as those words. "You're *demoting* me because I won't take off my clothes?" Nigel rushed over.

Rivers pulled us down a deserted hallway. "I'm giving you the opportunity to do the show *that's all yours*. The one you really want to do."

"The one I really want to do is in the daytime."

He continued with his sales pitch with more conviction. "I'm offering you a great slot. It's where Ariella made her name."

"Back when everyone was up all night doing drugs. Why not have the naked bitches on at night and *me* in the daytime?"

"Could you excuse us, Rick?" Nigel asked.

"I'll be in my office."

"If it were any other city," Nigel said in a comforting tone, "I could see why you'd be upset. It's late night in *New York*, love. You'll have your days free to pursue voice-overs and whatever. Bide your time at night. Make money, get benefits, build up your pension, while you find something else."

"It's late night until two in the morning! I signed on to do mid-days."

"Nothing is certain but uncertainty, especially in this business."

There was my chance to break off our engagement. "Talking about uncertainty..."

"We're waiting for you." It was Flavie's impatient assistant.

He patted me on the back. "You'll be glad you did this. That's my professional opinion."

I pulled the robe around me even tighter. "Nigel, there's something I need to tell you."

"I know you took your ring off for the shoot. It keeps the fantasy going for the reader."

"That's not it." His phone rang. "That fucking phone!"

"Let's talk about it over a dinner you'll never forget. I *have* to take this." He tried to kiss me. I pushed him away. He stifled a laugh. He enjoyed seeing me bitchy, the ass.

I followed the assistant as reluctantly as someone being called to the principal's office for bad behavior.

Soon I was watching Donna and Cat kissing a microphone as if it were a cock. A joke, right? The lights went flash, flash, flash.

"Cat, sit on the soundboard. Donna, I'd like you between her legs. And Jazmyn, take off your robe, get on your knees, and put your hands on Donna's ass. Then move your face in like you're going to—"

"Wait, I thought we'd just be, um, striking come-hither poses."

She put her camera down. "When was the last time you saw *Penthouse?*"

"I went on the site."

"This is for the *magazine*. When you pay for something, you get a lot more." She handed me the latest copy.

I leafed through it. "Shit, this is hardcore."

"Really, Jazmyn," said Cat. "Do you know how much is out there on the Internet for free? We're being paid a lot and we're not *fucking* anyone. It's no big deal."

I felt disoriented. Like I'd stepped onto the wrong movie set.

Flavie didn't hide her irritation. "I'll have you over here, pulling albums out of the shelves, looking very retro and wearing a see-through blouse."

"That's all?"

"Then take it off. You don't think baring your breasts is indecent, do you?"

Could she have made me feel any more prudish? Me. Ms. Queen of Rock Radio.

Soon Cat was leaning back admiring Donna who was stroking her leg that was lifted and pointed like a ballet dancer. Was she ever flexible. I was in the background. I moved closer.

Something really was shifting inside me.

"You look so hot, Cat ... let go, Jaz. Feel free ..." Flavie had one of the sexiest voices I've ever heard. "You're gorgeous, Donna ... head down, Cat, and look to your left .... open your eyes more ... you're so hot, Jaz."

For a moment, she had me. I *was* hot!

Flavie had me lie back on the table where we did our off-air interviews.

"How am I supposed to look turned on? This is hard as a rock."

"Not as hard as the dicks of millions of men," Cat said.

I began to detach. It wasn't me doing this. It was Jazmyn Brown, my alter ego. The person I really wanted to be.

The person I had become.

Just don't do anything nasty nasty, Ree had said.

My breasts were completely exposed. Delicate female hands caressed them. I wasn't turned on. I was sad. In my mind I was back in my bedroom in Richmond. Thirteen, fourteen. Secretly spying on the boy across the street who I had a mighty crush on. He was polite at first, then avoided me whenever I came into view.

Now I was walking into my first ninth-grade class and the most popular guys started chanting Fatty Patty, Fatty Patty.

Then I saw myself every weekend night staying home and binging on anything and everything in the kitchen, certain no one would ever love me or want to touch me.

Now here I was, with the body I had always dreamed of and men hot for me like I had always dreamed of, and I was burning with the same humiliation and shame.

That homeless man with the dog popped into my head. *No shame, big gain.*

Flavie had just said, "Are you crying, Jazmyn?" while rubbing my lower back gently (how did she know that was my hot spot?) when one of the bulbs blew out with a *boof.*

"I have to go to the bathroom again."

I grabbed the robe and my purse. I had to get this over with. Nigel, too.

The stylist pointed down a long hallway when I asked her where he had gone. Taking off the towering heels, I padded toward him in my black stockings. I heard him and Rick around the corner.

"Good job, Nige," Rick was saying. "Jazmyn wouldn't have done the shoot or agreed to nights without your help. You'll be hearing plenty of MGX on The Bear. And soon."

"Jolly good."

That Brit shit. And I'd fucked him!

"Hey, *Nige.*" At least they registered embarrassment when they saw me. "I think you dropped something."

I hurled a shoe at him and hit him smack on the side of his head with the spike heel, barely missing his eye.

"Jesus molly Christ!"

"*Fuck you* and the cockroach you rode in on backwards!"

I hurled the other one, then ran toward the elevators.

They caught up to me. Rick started in. "Everyone's going to be disappointed in you, Jazmyn. The sales department, the GM, your agent, and most of all, the *listeners*."

"You're just nervous, *darling*," Nigel said in the unctuous voice he used with misbehaving artists. "Flavie is the best. You'll *love* the shots. I wanted you to do the shoot regardless of whether my records were added."

They followed me into the elevator, Rick threatening me with everything from insubordination to breach of contract. Nigel, his temple starting to bleed, played good cop, but I could feel his temper rising.

We reached the street and I ran out to hail a cab.

"Maybe you shouldn't even be on New York radio," Rick said. "You're too small market in your mind."

"Nothing would please me more than to never say *THE BEAR* again! And maybe you've got a too small dick."

"After all I did for you!" Nigel dropped his nice-guy façade.

"*I* got this gig, and all of my gigs, because of my talent. You just opened a door here and there. You even said so."

"How do you think you got into *Page Six* and *The Star-Ledger* and *Billboard?*"

The cab coming toward me didn't have its light on. Ree jumped out, to my enormous relief. A van screeched to a halt behind him. Two cameramen appeared.

"Smile!" Ree said. "You're on *Ree-ality TV*."

Rick's demeanor completely changed. "Mr. Ree, man. I really *did* marry the stripper!

Me and my wife sing your song all the time!"

"Calm down, Rivers," Nigel said.

"Good for you," Ree said to Rivers. "You married a stripper. That's something to be real proud of."

"Was that an insult or a compliment?"

"You can't shoot us without permission!" Nigel yelled at the cameramen.

"They can shoot whatever they want," I said, and gave Nigel the finger. "You, you, jolly good fuckhead!"

Ree and I were in the cab and outta there.

24

SUGAR MAE'S

We rode to the Gramercy Arms so I could change into some real clothes.

"And pack an overnight bag," Ree said, real sexy. "I'm not letting you out of my sight." Peeking down my robe, he asked, "What are you wearing under there?"

"More what I'm not wearing."

He ran his hands over my black stockings, nice and slow. "I like."

I touched his hand, which led to an amazing kiss that took me all the way back to my virginal state when I met him, and then far into the future, our future, in a blissful pink cotton candy cloud spun from dreams that really could come true now that we'd grown up.

When our lips parted, in perfect imitation of me he thrust his middle finger in my face. "Jolly good, fuckhead!"

If I'd been drinking something it would have come out of my nose. Just like old times.

"What was that all about?" he asked.

"Just something he likes to say. Jolly good, that is."

No need to tell him it was Nigel's climactic punctuation. Knowing Ree, he'd start saying it to bug me.

I filled him in on the conversation I overheard between Rick Rivers and Nigel.

"I have to hand it to Tut-tut," Ree said. "He's slicker than an eel in an oil barrel."

"Are you worried he's going to screw you over now?"

"I'm not worried about anything now that I have you."

Oh, those words. Oh, those arms that could lift me up as easily as a pillow.

"My knight in shining Armani." I rubbed my palm over his soft shaved head.

He gently wiped away a tear from my face. "My Delicate Flower of Love."

"I used that handle in Atlanta."

"I know. And Marcia Mathers in Detroit."

A play on Eminem's name, Marshall Mathers. "I hated those names."

"Now you know how I feel every time I sing those stripper songs."

After a quick stop at my hotel we headed north on Madison Avenue.

"Where are we going?"

"Harlem."

I tried not to look like a scared white girl.

"It's the hippest place in the city now, Miz New York. You'll love it."

"MGX didn't put you up in some happening hotel in Manhattan?"

"They offered," he said, "but it's not me. Besides, they may pay the bill, but it comes out of *my* advance, so I'm really footing it. I'm never going to be stupid about money again."

The van pulled up next to us when we stepped out of the cab. The cameramen were super-young. The director, Joe Lumas, was somewhat older and disheveled.

"Need more reunion footage," Joe said, then turned to me. "I have a release form for you to sign."

"Now? I need to talk to my agent."

My agent. Sure felt good to say that.

Joe ran his hand through oily hair. "Sure, sure. Have your people call my people, yadda, yadda, it's all good. Now walk up the steps of the brownstone with your arms around each other looking like you're madly in love."

"That won't be hard to do," Ree said.

We went up and down the stairs five times before Joe yelled, "Cut! Fabu!"

Sugar Mae's Bed and Breakfast overlooked a beautiful tree-lined street. The gleaming wide-plank floors and freshly polished antiques had a wonderful scent. Later I'd notice the pale yellow walls, dark wood trim, old-fashioned radiators, and black-and-white photos of Duke Ellington and Ella Fitzgerald. All I could see now was a stately sleigh bed, freshly made.

It wouldn't stay that way much longer.

Silently, slowly, we undressed each other. It all felt familiar. The way he smelled, his touch. The way my legs wrapped around him. His holding back before he surged forward. Yet it felt different.

Deeper.

Why did it have to get so ugly before?

Get past your past, girl.

He still knew touching the back of my left knee turned me on. Not the right, only the left.

I remembered his sensitive spots, like his anklebones. If I ran my toe over one when our legs were entwined, it drove him wild.

He didn't want to use a condom. I insisted.

"I'm using birth control but I have no idea where you've been the last seven years."

"Do you know where Nigel has been? Did you use protection with him?"

"At first."

He shook his head. "It's okay. I can't hate the guy. He played a big role in getting MGX to sign me."

We didn't speak again for quite some time.

After we made love, we couldn't stop looking into each other's eyes.

"How are you feeling, Blondie?"

My answer was a long sensuous stretch, feeling muscles I hadn't used in a *long* time, even with Nigel. At this rate, Ree would have me in shape for the next New York Marathon.

"Like a piece of taffy pulled in every direction. In a good way."

"I do that, too," he said.

"What?"

"Rub my tattoo."

I looked down at my upper arm. "Didn't realize I was doing it."

"It's waiting for its other half."

He traced the grapevine with his finger. I pulled away.

"What's the matter?"

"That's where my birth control implant is. It feels weird if you touch it."

His eyes widened. "How can you put that shit in your body?"

"Easy for you to say!" I sat up. "You don't have to be pregnant. And it lasts three years. No remembering to take a pill every day."

"There are other forms of birth control, you know. IUDs, diaphragms."

"Diaphragms don't stay in if your weight fluctuates a lot, which mine does."

"What about an IUD?"

I had to think back to this decision a couple of years ago.

"The doctor thought with all the moving around I did, the implant would work better. I wouldn't have to look for a doctor wherever I went."

"You don't have to think about an IUD either," he said. "Doctors push drugs because the pharmaceutical companies work them the same way record companies work radio stations."

"I'll look into it. It's time to change it anyway."

He studied me a moment. "What's wrong with being pregnant?"

"I'm married to my job and single, in case you haven't noticed."

"Sure you're not afraid you'll blow up like your mom did and not get the weight off?"

"Every woman worries about that."

"Stop worrying."

He said it so gently, I nestled back into his arms. It wasn't possible to love another person more than I loved Ree.

However ... "About this TV show."

He stopped playing with my hair. "What about it?"

"I just want to talk it through. Will we have *any* privacy?"

"Who has privacy anymore?"

Howie Kamen would say the same. *Of course you shouldn't do it if you want to stay a nobody.* I had to prove I had spark, too, dammit.

I held out my hand. We shook. When I tried to pull my hand away his grip tightened.

"Let's shake on making a baby, too."

My stomach shot up somewhere behind my eyeballs. "Not this second."

He snuggled close. "Remember Freddie who had a kid when he was fifteen and couldn't hold a job at Burger King?"

"Vaguely."

"I ran into him a couple months ago. He handed me a cigar. He'd just become a grandfather at age thirty-three. That's only five years older than I am!"

"What are you saying, you have to have a kid to impress *him?*"

He moved even closer. "You don't think I've had plenty of opportunities to become a daddy?" He stroked my forehead to erase the frown that had appeared there. "I want a child with the woman I love."

"Can we talk about this later?" I tried to shut him up with a kiss.

"I'm not going to be strappin' much longer, Jazmyn Brown. I can't feel the *real* you. You want me to get an AIDS test? Fine. We can both get one for the show. But *get those chemicals out of you.*"

I smiled as I ripped open another foil packet. "I can sure feel you."

When I opened my eyes after a post-lovemaking power nap, Ree was doing push-ups. Naked.

"What time is it?" I asked.

"Four-fifteen Saturday afternoon."

"What a day." I flashed back to that morning's photo shoot. What had I done?

He climbed into bed. It was hard to focus on anything with an *au naturel* Ree close by. "What's up with the radio station now?" he asked.

"Rick sure sounded like I was fired."

"He's more worried he'll be fired."

"Even if I still have a job, I'm fed up with pretending I'm naked on the air."

He gave me his I-want-you-to-do-something-for-me-baby smile. I braced myself.

"If you don't have a job, why don't you be my manager?"

I groaned. "That's the worst idea I've ever heard."

"Come on, Jaz, this is *our* moment. Why should I be handing over twenty percent to a manager on top of what Howie is taking?"

"Maybe I charge more than twenty percent. Wait, you're with Howie now?"

Howie was an agent, not a manager. Agents broker specific deals for lots of clients and make a ten-percent commission. Managers oversee careers of a much shorter list of people and typically take twice as much.

Ree tickled my side. I tried to kick him off me but he was way too strong.

"You'll get half if we ever split, but that's never going to happen, and you know it. We're together *forever.*"

"I want that in writing."

His arms wrapped around me.

Yet another orgasm later I agreed to think about it.

After our own workout, he hung off the bed, I sat on top of his lower legs, and watched as he did ab crunches.

"Seriously," he said. "I'd love for you to manage me and come to Europe, but I don't want you to mess up your career either."

That floored me. So did his six-pack. "

"Jaz, I've met enough older people in this biz to know we have to milk the next few years for all we can. I also need to get beyond the stripper bullshit, broaden my image."

"It's not bullshit. It's pop art."

"Like what you do for a living. Come on, Jaz. DJ-in' ain't brain surgery."

I released his legs and he toppled onto the floor.

He moaned. "Why did God answer my prayers? I forgot what a pain in the ass you could be."

I followed him into the bathroom. Soon we were snuggling together in hot water and white fragrant bubbles in the old-fashioned claw-foot bathtub.

His hands snaked around my thighs.

"Ree, I'm still recovering from the last three rounds!"

"Just saying hello to my little honey pot."

As we lay quietly parboiling and turning wrinkly as prunes, I conjured up all our good memories. It hit me that Ree was taking as big a risk getting back with me as I was with him. How did he know I would stick around if times got tough again?

"I can see us in our dream house, baby," he whispered. "Or house*s*, if you want a crib in New York. We'll have a gym, steam room, gourmet kitchen."

"A couple of white rocking chairs on the porch for our old age?"

"To go with our white hair."

I said no more. If all I hoped for wasn't finally coming my way, I didn't want to hear it.

What I did hear was a loud fart. Right in the tub.

"Ree! That's disgusting!"

I tried to get out. He wouldn't let go of me.

"It's a love fart, baby! A love fart! You think I'd do that for just anyone?"

I laughed so hard my stomach hurt. Yep, just like old times.

25

Ree and Chee

Amsterdam. London. Berlin. Paris. Milan. Rome.

Sounds exciting, doesn't it? About all we saw of Europe was glimpsed from the plane or riding in a car to our next destination. A hotel room in Berlin felt a lot like a hotel room in America, except for how the phones rang, what snacks were in the mini-bar, and what was on TV — not that we had time to watch anything.

Howie had run interference with WBRR. I was still employed, officially on vacation. Only Howie knew I was testing the waters about being Ree's manager.

"Go to Europe with Ree," he'd said. "See how you feel about doing that and being off the radio. Doesn't hurt to play hard to get if you do want to come back. We'll also hear how Cat and Donna sound without you. I predict not good." Twisting the knife. "But maybe not."

To my surprise, he had no problem with me doing the TV show when I learned the pay was nowhere near what I had expected.

"The women on *The Real Housewives of New York City* only made ten thousand each for the entire first season," he said. "If it's a hit, you'll make a lot more." He added something else that stuck with me. "The key to success is not caring what other people say as long as you're being talked about. The key to failure is trying to please everyone."

He'd said that after telling me *Penthouse* was going to use the photos of me.

"Fifty grand for showing my boobs and having them fondled," I told Ree later. "Cat and Donna went a lot further."

He hugged me. "We all have to do shit in this life we don't want to do. At least you were paid well."

"How can I ever work with those girls again with those images in my head?"

That caused me to think of Darla Sharp, the TV coach. I replayed to Ree my encounter with her and her rebellious kid.

"I hope no batons were injured in your photo shoot," he said.

"I hope I can look back on it with the same misty nostalgia she does. Shallow, I know. But I didn't go to college. I chose to say ridiculous things into a microphone for a living. I *am* shallow."

"At least only one of us is onstage doing an inane act now."

A typical day with Ree went like this: Rush to airport. Wait in security lines while Ree made soft mooing sounds and entertained everyone around us. Try to sleep on the plane. Act as air traffic controller to hundreds of texts, emails, calls. Fend off women (and men) tracking Ree like big game on a safari. Rush to an interview. Another. Tweet, tweet, Instagram, tweet, Facebook, Tumblr, tweet. Do a radio or TV show. Or four.

Go to a nightclub or small concert venue for a sound check, rehearse with dancers we'd never met before. I'd step in if one didn't show up or cut it. Back to the hotel to freshen up and eat. Back to the club. Perform three songs to a recorded track: his two hits, the next two singles, a cover of Barry White's "My First, My Last, My Everything" that made me weak-kneed every time he sang to me "Girl, you're my *reality* ..." — then back to "I Married the Stripper."

Crazed women would surround his table, thrusting CDs, T-shirts, and Mr. Ree zebra-print thong panties at him to sign. I tried to keep track of the sales and thefts. A few pulled down their pants or hiked up their dresses so he could sign their butts.

One woman offered the site of her latest Brazilian wax.

"Booty only," Ree said.

Back at the hotel, I'd count the money, then have him double check. The adrenalin took hours to wear off. On a good night, we'd crash around two a.m.

The phone didn't stop buzzing with calls and texts. The requests I fielded ranged from hosting a charity benefit to a six-figure offer to be the spokesman for a line of all-natural, preservative-free edible underwear. He was already selling thongs, but *spokesman*?

"Where can we send samples so you can try them for yourself?" the rep said. "You might change your mind."

We put them through their paces when they arrived the next day. It was a no-brainer. Take the money and run.

Meanwhile, I barely thought about food and when I did, I ate whatever I wanted and didn't gain an ounce. Whoo! Did I love that. I also loved helping Ree, and I felt challenged. What could be bad about this?

My moments of serious doubt, that's what.

When we did radio interviews, I'd check out the equipment, analyze how each personality handled the situation. More than once I longed to be in the announcer's place and put words in his or her mouth.

One of the female DJs we visited in Berlin must have sensed it. "Care to take her for a spin while we take photos in front of our station banner?"

How many times had a star stopped by one of my radio shows with a companion we'd brushed aside? I hadn't given it a second thought.

"Sure."

When she stood, her short skirt barely covered a knockout body.

A cameraman grabbed footage of me playing DJ, then left. I got a hinky feeling that grew into a devious one. Having worked at so many stations, I knew how to override the autopilot on the soundboard. When the next song was more than half over I went looking for the host.

She and Ree were being filmed. His back was to me. She sat all sexy on a desk, legs crossed, feet clad in fuck-me pumps, her top leg bobbing up and down.

I stood there, arms crossed, as she ignored me. The overhead speakers went silent.

"ACK!"

She kicked off her shoes and raced back to the studio. We never saw her again.

I soon understood how easy it was to make an ass of yourself on these TV shows. You got caught up in being the star of your own movie and giving the director the entertainment he wanted. The moment the cameras were gone, I felt lightened, liberated.

Ree and I took full advantage of our private moments. Condoms? What condoms? Before we'd left New York we'd taken HIV tests at a clinic.

"It's a public service as well," Joe Lumas said, uncharacteristically serious. "People today are so damn stupid about this. They think they won't get it if they're straight. And even if they do, 'Oh, I'll just take the drugs for it.' They're expensive as hell and will knock you on your ass. I know. My sister has it. Her rotten husband cheated on her with a woman who didn't know she had it. So she says."

After that, Joe became more human to me. I still didn't trust him as far as I could spit. And his lecture did freak me out. I had to believe Ree was faithful.

The clinic said we should use condoms for another six months, then get tested again, to make sure our negative results were true. Then we could have unprotected sex provided we'd been monogamous and would continue to be.

"To hell with six months," the camera caught Ree saying as we left the clinic.

"What kind of role model are you?" I said. "Of course we'll do it."

We didn't make it to six days.

Ah, sex. Glorious, mind-numbing sex. The glue that binds lovers together. There was nothing like it to completely cloud my thinking. Ree let down his defenses and still showed me his strength, his ability to protect me. I felt like the sexiest woman alive.

Honey, you do not walk away from that easily. The rest of it though...?

I'd often wondered about stars who turned their romantic partners into their managers or assistants or aides. At least they knew where their lover was at all times. But it was a lot of work for a short blip of sheer mania on stage.

When the music thumped, the lights pulsed, and a packed house screamed the words to Ree's songs, "It's the greatest high I've ever known," he said.

My contact high wasn't too shabby either. Those moments (and the rare romantic private ones) were what we had to remember when the rest became a crashing bore. Or made my blood boil.

I fielded a call in Milan that went like this: "Mr. Mack would like Mr. Roberts to come to his suite at the Ritz-Carlton for lunch."

"To whom am I speaking?"

"His *personal* assistant, Cheetaya. Who are you?"

"Jazmyn Brown. Ree's *manager*. I believe we've met."

"Sorry, I don't remember you."

I nearly said *Ms. What's He See In Her from the photo shoot in the Flatiron Building.*

"Ree's on tour. Every minute is filled. No time for lunch. Let me see if there are any V.I.P. passes left for his show tonight. Oh, darn, all gone. You'll have to call the club. 'Bye."

That night, before Ree's show, Big Mo' Mack strutted in with shoulders rockin', bling flashin', grill sparklin', and five people in tow trying their best not to look like lost sheep.

Stunning Cheetaya was glued to his side. I was glad she was with him until I caught her send Ree an admiring glance with an added back arch, just like the groupies lurking at sound checks. I could sense their presence without even turning my head.

Big Mo' and Ree nodded, grunted, slapped each other's back.

"This club ain't my style. Too low," Mo' said. As in *low-class.*

No lower than your testicles, I wanted to say. Women still loved him, though. When he took the stage, I swear he grew a foot.

"Get with my manager, Ree. We'll tour together." He glanced at me. "Hey, Wild Wendy. Long way from Richmond. How's it goin'?"

"It's Jazmyn Brown and I'm fine."

"You got a problem with me?" He tried to sound charming when he said it.

Ree stepped in, putting his arm around me. "She's my manager now."

"So I heard. Good luck, man." He put his arm around Cheetaya. "This is the mother of my next child."

It was as if he's said, "I'll see your 20 and raise you 200."

She would no doubt be looking rail-thin one week after giving birth, the heathen whore.

"When's the big day?" Ree asked.

"She's due in seven months."

"I mean the wedding."

He waved a hand. "Who gets married these days?"

"Me."

Chee wasn't happy about Mo' brushing off marriage, but she sure liked Ree's take on it. She looked at me, then Ree. "Are congratulations in order?"

I looked at him, as if to say, "Well? *Are* they?"

"Where's your camera crew?" Mo' asked, obviously the real reason he showed up.

"Took the night off. What brings you to Rome?"

"Performing for a private party. Rich fuckers. A cool half mil plus expenses. Come by after your show. Chee, tell him where it is."

"Give me your cell number, Ree, so I can text you the info."

"I'll give you mine," I said. "Ree doesn't text."

Big Mo' made a quick jerk of his head. "Ciao."

As his posse trailed behind him, Cheetaya gave Ree one last sexy look and an extra wiggle of her ass.

"She's pregnant and flirting with you?"

"Half a million dollars to play a private party. He probably added a zero."

"He didn't even stay for your show and he's asking you to tour with him."

"It's all bullshit," he said. "View him as the cartoon that he is. Don't let anyone know you feel that way. He's a powerful player for the moment, but I guarantee you he's shitting bricks."

"Why?"

"His last single didn't crack the top twenty. His supernova is about to dim faster than you can say M.C. Hammer." Ree stood to leave the V.I.P. area and hit the stage. Before he left, he said, "He'll deserve it, too, treating his woman that way. I feel sorry for the kid. He'll be a lousy father."

Nothing funny about that.

The Mo' private party took place inside a massive villa hundreds of years old, with tile and marble everywhere and flowering vines crawling up the walls. No one knows how to do over-the-top like the Italians. The fabulous clothes, the rapid-fire accented speech that made me feel like I was in the midst of a flock of exotic birds, the incredible food. And no interviews. No photo shoots. We could actually see the sights in this under-the-radar way.

Note to self: Tap into the private benefactor mother lode ASAP.

I found Mo's show lame, but the crowd loved hearing his hits. They'd gone berserk when he asked Ree to join him on stage. I was pissed the *Ree-ality* cameraman pulled into duty at the last moment missed filming their duet because he was too busy pointing his camera at the gorgeous women swarming around him.

He did, however, nail a shot of Ree rubbing Cheetaya's belly, then putting his ear against it, his face aglow with baby envy.

I pulled Ree away. "She's not even showing yet."

I knew how it would come across on the show, which may have been the reason Ree did it. For the show.

Or maybe he really did want to be a daddy. Now.

Why didn't I feel the same about motherhood? If I were going to have a baby, sure, I'd want Ree to be the father. I just didn't feel what I thought you're supposed to feel before bringing a human being into this crazy world. I didn't cry over Pampers commercials. I didn't look at babies in strollers and wish I had one.

When that happened, I'd stop using birth control.

26

THE BIG QUESTION

After a very creative shower in Rome, I watched Ree run a thick white towel over legs that belonged on a professional athlete. My eyes moved up to his face. I couldn't help it. I had to touch his shaved head.

"It's like touching a baby's butt," I said.

"Save that."

More unreality. Saving conversations for the cameras.

"Don't give the performance in the dressing room!" Joe Lumas kept saying.

I told myself it was no different than filing away bits to use on the radio. But it *was* different. Those were observations. This was our relationship.

"Lovebirds, this is the same day over and over," Joe also said. "We need conflict!"

Once the cameras were running and we were back in the bathroom (me wearing a fluffy white hotel bathrobe, Ree with a towel around his waist), I lovingly shaved his head.

I ran my hand over his dark dome. "Soft as a baby's butt."

"Women can't resist touching it."

My demeanor radically changed. "I *know*." He made a face, too. "Don't say I'm being paranoid, Ree. Any woman who isn't protective of her turf isn't that into her turf."

He smiled, "That's right, baby."

"Baby. You remind me of that Destiny's Child song 'Say My Name' where the guy never calls her by her name because he's juggling so many women."

"How could I be juggling a lot of women when I'm chained to you?"

"For that remark, my little pepperoni, you need to bring me some gelato. I'll stay here so you won't feel *chained*."

"Only if you eat it off my big pepperoni."

I rolled my eyes.

"Jazzamina, my little linguini-etta, take a taste-ah of my bigg-a pepperoni."

"You're not getting out of the gelato run."

Joe hissed, "More conflict. Way more."

Ree scowled.

"What *now?*" I asked.

He faced me. "Your father not liking me had a lot to do with your leaving."

Had this been bothering Ree or had Joe asked him to say it? I opened my cosmetic bag and grabbed a lipstick while I thought of a response.

"I would have left a lot sooner if that had been the case. *I* love you. Is there a problem?"

"We'll see if he's changed."

"How's *your* dad?" I asked.

"Disappeared again as soon as I was broke." I could hear the hurt in his voice. "Anyone who tries to put their fingers in my pockets now will be sorry. Except you, of course."

"That's because I'll be reaching for something other than your wallet."

He admired himself in the large mirror. "If having another hit and handling it right doesn't impress your father, I don't know what will. How can he not like me?"

He sucked in his cheeks, puckered his lips, pulling a goofy Zoolander "Blue Steel" model face. He did a few spins that caused his towel to fall off, and sang a falsetto imitation of Prince's "You sexy mothah-fuckaaaahh!"

My lipstick shot up the side of my cheek. "Shit!"

"Cut! Fabu!"

Joe Lumas had exploded out of NYU's film school ten years before with an indie documentary about a nutty, sad, pretty model who was too flaky, damaged, and drug-addicted to make it. Hollywood and Madison Avenue threw money at him, and the model straightened up enough to have some success for about a minute.

Joe didn't turn out to be the next Martin Scorsese, but he did have a quirky sensibility and depth that Ree and Howie assured me would make this reality show different in a good way. Personally, I thought Joe was losing his mind. He barked at anyone over the slightest thing.

Ree joked, "Just how much caffeine are you drinking, Joe?"

"Caffeine? What I need is heroin. Massive, *massive* amounts." He grabbed the hair at his temples as if about to rip it out, shrieking, "I'm kidding!"

Ree thought he was sexually confused. Joe did stare when Ree took his shirt off, but who wouldn't?

The contract allowed VTV to do anything they wanted with the footage and our likenesses — standard reality TV rules, according to Howie. We had to trust Joe. Who knew if this show would even make it on the air, and if it did, if anyone would find this shit interesting.

While an Italian magazine interviewed Ree, I ducked into a wi-fi café to check the news and stream WBRR. Donna was talking about getting drunk using tampons soaked in vodka. Where was the insecure girl I'd met not long ago?

Donna: "The best part is no calories, you don't get drunk enough to puke, and no alkie breath. It's a myth that you can't smell vodka on someone's breath if they've been drinking it."

Cat: "Really?"

Donna: "Oh, yeah, I know that first hand. I was fifteen when my dad grounded me for a week when I got sloshed on it."

Cat: "Back to the tampons. Doesn't it hurt? It's no different than rubbing alcohol, no?"

Donna: "Haven't tried it. Why don't I do it on the show tomorrow?"

Oh. My. God. Women doing the same crass crap as men felt like a big step backward. Still, it was bring-'em-back-day-after-day radio, all management wants.

Cat: "Right now we have a new contest on the Barenaked Radio Ladies. What Rock Star Will Drop Dead Next."

I groaned, prompting the handsome young man behind the counter to ask me something in Italian. His concerned look translated for me.

"No, I'm fine. *Eccellente, grazie.*"

He gave me a wink. I smiled. At this moment, I loved being in another country. And flirting. What's good for the gander is good for the goose.

Donna: "Of course we don't know who will die next, but tell us who you think it will be. We'll give you the chance to win one thousand dollars!"

Cat: "Be the ninety-ninth caller, give us your guess, and win a Bear T-shirt."

Donna: "If your guess actually does die in the next month, you win a *thousand* bucks!"

Cat: "And now the latest from U2."

Silence. More silence. Then the song began.

Flat as a pancake. *I* would have added while talking over the song intro (to give it more forward motion), "Let's hope it isn't anyone from U2. Still knocking it out of the park, here's their new one."

I mean, *really*. Show some enthusiasm.

I checked my email, read one from Shane. He asked how my vacation was going.

Vacation??? Never worked this hard in radio. Ever. But it beats playing What Dead Rock Star Will Die Next. How's Charlie?

He answered right away. *Not good.*

I could barely see to type. *So very sorry, Shane. I'm in Rome for two days. I'll go to the Vatican and light a candle for him.*

He wrote: *Thanks, Jaz. At this point, I'm ready to let him be with God.*

I looked around to see if anyone was watching me cry. *Shit!* A TV camera was pointing at me through the window. My phone had an app that showed where I was at all times, part of my contract. Standing beside the cameraman was Ree putting on his wounded puppy dog look.

"What are you getting emotional about?" he asked.

"Shane's little boy, the one with brain cancer, probably isn't going to make it."

"Man, nothing's rougher than that. But why'd you have to sneak off?"

"Can't I get away on my own once in a while? Geez."

Bring on the conflict.

In a hired car on our way to that night's club gig, I started to doze off in the backseat, my head resting on Ree's lap as he gently massaged my neck.

"Have you had enough of New York yet?"

I mumbled, "Not even close." His hand stopped moving. "Are you expecting me to move back to Richmond?"

"I'm just thinking this manager business may not be you."

That opened my eyes.

"I don't think you're happy. I see how excited you get when we go to radio stations, how annoyed you get with a lot of the rest of my life. I'm not crazy about it either, but I can't change it. You could be on a station in Richmond and have a lot more fun and influence. In New York, you're at the bottom of the food chain."

I sat up straight. "It's the number one market. Being there means you're at the top of it."

"You are one elitist chick. And New York is too damn expensive. You want to be smart about money? Live in Richmond, visit New York."

I said our hometown had little going on, and racism still ran deep. He said New York cabbies were famous for not picking up brothers. If that wasn't racist, what was? As for New York having more going on, he said, "Yeah, more crime, pollution, ridiculous prices, and bitter attitudes. At least Southerners act nice even if they hate you. What's that smile for?"

"I love arguing with you."

"Who's arguing? I'm stating the truth and you're refusing to accept it."

"Cut! Fabu!"

Howie called during our last day in Rome. The cameras were banned from the room as I turned on my cell speaker so Ree could hear. (Later, when the show aired, I saw they were taping the audio from the other side of the door.)

"The Bear is offering you three hundred thousand a year if you rejoin the Barenaked Radio Ladies." He waited a beat before saying, "Afternoon drive. Maxx is leaving to explore other opportunities."

Three hundred Gs because of a *Penthouse* shoot and a reality TV show?

I wasn't crazy about seeing Rick Rivers again, or Cat or Donna, but I was being offered *drive time in New York*. I could die happy. Ree didn't look happy at all. My heart sank.

"This is my dream, Ree. How can I not give it a shot?"

"That's not what's bothering me. Why does Jaz have to share the spotlight, Howie? She's good enough to have her own show."

That made me feel a lot better.

"One step at a time," Howie said. "There's a good chance the station will change formats soon. Then the major shakeout will follow. I'd hang in."

What I really wanted to ask him was how much they were paying Cat. It was probably for the best I didn't know.

"If *Ree-ality* hits, I'll renegotiate," he said. "Take the bird in hand. Now, I know this means Jazmyn can't manage you, Ree. The radio show has to come first professionally. She's spent over a decade building her radio career. What if you break up? It wouldn't help your image if she blew her chance to do afternoon drive for your career."

Any mention of our relationship not lasting only deepened our resolve to make it work.

"Ree, female viewers will love you moving to New York to accommodate your woman."

"All right," Ree said, "take your juicy bite out of the Big Apple, Jazmyn Brown. I know this is what you've always wanted."

I let out a whoop. "Afternoons in New York!"

As much as I loved him, I loved being on the radio, too. But once again, we'd be planets in two separate orbits.

Was I any different from the stripper in his song?

"The Vatican, *per favore.*"

As we got closer, the traffic was at a near standstill. The driver communicated in his broken English that 10,000 people a day visit Vatican City. We paid him and started to walk.

The camera crew appeared.

"I wanted to light a candle for Charlie by myself, without cameras," I muttered.

Joe Lumas lit into me. "Are you insane? This is going to be one of the most touching moments we've got in between all this other crap."

At the entrance to the Sistine Chapel, the guard pointed to a sign that said no bare legs or arms allowed on men or women. You couldn't light candles there either.

"St. Peter's Basilica will let you in if you cover your arms," a man going in told me, pointing to a church not far away. "There are vendors who can help you."

"Can you light candles there?"

"*Si, signorina.*"

It felt wonderful to sightsee like normal people. Then we noticed the stares, people following the camera crew that was following us.

I was thrilled when we found that St. Peter's did not allow cameras! We removed our microphones. It felt like taking off a pair of shoes that were giving me blisters.

Ree put his arm around me. "See you guys later."

The basilica was breathtaking. The crowds faded from our sight and we fell silent in awe.

Holding hands we slowly walked around, taking it all in. The great shafts of celestial sunlight pouring in through the dome, the massive ornate arches, the cool marble floors with groups of people kneeling in prayer.

I lit a candle for Charlie and prayed for him and Shane. Charlie's mom, too. I lit another and prayed for me.

Dear God. Thank you for all the blessings you've bestowed on me and Ree. Please give me a sign that I'm on the right path with Ree.

We wandered into a smaller room where more people were praying. We were transfixed by the feeling, artistry, love, and dedication that had gone into making this sacred structure.

Ree took my hand, giving me the look I couldn't refuse.

"Marry me."

I held back tears that had appeared from nowhere. "That was fast," I managed to say. "I was just praying for a sign we were going to work."

His look made me realize what I'd said.

"You have *doubts?*"

"Not anymore. I didn't realize how much I needed to hear those words."

Our lips rushed to meet. If it was sacrilegious to kiss here, I didn't care.

"How soon, Ree?"

"Soon. Joe will be angry I didn't ask you on-camera," he said softly. "I'll do it at the end of shooting the show. I wanted my proposal, my *real* proposal, to be just between us."

"I love you so much, Ree. I'll never forget this moment."

He leaned closer. "Me neither, Mrs. Roberts."

27

WOULD THE REAL JAZMYN BROWN PLEASE STEP FORWARD

In the wake of Madd Maxx's departure, a palpable fear had spread through the station. Only the cool-headed Ariella was unfazed. She had been right about him being snapped up by satellite radio.

"Two things always float to the top," she said when I called her. "Cream and crap."

The Barenaked *Afternoon* Radio Ladies should have been called Ego Central. The jealousy oozing from Cat and Donna toward me was so thick I could have floated to Siberia on it — exactly where they wished I would go, I'm sure. I was co-star of a coming reality TV show *and* dating someone famous. The listeners were bursting with attitude as well, some positive, others definitely not. "The whole station's gone down the freakin' tubes. Just pull the plug already."

"Madd Maxx was like family to me. I feel like my own brother has died. This is corporate anything-for-a-buck bullshit!"

"Maxx should consider it a blessin' he got outta derr. He gots too much class for youse guys."

"Cat's a fake and Donna's an airhead," was Krazy Karl's contribution. "Working with them drags you *down*, Jazmyn *Brown*."

Donna fought back. "I am not an airhead, you gross, smelly nut with holes in your organs."

"But with an amazing body, as you pointed out, Donna D.," I commented.

"You're damn right I have an amazing body, but you won't see it. Only Jazmyn is worthy."

Donna squeaked, "But she doesn't want to show it to anyone but her boyfriend. I on the other hand ..."

Enough with this boyfriend biz. When would I get to call Ree my fiancé?

Next Donna was threatening to climb the radio tower of One World Trade Center *naked*.

"Won't happen," Karl said. "Security issues."

He offered another location. Titus, who was guiding us through our initial two weeks on afternoon drive, put him on hold while we played commercials. *Lots* of commercials at higher rates than Maxx's show, I heard.

"Don't want to divulge too much over the air," Mr. I Call The Shots said.

Karl said he would find a tower for Donna to climb. If she managed to reach 300 feet he would strip naked and climb the whole thing.

"Donna, don't do it," said Cat.

"I agree," I said. "This is crazy."

"There you go again, not having any faith in me. I do this for a living."

"That's right," I said. "You do it *for a living*. Donna doesn't."

"It's just climbing a tower! I won't be *fixing* anything."

Positively gleeful, Titus scheduled Donna to do the tower climb challenge right after Labor Day, when the important fall ratings would be on. He was also going to figure out a way to raise money for a charity at the same time.

"I wouldn't climb a flight of stairs for that guy," said Cat after Karl hung up.

I didn't have a good feeling about this stunt. But then I didn't have a good feeling in general. I hadn't had a decent night's sleep in ages. If I did drift off, dreams woke me up.

I was either flying or I was trapped. In one I was flying upside down. What did that mean?

"I can't decide if the Napoleonic Titus Tucker is brilliant or leading us to our Waterloo," I told Ariella in another late-night call.

"It doesn't matter," she said. It was her favorite response to just about anything. "If the radio show goes away tomorrow, you've arrived. It's your decision how far you'll let yourself be sucked up into the madness."

"You mean how long I can pretend to be Jazmyn Brown?"

She paused a beat. "Are you pretending?"

I had no answer.

Marcie Lauffer was middle-aged and motherly, instantly putting me at ease with her comforting smile, big cushy couch, and earth-tone décor. A box of color-coordinated Kleenex sat beside my chair. I was nervous. Was this going to be like I'd seen in the movies? I reveal things I don't want to tell anyone. She makes a pithy remark. Light bulb goes on in my head. I leave with my self-awareness higher and destructive ways conquered.

I rambled on, I cried, I made her laugh. I recapped my childhood, went on about my parents, weight issues, radio, Ree, Nigel, more Ree, Shane and his son, even more Ree, the TV show, Howie, career, babies, the future, and the fact that sometimes I thought about quitting radio and becoming a veterinarian, if I could attain such a lofty goal.

She nodded, smiled, jotted notes.

"Have you ever heard of the fear of success?" she asked.

"No. Fear of failure, yes."

"We often feel guilty surpassing our parents, siblings, and peers. It holds us back from attaining, or at least enjoying, success."

I considered her statement. Was that what felt off to me?

"Maybe you're right. It's the weirdest feeling to be at 'the top,'" I said. "There's always someone higher. It's like climbing a glass wall. Some unseen force is holding me there. At any moment I could slide right down."

"Unless you grow suction cups for your feet and hands."

We were out of time.

"You're at a very exciting age," she said. "Life is ripe with potential in all directions. Why settle down with one man? A baby? Your sense that you'll be ready in a couple of years might be right. However ..." She sat up, palms on her knees as if she was about to stand and looked at me. "Life usually doesn't happen according to our timetable."

She went to her computer. "Weekly sessions would be good, Jazmyn. How does next Wednesday look for you?"

"That's it? You aren't going to tell me what I should do?"

She smiled.

"Am I being like Dorothy in *The Wizard of Oz* asking the Good Witch to get her home?"

"Somewhat."

"Can you at least give me a prescription that will help me get some sleep?" I asked. "I'm awfully cranky without it."

She told me to drink Sleepytime tea, take an over-the-counter melatonin tablet before bed, "And keep a log of your dreams."

As I walked briskly down Columbus Avenue, I called Ariella.

"Two hundred bucks to hear myself yak for fifty minutes!"

"That's nothing," she said. "I know people paying more than twice that."

"If they weren't crazy before starting therapy, that's certainly proof they are now."

"Are you going back?"

"Why? I have the job I always wanted, the man I always wanted, I'm thin. What's the problem?"

"Knowing that is worth a lot more than two hundred dollars."

I passed a sad homeless woman rummaging through the trash while I squawked on a cell phone worth $500. For the moment, Ree and I were living in a large designer-furnished Tribeca loft with a landscaped wraparound terrace overlooking the Hudson River. It was essentially a set. Very little in it belonged to us. We split the rent with the production company. Our *half* came to ten grand a month.

How did this woman end up on the street? Could that happen to me? What was the point in having it all if I constantly worried it would disappear?

Back to *Ree-ality*.

The cameras caught us arguing over my wanting Ree to turn his phone off at midnight and him telling me I was acting like a jail warden. Great sex did not follow. I was so sure Joe had hidden a camera in the bedroom that I didn't make the slightest overture.

Neither did Ree, which bothered me more. What bothered me the *most* was the posse.

Toward the end of our time together way back when, our Richmond pad would be crowded with perpetually high, glassy-eyed dudes who stayed up all night with Ree pontificating about nonsense like colonizing Mars. I'd go to bed early to the familiar sound of Ree and his companions' coke-induced post-nasal-drip hawking. Often I'd wake to the sound of a pot-generated coughing fit, just in time to get ready for my radio job.

When I put my foot down he stayed out all night, which made me crazier.

It was creeping into our life again, this time with expensive liquor and louder talking and laughing. Provocatively dressed women lounged around like hood ornaments as their sloppily dressed men went off on various conspiracy theories. Ree was especially keen on how the government and Illuminati were controlling the stock market and the price of oil. More than once the cameras caught me shaking my head in disbelief. Or falling asleep.

Ree hardly touched alcohol, but when he did (only when the cameras were off), he'd go too far. One night I found him nodding off in a bath overflowing with suds. All I could see was his dark face poking through a cloud of white.

"You're drunk!"

"I'm shelf-medicatin', Jazzy. I need a mental cavation, I mean, vacation. Can't take a real one. Come on. Drink up'n geh in here wiff me."

I did. I needed a mental cavation, too.

In fairness, we socialized with movers and shakers far more than the losers. We hosted a benefit dinner party to raise money for a school that had lost all of its musical instruments in a fire.

It ended up filling one whole minute of airtime.

I had a far more visceral response to the lowbrow hangers-on. Joe tapped into that.

When a few of them showed up with guns, I exploded. Joe would edit their one visit so it seemed like they were there regularly.

All the things that upset me, according to Ree, were done for the show.

"Who wants to see two people getting cozy in front of a TV watching shows about cooking and renovating," he said.

Both he and Howie reminded me that this show would make our stock soar on the show-biz equivalent of the New York Stock Exchange.

"You're in the big leagues now," said Howie, "as long as you handle it like a pro."

One night, Joe Lumas showed up without a camera crew when Ree was in Boston doing a benefit for KISS-108. What new way had he found for me to sell my soul to the TV gods?

"I left my cell here," he said when I let him in. "Can't live without that."

Suspicious, I kept the front door open. I rubbed my neck, watching as he looked around.

"You look tense, Jazmyn. I give excellent massages."

"I'll be sure to tell your wife that if I ever meet her."

"If I wasn't married?"

"I'm in love with Ree, in case you hadn't noticed. And he could, and would, beat the shit out of you."

He looked me up and down. "Sure Ree's keeping you satisfied?"

"Of course."

"You said you haven't been getting enough sleep." He reached into his pocket. "Maybe these will help you relax."

He handed me a vial of a prescription medication. Percocet.

The rattle of the pills inside was like an old familiar toy I hadn't played with in a while. Was it a coincidence that he'd brought them along, or did he know about my love affair with painkillers?

I hesitated too long.

Smiling, he said, "Our secret."

"No, thanks."

Throwing them on the couch with a devious smile, he left.

A million lights of gold beckoned outside the window that offered a fabulous view of Manhattan. I sat there turning the vial around. When I opened it, the chemical smell made my stomach turn.

But, oh, was it tempting to float on that temporary cloud of happiness.

Flushing the pills down the toilet, I tossed the vial. I waited to feel good, proud of myself, but instead I felt a terrible ache inside.

Bringing up WBRR on my phone, Jimi Hendrix's "The Wind Cries Mary" was just starting. I remembered Ree playing it for me early in our romance. I'd never heard anything like it and was transfixed. He explained the technical genius of the song. Something about chromatically ascending "five" chords with a missing note, and a syncopated something that created an odd downbeat. It all added up to an eerie, disorienting song that sucked you right in and made your heart break.

Its effect had only deepened with time.

28

Long Way to the Top. Short Fall Down.

Titus Tucker posted an ongoing poll on the WBRR website. Listeners voted for their favorite Barenaked Radio Lady, pitting us against each other even more. He'd probably hired elves to spend all day voting, the way some record companies hired kids to barrage radio stations with requests for their latest releases.

The day Donna D. was to climb the radio tower she was way ahead. For every rung she climbed, a listener had donated $100 to the Red Cross. We'd raised $30,000. Donna was committed to reaching the 300th rung.

"How hard can a measly three hundred be?" she quipped. There were 1,112 rungs in all.

Titus had found a company that would let Donna climb the outside cross rungs provided

1) Fire & Rescue were on hand, 2) she was tethered to a pulley that ran the length of the tower, and 3) we gave them lots of plugs.

I was stationed to do play-by-play at the mammoth metal structure in the middle of a New Jersey field. The Manhattan skyline was so far in the distance it looked like a toy train set. Titus was producing in the studio with Cat on the mike there.

What no one considered was that it would be so hot. A September heat wave had the thermometer climbing into the nineties that Thursday. Karl recommended not doing it, especially with thunderstorms in the forecast as well. But with the media coverage, ads sold, $30K in donations, and listener momentum cresting during a critical ratings period, there was no backing out on the *chance* Mother Nature might throw a few thunderbolts our way.

The square-shaped big yellow safety air bag on the ground looked to be about two stories tall. No worries about bouncing off that once you sank into it.

The tower, with its masculine lattice of interconnecting thick steel, was a work of industrial art. I'd never really thought about these monolithic steel structures essential to radio and TV. Standing at its foot, I had to bend my head all the way back to see the top of it.

This was insane.

True, I'd done crazy stuff when I was trying to make my mark, like riding a mechanical bull at a county fair and roller skating in my PJs at a late-night roller rink pajama party.

Posing practically naked for *Penthouse*.

They didn't hold a candle to this.

Sweat was already coating my face, and my shirt was sticking to my back. It felt like July. I made sure Donna put sunscreen on and drank plenty of water. She'd been working out constantly. Since doing this stunt naked turned out to be illegal (Karl agreed if he lost the bet he'd climb the tower in the smallest G-string made), she decided to climb in a microscopic day-glow orange thong bikini.

The nerdy male EMT couldn't take his eyes off her ass. He asked if she'd hydrated.

"Absolutely. And you can hydrate me when it's over."

He literally walked into the side of his van.

She flirted with him some more when he came back to hook a bottle of water onto what little she was wearing. She already wore a meter strapped to a belt to alert her if the RF output was too high (what had caused the holes in Karl's organs).

Then the hunkiest, bicep-bulging fireman I'd ever laid eyes on swaggered in her direction. Did he work out his facial muscles as well?

She twirled away from the EMT and looked right at him. Please don't throw yourself at this guy, I thought. Like he doesn't get that all day long.

"Now here's a man who knows all about water," she said. "Mr. Fireman, what's *your* name?"

"Bryce."

She struck a sexy pose, said, "Yo, VIP, let's kick it!" and started singing the song "Ice Ice Baby," substituting Bryce for ice.

Oh, boy.

Karl stepped in, handing her a water carrier on a shoulder strap. "Put the bottle in this, then over your head and across your body. We can drop the RF meter. That's ridiculous. I checked the level. It's fine."

"What do you think, Bryce?" The only opinion that mattered to her.

"This gentleman knows a lot more about climbing towers than I do, miss," he said in a damn sexy voice.

The RF meter was history. I had a momentary image of Titus Tucker deviously overriding the system so the signal would send this stunt far beyond where it should go. It disappeared as I listened more closely to Bryce while he and Donna flirted. No discernible accent.

I almost asked him if he'd ever done voice-overs. Shane had told me some of the biggest guys in the biz were discovered simply by being in the right place at the right time. One was in a bar band, couch surfing with anyone who would put up with him. A talent agent heard him talk on stage between songs and approached him about doing VOs. He had no idea what she was talking about. A year later he was buying a million-dollar condo.

"I love your voice," Donna said.

"Thanks. Yours is cute," he said, "but you need to pay attention to what Karl says."

Karl backed off. "No, sir, rescue is your wheelhouse. You can hook her up. And make sure she puts her helmet on."

The fireman looked at her closely. "How much do you weigh?"

"One-ten."

"Do you mind if I lift you up for a moment? Just to double check."

"Not at all!"

Up she went in the air like a gleeful little kid. I snapped a photo and caught Karl scowling.

"I think you're a hundred five," Bryce said.

Karl handed him a hook to put on the belt. "Use this one. It'll hold over a hundred pounds." He briskly walked off, conceding defeat.

I could feel his I-never-had-a-chance rejection, like when I was pushed aside by cute girls in school when I showed an interest in someone. Eventually, you just stop trying.

We looked at the huge metal contraption Karl had handed her. Donna's hand dropped.

"It's so heavy! Isn't there something lighter?"

"Let me see," I said as I tried to hold it. "Yeah, this weighs about as much as you." I asked Bryce, "How can she climb with that?"

"I'll take a look in the truck."

He came back with a much smaller one. "I used this to get a Newfoundland out of a burning building. She weighed more. Should be fine."

"Should be or will be?" I queried.

"*Will* be."

A thick belt with a loop was put around Donna's tiny waist, the hook attached to the loop.

She walked to the base of the tower (shaking her skinny ass most of the way) and Bryce attached her to a pulley on a steel cable that ran the length of the tower. Donna placed a bright red rock climbing helmet on her head and rubbed her hands together before clasping the first rung. She was wearing Karl's black cowhide climbing gloves with the tips missing.

"Piece of cake!" Donna crowed. To Bryce, "You can tie me up anytime."

He lowered his deep voice and whispered something to her that caused her, I swear, to blush and nervously titter.

I rushed in. "No distractions, buddy. She's never done this before."

"What are you, my mother?" she said, in a vicious tone I'd never heard from her before.

She put her right foot on the first rung. It was impossible to miss her nipples hard as jellybeans. Neither did Bryce.

The crowd cheered and whooped. Karl was above us wearing only a zebra print G-string. I had to smile. What a body he'd been hiding. He started scaling the tower with no belt, hook, tether, helmet, or pulley. Go, Karl. Take that, Bryce.

"I can't wait to prove you wrong, *Sieve* Vicious," Donna called out to him, her tone friendlier.

Scattered laughter momentarily lightened the mood.

I guessed the crowd that had gathered to be around fifty people. Maybe. Most of them had some tie to the station or promotion. This wasn't the most populated area and most people were at work now. At least one TV station truck was there. The VTV crew was missing. They were following Ree on his *Rolling Stone* interview and photo shoot. He had made the cover of *Rolling Stone*. Nude, of course.

"If *you* were climbing the tower, *maybe* we'd send a crew," Joe Lumas had told me.

He was always making digs that I was a lowly radio DJ. When I had to cut out to do my show, he'd say things like, "Yeah, don't want to miss that ninety-ninth caller for tickets to the monster truck show." I kept waiting for the day when those remarks, from him or anyone, would roll right off me.

Come to think of it, when was the last time Ree had listened to my program? How many hours had I spent listening to his songs as he created and performed them? I couldn't focus on that right now. I was working. And I'd accepted a long time ago that recording artists mainly liked listening to their own music, preferably when freshly recorded.

Donna talked into her headset as she began climbing, describing the sun on her back, the heat of the metal rungs.

"This water bottle's heavy and getting in the way." She pulled it off and tossed it into the air. The EMTs, firemen, and Karl did not look happy.

"If she gets heatstroke she'll become confused," the female EMT said. "I think she's been pretending to drink water. The level in the bottle looks unchanged."

"This helmet is hot and making sweat pour into my eyes!" Donna cried.

"Try loosening it a tiny bit," I said.

"Then I won't be able to see!"

I was about to say, "Whatever you do, don't take it off," when it went flying through the air. A few jerks in the crowd applauded.

The EMT nodded to the south. "This is not going well. And I don't like those clouds."

Karl whipped around. "Shit!"

He had a headset on too and could hear what was going on where I stood and in the studio, as well as from Donna. He shot down the tower like a monkey, holding a water bottle to her lips. Through binoculars I could see her legs and arms trembling.

Again I marveled at his physique. How could anyone not?

"Don't leave me," she whispered.

"Donna, come down," I tried to stay in my cool, low radio voice. "This isn't worth hurting yourself over."

Back in the Manhattan studio, Titus was in control, not Cat, but I wasn't sure how much he was putting on the air. I had to assume everything.

"I know I can do it," she said. "I have to! The Red Cross and listeners are depending on me."

"You've done enough," Cat said.

Donna moved up another twenty rungs.

Karl was right underneath her now, frequently taking one of his bare hands off the blazing hot metal and shaking it.

Squinting through the binoculars, I could practically see sweat pouring into her thick ankle socks. It must be pretty wet inside her gloves by now. The crowd was going wild, yelling, "You can do it!" and urging her on. Only a few said, "Get down!" Some left, freaked out.

"Where's King Kong when you need him?" Donna said, out of breath.

"I'm right here," said Karl. "I'll protect you, not that fireman. Dammit. Where's the hook I gave him? "

"It was too heavy. You know, Karl, you're all right. Just take a shower every day."

"I do! My job is very physical, in case you didn't notice. It's *normal* to sweat."

"How high am I now?" she asked.

"Two hundred feet. Now be careful. I'm not sure about that hook."

"He said he rescued a dog with it that weighed more than I do."

"From how many feet?"

"Stop being negative. Only one hundred more to go."

I heard a rumble in the distance that I thought was a jet.

Karl yelled, "Abort! Lightning can strike from miles away! Abort!"

"Yes," Cat and I chimed in. "Come down now!"

"I'm not going to be hit by lightning."

Karl tried to grab Donna's foot. She kicked away his hand and kept climbing.

"I mean it," he said. *"You have to get down now."*

"Leave her alone, Karl," hissed Titus.

She grimaced and moved up the ladder.

"Donna. Get off that thing!" I was screaming, no longer cool.

"Get up offa that thing and dance till you feel bettah!" She was bumping and grinding to the James Brown song. "AH!"

She almost fell off. The crowd gasped.

"Karl, you don't want me to make it so that I'll lose the bet," she huffed. "Just for that, I'm climbing all the way."

She kept going, bouncing up rung after rung another fifty feet until she yowled, "My leg!"

"Uh-oh," said the EMTs. "Heat cramp."

The fire truck moved in. Bryce hurried up the ladder, calling out, "It's okay, Donna. Take deep breaths. Don't panic."

The ladder only came half way to where she was. Titus yelled into my headset to say something. Nothing would come out.

"What are you doing?" Karl screamed at Donna. "Put that back on!"

She had unhooked the tether. "I'm just getting my water."

"That's not your water. This is." He held up the bottle he'd taken up with him. "That line is what's going to save your life if you fall!"

"AHHH. My *leg*."

I could hear Cat and Titus going at it in the control room. Cat was screaming, "Go to music! This is too horrible to listen to."

"Are you crazy?" he said. "This is the best radio this city has heard in years. It's drama! Say something, Jazmyn!"

"Not live."

"Okay, you're off the air. Now, talk to me."

"It's drama, all right, of the sickest kind. She could die, Titus!"

"She's going to be fine."

"No, she's not!" said Cat.

"No guts, no glory, girls."

Just as Karl was about to reattach her to the tether a big gust of wind came up, so strong I thought it moved the air bag below. No, they *had* to have that thing tied down. But Donna was no match for the blast of air and lost her footing again. Karl reached for her. She fell back, him with her. The air bag didn't seem wide enough to catch them from that high of a fall.

Screams rose around me. I was told mine was the loudest.

He turned her toward him, yanked off her headset and yelled, "Put your hands in front of your face!"

I would later find out he was trying to land on his feet with a little give in his knees, the best way to land from a steep fall. Also, that falls from over 100 feet are almost always fatal. This was more than twice that distance.

He hit the very edge of the airbag feet first. Donna instinctively grabbed him around the neck. I will never forget the sound of his body slamming into the ground back first, Donna clinging to him.

When the emergency crew lifted her, she was limp and unconscious. Or dead.

I recovered my ability to move and rushed over. Karl's headset had lodged into the side of Donna's head and the microphone had impaled her chin. Blood spread over that side of her face.

The female EMT pulled me aside. "You have one second to reassure her she'll be okay. Do *not* tell her what happened." She rushed over to Karl.

The other EMT wheeled up a gurney and barked, mainly to Bryce, "No room for anyone else in the ambulance."

Bryce leaned over her. "Donna, you're going to be fine. Karl knew what he was doing in that fall. He saved your life."

Needing to lash out at someone, I said, "Did *you*, pretty boy Floyd?"

He threw up his hands. "Hey! She unhooked it. I didn't!"

I held Donna's hand as long as I could. "I'll see you at the hospital. They have to do a routine checkup. You'll be back on the radio tomorrow. You just had the wind knocked out of you. That's all."

She tried to say something. I think it was "How is Karl?" but it was impossible for her to talk clearly. That's when the fear set in for both of us.

I ran to Karl who was still conscious and in shock.

"It's my fault," he said so softly I had to put my ear next to his face. He could barely take a breath. "I'm a fuck-up."

"Karl, calm down. You'll be fine. You just fell from the edge of the air bag. And you're not a fuck-up. Not at all. You protected Donna."

It was the way he had landed and from how far he had fallen. That thud and crack. He wasn't fine. He had to have serious internal bleeding. Blood was seeping from the back of his head, forming a pool around him.

He smiled as if he were seeing me for the first time in years. "I'm your number one fan, Patty." His eyes turned funny, like he was seeing through me to something wondrous.

"Karl?"

Another bolt of lightning fanned out into several spikes across the sky, followed by a deafening boom.

When I turned back to him, he was no longer of this earth. A man who had easily climbed towers over a thousand feet was foiled by a twenty-foot air bag.

He was loaded into the ambulance with Donna. How the sobs welling up in me didn't crack my ribs I'll never know.

The firemen urged everyone to retreat to a protected area. I was in a fog looking for my Cruiser. I climbed inside, numb, and heard Titus yelling, "What's wrong, Jazmyn. What happened?"

"Karl is dead."

"SHIT."

As I relayed what had happened into the headset, one more streak of white lightning ripped through the sky, then a long rumbling. Norman Greenbaum's "Spirit in the Sky" started playing on WBRR.

"That is in *really* poor taste, Titus."

I turned off the headset and flung it onto the passenger seat, leaned on the steering wheel and bawled. Light rain turned into a downpour.

A man in rain gear with a TV camera on his shoulder pounded on my window, yelling something. His voice sounded like it was under water. I locked the door, found my keys, and managed to start the ignition, my hands violently shaking.

My cell rang as I drove. It was Shane. "Are you all right?"

"No! I have to call you back."

"Wait! I think I can help."

"There's nothing you can do now." I hung up.

I didn't know where I was, I realized. The ambulance was long gone. I searched for the closest hospital on my car GPS. The TV truck followed closely.

I called Ree, hysterical.

"Hey, hey, it's okay. You have every right to be upset. I wish I could be there. Let's talk later. I'm doing my *Rolling Stone* shoot."

"Oh, right."

Another call came in. It was the big boss, Ken Crewett, the calm eye in the center of the storm. He asked how I was.

"Terrible."

"You handled it fine. But we have a catastrophe on our hands. I'm hiring a top PR firm specializing in this kind of crisis. Don't go to the hospital. Donna's family is on the way there. Come to the radio station. Fend off all questions from anyone about what happened. Say nothing on social media."

Howie was on his way to the station, he said.

Traffic on the Jersey Turnpike was moving fast even in the hard rain. A semi swerved in front of me. I jumped on the horn and watched a hairy hand flip me the bird as I fought not to flip over. At least the TV truck wasn't on my tail.

There was a long backup at the George Washington Bridge toll. I called Ariella. She sounded out of breath after my news.

"Karl is in a better place now. But Donna. Poor girl."

"Has anything like this ever happened to you?"

"Not where someone died."

"I hate this business right now."

"I've been there." She said she was at her place in Montauk. "Come out. Take a walk on the beach."

I knocked my fist on my head. "I forgot you took time off. No, I'd be ruining your vacation."

"You would have ruined it if you hadn't called. Come."

"The beach does sounds great right now. Let me get back to you."

Inching along in traffic allowed me to go over the events of the day. I should have done this. Shouldn't have done that. Why hadn't I …

The car in front of me had two kids in the back waving and making faces. I thought about Karl as a child. At what point did everyone know he was different? What a sad life he'd had.

Driving across the GW Bridge, I took in the Manhattan skyline. It didn't look so glorious now.

29

DAMAGE CONTROL

When I reached the station, lots of office doors were closed. When I saw a wiped-out Cat, I knew I must have looked a wreck too.

I joined her, Ken, Rick, Howie, Titus, and a lawyer named Henry in the same room where I had attended my first WBRR jock meeting. This time the room was more like an inquisition chamber than a locker room.

Rick Rivers' goatee was nearly gone from picking.

Titus twitched in his seat as his father yelled over the speakerphone. "Don't blame this on Titus. He's the best producer in radio."

"Then whose fault is it?" I asked. "We told him to stop the live broadcast when it was obvious Donna was losing it. And again when lightning wasn't far away, as per Karl's instructions. Titus said to continue."

"Not true!" He pounded his tiny fist on the table. "There's no proof of that!"

"That's because it was off the air," Cat said, "but we both heard you say it."

"Karl told Donna to come down. *She* wouldn't do it." Titus paused. "Maybe I kept it on the air a *fraction* too long."

His father's booming voice cut him off. "He thought she was going to change her mind. Naturally he let the bit run. Karl is the one solely to blame for this. He must have done something wrong in setting up Donna's gear. May have even *planned* it. Everyone knows he was crazy. This was his way to make history, like a suicide bomber."

Ken Crewett's fury was building. "Easy to blame someone who's now dead. You didn't think the moment she released her tether was the time to bail out?"

Tommy bellowed, "We were given a hell of a challenge to put your piece-of-shit station back on the map! Look at the trends for the month. They doubled in all key demos! Your rate cards, too. Imagine what we can do over an entire book."

Only Titus wasn't shocked.

"The image of this station has been tarnished forever," Ken said. "Advertisers are canceling schedules. This is being called the Hinden*bear* Disaster online. Someone died. Another may be permanently disabled, and at a very young age. Your son used extremely poor judgment. I put the blame squarely on his shoulders."

"What?" Titus seemed to shrink even further. "It's Cat, Jazmyn, and Donna's show. They have the ultimate liability!"

"You know damn well you said *you* were the one to decide what was over the line!" Cat yelled.

"I don't recall him saying that," said his father. "Do you, Titus?"

"I do," I said.

The phone nearly vibrated from the growl in Tommy Tucker's pipes. "Titus, you edited that session up, right?"

He paled. "I did some of it and handed the rest over to Shane. Donna was a ditz, Dad! I couldn't teach her anything!"

"It just so happens Shane is here," Ken said, "looking for that session."

That's what he meant by being able to help!

Within minutes we heard Titus's recorded voice saying, "If something's questionable, run it by me. I'll make the call."

"Like broadcasting two listeners screwing at St. Patrick's Cathedral," Tommy had added, laughing.

Cat gave me a thumbs-up.

"I rest my case," Ken said. "The services of Tucker Transformational Talk are terminated." He turned to the lawyer. "Our contract is null and void, right, Henry?"

"You'll hear from *my* lawyer, you fucking jerk!"

Ken wasn't done with him. "You should really clean up your language and your act, Tommy. It's your only hope for salvaging what little business you'll have left after this. Radio is as corporate as Dow Chemical now. You're a dinosaur."

He clicked him off the speakerphone. Titus fled.

"Those mother*tuckers,*" Ken said. "Ladies, I need to convene in my office for a few minutes with these gentlemen. Would you please stay on the premises a little longer?"

As the lawyer and brass conferred, Cat paced the hallway, cursing under her breath.

"Cat." I opened my arms. We embraced. "Let's go thank Shane."

We went to his studio, hugging him. He insisted he'd done nothing special.

"I need to freshen up." Cat left, throwing a smile my way.

"You two friends now?" Shane asked.

"War buddies. Not sure about friends yet."

He went back to his control board. "Ken asked me to stay to do some emergency production but wouldn't say what it was. Something's up."

I plopped onto the funky sofa. "What a day."

"I'll say. How do you feel?"

I spilled my guts about how guilty I felt over what happened.

"Maybe doing voice-overs isn't so bad," I said. "Nice and safe. You work normal hours, you don't deal with wackos, and the pay is phenomenal."

"I hope this doesn't come off the wrong way, but not many men in this business make the kind of money I do, much less women. I count my blessings every day." He pulled up a chair. "Every DJ hits the wall at some point, Jaz. You could focus on announcing like I did, but it's more competitive than being a DJ for just the reasons you mentioned. Plus, in New York, you're up against thousands of extremely talented actors." His voice shifted to cautious curiosity. "How's it going with Ree?"

"Up and down." Shane had a stubbly beard again, I noticed. I was afraid to ask, but had to. "Enough of my problems. How's Charlie?"

His smooth voice tightened. "Thanks for asking but I really can't talk about it."

"I understand. If there's anything I can do?"

"They're recommending just immediate family visit. It tires him to have company."

"I'm so sorry."

Not knowing what else I could say, I excused myself to walk around the station. "Might be my last look." I held up my cell phone up and took his picture. "Might be the last time I see you, too."

He registered surprise. "I hope not."

"Me, too. I feel like we'll be friends forever, Shane. But I could be back in Richmond after this." I grinned. "If you ever date again, be sure to shave your beard before you go out."

He was rubbing his chin and smiling as I left.

Passing the wall of rock star autographs, I ran my hand over the Beatles' signatures. I snapped photos throughout the station, making sure to capture Victor's Vendetta. I'd never see another studio like it.

The station was running on autopilot out of Dick and Dork's studio. There was no one on the air, just Shane's generic sweepers between songs. It gave me a chill.

I ran into a worried Cat. "Ken wants to see us," she said.

I barely noticed the spectacular view of lower Manhattan from his office.

"We need to suspend you with pay pending an investigation."

Howie assured us it was the best possible outcome and merely a formality.

"Is there any chance we'll be charged with something?" was Cat's question.

"Highly unlikely," Ken said, "though if Karl or Donna's family files a suit, you might be included. There's no way to know at this point. Just lay low for two weeks and do *not* talk to the press. Stay off *all* social media. And Jazmyn, we have to speak about the TV show you're doing."

Cat took off, on the verge of tears.

My ironclad obligation to *Ree-ality* was in place for another week of shooting.

"Since we don't know how this will all shake out," Howie said, "only touch on it for the cameras in the broadest of strokes. It could very well act as a springboard to a serious segment that Ree could add to as well."

I nodded blankly.

Ree called when I was on the road to Montauk to see Ariella. I told him what had happened and why I needed to escape.

"It'll do you good to get out of town, take a break," he said. "I'm workin' on some new tunes wit' Mo'. Got a motherfuckin' cool idea for my next album. *Rootin' Tootin' Rappin'*. I'm gonna sample Country and Western hits. Whatcha think?"

His "hood" speech was creeping back, Mo's influence. And what about him getting away from rap? I was in no frame of mind to discuss it.

"I love it."

"You don't sound it."

"This is only about the worst day of my life!"

"Okay, okay. Chill."

"Chill my ass."

Music thumped in the background. I heard female laughter. The eternal viperesses I would never vanquish. I also heard the unmistakable sound of post-nasal coke drip.

"Please tell me you're not doing that shit."

"What shit?"

I told the voice screaming in my head that he was doing drugs again to shut up.

"Forget it. I have to be in hiding anyway."

"The outlaw Jazmyn Brown," he said, in a movie preview voice.

"Why don't you come out to Montauk and tie me up until the authorities arrive?"

"We're going to Atlantic City when we wrap here."

I smelled trouble with a capital T. "I've never been there. I'll come with you."

"This is a male bonding thing, baby." Smooth as a snake. "Do your quality time with Ariella. Take a break. You need one."

Though it sounded like there was plenty of female bonding going on there, I scratched "policewoman" off my résumé for now. I was too beat.

"Fine." Click.

I called Shane somewhere near Ronkonkoma, Long Island. "I wanted to tell you again how thankful I am for what you did."

"I wish I could talk but I'm slammed with work."

There was something in his tone. "What's up, Shane?"

"You're always welcome to stop by and take my pirate station for a spin. I'd love to hear your uncensored playlist."

"Shane. What's going on?" Silence. "Are you okay?"

"I can't talk about it, Jaz."

Had to be Charlie.

"Sure, I'd love to come see your pirate station. *Arrr!*"

30

BUNGALOW OF BLISS

The soothing low tones of a large bamboo wind chime greeted me as I approached Ariella's house. The Indian summer air was noticeably cooler at the tip of Long Island. Nestled on a private lot overlooking a large pond, her cottage was white-trimmed, saltbox, cedar-shingled, and weathered to the color of driftwood.

Inside her home was bright and airy with several skylights. The mix of Eastern Indian and American Indian décor, plump chairs, inviting sofas, and patchouli-scented air banished the outside world. We wasted no time opening a bottle of white wine from the nearby North Fork.

"Cat's joining us for dinner," she said. "She has a place in East Hampton. I had a feeling she'd go there to hide out. She's pretty shaken." She squinted toward her serene pond. "I have a vibe she's hiding something. The truth always comes out here."

"Do tell."

"We'll see. Meanwhile, I'm marinating tuna caught this morning."

"I wish I had more of an appetite."

"I know how to remedy that. Maui Wowie."

"Why wait?"

"Because it's so potent, you'll be out cold before dinner is ready."

Dressed in jeans and a white linen shirt, Ariella glowed with a light tan. Her short hair was gray. It was the first time I'd seen her without a wig or makeup.

"You look serene as a Buddhist monk," I said. "Why wear those wigs? Aren't they uncomfortable?"

"As long as I'm on WBRR, I have to keep up the Ariella act."

She put an irresistible bowl of fresh-made guacamole rimmed with tortilla chips in front of me and I dug in.

"I don't need a joint after all."

She rubbed her stomach, then popped a chip in her mouth. I didn't think it was just a nervous tic, but I knew better than to ask. She'd say she was fine.

My frayed nerves quickly vanished as we walked to the beach and I inhaled the salt air.

Sitting in a bright green Adirondack chair, I watched the waves break until I drifted off. I dreamed about Ariella and a house that wasn't her house. It had a wide front porch with white rocking chairs. I was sitting there slowly rocking when a man came out from inside. I couldn't see his face.

When I woke up, I tried peeling back the layers of what the dream meant. Ree and I once had an exchange about white rocking chairs to match our white hair when we grew old together. I asked Ariella what it meant that I couldn't see who the man was in my dream.

"You don't know which man to be with—if any—would be the obvious interpretation," she said. "But most dreams, I think, are just scrambled signals from a weak antenna. Some, though, are epic. You know in your heart exactly what they mean." Seeing that her answer was confusing me even more, she added, "Don't get stuck in the paralysis of analysis."

"How about we get stuck in some Maui Wowie."

"Not yet," she said with a naughty finger wag.

Cat managed to look angelic in tight white pants, a white tank top with a flow-y white shirt over it, and high-heeled sandals. She deemed Ariella's place "charming, in a new-age way" and said she wouldn't be staying long.

"Today made me realize how precious my son is. I took him out of school for a few days and brought him out here. He's with friends now."

"Take off those shoes and relax," I said lightly. "My feet hurt just looking at them."

Ignoring my suggestion, "Let's get a status report on Donna. I'm worried sick."

We reached Donna's mother, a true Long Islander (with a hard "g" on Long). I was afraid she'd be angry at us and plotting a lawsuit.

"Thank you for believing in her," she said, to our relief.

Miraculously, Donna *only* had a broken jaw, a punctured Eustachian tube, and a couple of broken fingers and ribs. Her hearing in one ear could be permanently diminished. Her jaw would be wired shut for a few weeks. Then they would know if she'd need speech rehab.

"She'll get braces at last," her mother said, "and a more natural smile. Most important, she still has her sense of humor and love of radio. When the doctor told her the headset and microphone had been removed, she snapped her fingers like, 'Oh, darn.'"

We hadn't lost a member of the radio sisterhood, after all.

"Did our flowers arrive?" asked Cat. "The ones from me and Jazmyn."

"The most beautiful arrangement I've ever seen. Thank you! Donna loved them."

After we hung up, I thanked Cat. "What do I owe you?"

"Don't be silly."

"This calls for a toast." Ariella freshened our glasses. "To Donna's full recovery."

"And to Karl's memory," I said. "In a weird way I'm going to miss him. He was blunt, but honest." And often right, something I wasn't going to say in front of Cat.

"Did you hear what Donna called him, because of the holes in his organs?" Cat said. "Sieve Vicious."

Ariella didn't laugh. "I met Sid, all of the Sex Pistols." We leaned in for more. Wistfully, she said, "Beneath his rebel posing he did have a porous quality about him, like he never stood a chance of surviving. How sad he died of an overdose from heroin his mother scored for him."

How do you get past *that* past? At least Ree's wasn't as bad.

I thought about how many people Ariella had known in this business who were no longer here. After a while, I guess you have to get Zen about it. I would have to do the same with Karl.

"You know what I'd love right now?" said Cat. "A joint." When she heard about the Maui Wowie, she said, "I better see if my son can stay overnight with his friend."

Setting another place at the dining table, Ariella put her CD jukebox on "random." The house filled with great music from Motown to Metallica.

"Ladies, I have a collection of vintage clothes that need new homes. Would you like to take a look, see if anything speaks to you?"

First, we indulged in the triple-grade-A ganja. Loosened up, Cat strutted about in a vintage Gucci paisley halter top and a micro-mini plastic pink skirt, dissing rockers she thought were asses.

"He gave me no chit chat whatsoever," she said. "Just a jerk of his head and (with a British accent) 'Come with me, love, on my Canadian tour tomorrow.' I said 'Dude, I wouldn't travel to the Riviera with you.'"

We were in stitches, though we would have laughed at the recitation of a grocery shopping list. Damn, that stuff was crazy strong.

As the cool night descended, Cat wrapped herself in a flower power fringed shawl. I tried yellow cotton yoga pants with an Indian dashiki of orange, red, and gold. We set aside a few numbers for Donna.

In our stoned state, Cat and I helped Ariella prepare our gourmet feast. Bumbled along was more like it, often forgetting what we were about to do. Somehow we turned out a fabulous dinner of fresh tuna marinated in lime, cilantro, and vodka, and topped with a mango salsa. Also a tossed salad with lettuce and herbs grown in a neighbor's greenhouse, grilled local veggies, and multi- grain bread from a bakery down the street.

"Come on, Cat," I said as I carefully sliced the bread. "Who have you slept with at the station? Ken Crewett, right?"

They both answered. "He's gay!"

Cat tossed her head. "Only Chopper, right after Vee died."

"And ...? How was he?" Ariella asked.

"I couldn't stop crying. That's the real reason I avoid jock meetings. I'm still embarrassed all these years later."

Cat, embarrassed?

"What about you, Ms. Sex Goddess?" she said to Ariella.

"Maxx. Years ago."

I threw the bread knife down. "Shit! I almost cut my finger off!"

When that guffawing ended, Ariella said, "He was incredibly handsome in his younger days, and he wasn't dousing himself in cologne yet. I *had* to give in. I was messing up on the air too much in my distracted state. One night he just showed up." She shrugged. "I did it for the show."

"Don't leave us hanging," Cat said.

"He was wearing a Mexican poncho the first time." Ariella was relishing the memory as she tossed the salad. "He gallantly placed it on the floor of the studio for us. He lasted through all twenty-one minutes of Rare Earth's 'Get Ready.'"

I had no idea what song she meant. Cat sang, "Get ready. Cause here I *come!*"

We laughed so hard we couldn't make a sound, just grab our stomachs and pound on whatever surface was nearby.

When we were breathing normally again, Ariella added, "By the third time, he was done before the end of Zep's 'Good Times, Bad Times.'"

"That's under three minutes!" Cat cried.

Another round of hysterics followed.

Ariella said, "I used the 'I'm seeing someone' line and that was that." She took a beat. "And I never played 'Get Ready' again."

I couldn't hide my shock as Cat and Ariella talked about the groping and inappropriate behavior they'd dealt with in the past from men they'd worked for. That was one thing today's corporate radio had going for it. You couldn't get away with that behavior and keep your job. Rick Rivers knew how to walk the line just so ... for now.

We moved to a rustic pine table to eat our dinner. I admired the vase filled with flowers from her yard.

"I picked that up in Taos," Ariella said. "It's yours now."

I joked, "Do you have some incurable disease and you're giving everything away before you die?"

She stiffened as she divvied up the salad onto beautiful hand-painted plates.

"I have an abdominal aortic aneurysm," she said quietly. "It's been slowly growing for years. Watchful waiting they call it. Now they want to take it out because emergency surgery is very risky. I have a morbid fear of operations ever since my father checked out for good during one. Hey, I'm ready to go. I'm sixty-six, had a life beyond anything I ever imagined possible, and I am *not* cut out for a nursing home."

"Don't say that!"

"You have to do something!"

"After what I've been through already with cancer? Plus, I hate hospitals, doctors, anesthesia — and, most of all, being dependent on other people to look after me."

"You won't be out of commission that long," Cat said. "I'll hire a private nurse for you and you can recover out here."

"If I live through the surgery."

I broke down in heaving sobs. Ariella's eyes welled up with tears. Everything would be fine, we told her.

"I think you're going to meet a great guy once you get this operation out of the way," Cat said. "It's been holding you back."

"No more men!" she vowed.

The rest of the meal was subdued. I felt lucky to be healthy and young. I could imagine Ariella at my age, seducing men left and right. Seeing her now was another jarring wake-up call to grow up already, get a family going, find a "real" career. Beauty fades. Then what?

"I'll help you in any way," I said. I wanted to spend as much time with her as I could. I would ignore her protests that she didn't need help. She was just being proud.

"How's Ree?" Ariella asked cheerfully, changing the subject.

"Oh, you know, everything revolves around the TV show and his career pretty much. But I can't imagine being with anyone else."

She and Cat exchanged a look. Cat searched my face. "Everything okay?"

"I have nothing to complain about."

Ariella pulled back, crossed her arms, and gave me an I-don't-believe-it look.

I confessed that when it was just the two of us, I was crazy about him, but the rest of the time I had to be on guard against women, moochers, drugs, and the media. It was like being inside a bad dream. Once the show aired, things would only get worse.

Yet, if all that wasn't happening, it would be a sign *he* wasn't happening.

"Anytime I think about leaving him, my throat tightens, my stomach ties up in knots. I've had panic attacks where I can't breathe."

They shook their heads. "You've got it bad," Cat said.

"Perhaps you've broken the Eleventh Commandment."

"What's that?" I asked Ariella.

"Thou shalt have only one diva per household."

I laughed, but it was the rueful kind.

"We've known plenty of recording artists," Cat said. "Most of them act like children and need a lot of attention. It's all about them."

"Ree's different." It came out too forceful.

Ariella's head cocked in the direction of the music. The Beatles' "A Day in the Life" had hit its final crescendo. As its last note hung in the air for what would be almost a minute, Ariella said, "The ultimate cold fade."

Were Ree and I in a cold fade as well?

"Where's Ree now?" Cat asked. When I told her, she looked at the time on her cell. "It's eight-fifteen. Call him this instant."

"Why?"

She looked at me incredulously. "To see if he's with anyone."

My fingers lightly shook as I called.

A sexy woman's voice said, "Ree can't come to the phone now." Click.

I ran to the kitchen sink, afraid I might puke. Ariella was at my side with water. I hobbled back to the table, feeling like I'd been hit by a truck.

"That was Chee. She flirts with Ree right in front of me. She's pregnant with Big Mo's baby. No way she's fooling around with Ree, right?"

"Are you crazy?" Cat said. "Big Mo' is one of the most unattractive fuckers I've ever seen. And an asshole. She'll get his money and have your gorgeous Ree on her arm. Then have *his* baby!"

Ariella added, "If Ree wants to be a daddy, like you've said, and Mo' is his rival, what better way to one-up him than to be the one Mo's child considers his father."

I bolted up from the table. "I have to go!"

Ariella stopped me. "Not in your condition."

"I'm totally sober now."

"No, you're not."

"Yes, I am."

Cat's cell rang. "Oh, shit. It's Howie."

She slapped her face a few times and took the call outside. I grabbed my purse and car keys and waited to see what that the call was about. When Cat returned, something was very wrong. She slowly lowered herself into her seat at the dining table.

"As of midnight, WBRR will be playing Latin ballads."

I dropped what I was holding. Ariella and I both cried out, "Latin ballads?!"

"That was some damn good subterfuge," said Ariella, "generating the Edgy Talk rumors. The Latin stations were looking the other way."

"Why did they put us on in afternoon drive?" I wondered. "They had to have known about this. You can't change a format in a few hours."

"They probably were ready to roll it out after the next rating book," said Ariella. "The tower stunt forced their hand."

So putting three women on afternoon drive on a rock station appealing mostly to men hadn't been the big leap forward I'd thought. It was just for show until the switch.

"I'm sure Maxx knew," Ariella said, "and found a new gig fast instead of going down with the ship."

The flip. That was what Shane hadn't been able to talk about. He had to be doing production for it.

"Guys, help me!" cried Cat. "They want me to do *morning drive*. Not as a sidekick, *my* show as Catalina Cruz speaking Spanish!"

"And the problem with that is ...?" I asked.

Cat struggled to get out the next sentence. "I'm Romanian."

Ariella and I stood in stunned silence as she told us she didn't know until she was twenty-one, when she anonymously received a copy of her parents' marriage certificate. Her father's last name was Cruzmina, not Cruz. Her mother's was Arghezi. They'd wed in Bucharest.

"When I confronted them, they said Vee told them that in New York City they would have more opportunities and access to social services, grants, loans, and such if they were considered Hispanic. They spoke some Spanish and faked the rest. They had balls, I'll give them that. They changed my first name from Katrina to Catalina. I was one when this happened."

Cat said she always felt something wasn't right because she knew no living relatives. It also seemed odd that her family didn't speak Spanish.

"They said they didn't speak it around me so I would be more American. I can speak some, but not well enough to do a radio show."

"I see what a fix you're in," Ariella said.

"I'd just joined 'BRR as a Hispanic when I found out. What could I do? A big reason they'd hired me was to fill their minority quota. What I hate is how this affects my son. I can't stand hiding it. Vee advised me to keep my mouth shut, but he was from another era where family secrets were taken to the grave." She pushed her plate away. "I shouldn't have told you."

Ariella raised her glass. "If it's a crime to reinvent ourselves then we should all be thrown in the pokey."

Cat wouldn't be cheered. "I wanted to tell Howie the truth but couldn't. What do I do! I *need* this job because …" She looked away. This was even harder to say than her last confession. "I'm broke."

Ariella took it in stride and replied with another lift of her glass, "Join the club."

"No, I'm *really* broke.

"Wait," I said, "how can that be if you're making a quarter million a year and have all the money your husband must have left you?"

Ariella was as curious as I. Finally Cat said, mustering as much pride as she could, "First, a quarter mil in New York City isn't that much, Jazmyn."

After living here awhile, I had to agree.

"Second, I haven't made that in awhile. I had an amazing investment guy. Amazing! Twenty percent return year after year. My portfolio barely dropped after the crash in 2008. I should have known that simply wasn't possible. Howie said my job was in jeopardy and negotiated a big salary cut. I was fine with it. I was set.

"Turned out Mr. Amazing had a lot in common with Bernie Madoff. Overnight I went from being worth millions to hardly anything."

"Oh, Cat, that's terrible," Ariella said.

"I was best friends with his wife! I trusted him! They fled to South America. I took out a second mortgage on my apartment and house. Sold every piece of memorabilia and designer clothes that I could. I hang out with anyone willing to dinner because I'm a celebrity or they want to sleep with me." Why do you think I did that trashy shoot!"

I was shocked and, I had to admit, filled with delicious *schadenfreude.*

I didn't ask why she still kept a maid, or hired a limo for station gigs, or didn't sell her two places and buy one apartment for less. Cat had been living a lie for so long and been treated like royalty for so long, she couldn't be any other way.

While Cat chewed on her thumbnail, Ariella said softly, "It's over. It's really over."

"They're not even letting anyone say goodbye," I said. "Typical."

I gave Ariella a hug. Cat joined in.

Then our cells rang.

"Sit tight, Jazmyn." It was Howie. "Another rock station will emerge. Or another situation. Hold on until *Ree-ality* airs, you'll be in a better position. It's already generating great buzz." Rick Rivers called Ariella.

I called Ree and reached his voicemail this time. To hell with Chee. Ree had probably been nowhere near his cell when she'd picked it up, screwing with my head.

I called Shane.

"I'm going to work from home full time." He tried to sound upbeat. "No more commuting."

"You'll be a hermit."

"You think there isn't life in the exurbs?" A less crowded version of the suburbs, he explained. "Door's always open."

I wished he were with us. Ree wouldn't have understood how huge and heartbreaking it was for 'BRR to die anyway.

I texted Ree: *In 3 hours The Bear is officially dead. Can't believe it.*

He didn't answer.

Ariella put her arm around me. "You're in no shape to drive anywhere. Stay the night."

"At least he can't get Chee pregnant," I said.

WBRR stayed jockless. We didn't touch any more weed or wine. We were in mourning, listening to the station for its last hours of existence.

We all jumped when someone knocked on the door. Who could it be at a quarter to midnight?

"I rushed out here after Ree got your message." It was Todd, the cutest, youngest cameramen from the TV show, out of breath and with tape rolling.

"Why didn't he come with you? Or at least text me back."

Ignoring me, Todd asked Cat and Ariella for their permission to film them for the show. They both fled to the bathroom.

"After we put on make-up!" Ariella called out.

I hoped she had some eye drops handy, too.

"You look gorgeous already!" he yelled. To me, he said, "Cat Cruz is even hotter in person."

I faced Todd and his camera squarely. "Is he doing drugs?"

"Uhh … I can't answer that."

I pushed him against the wall, grabbed his camera and tossed it on a chair.

"Hey! That's expensive!"

"Tell me."

"No!"

"No, he's not doing drugs or no, you won't tell me?"

"Just no!"

Ariella pulled me off him. "Easy, Jaz, he's only doing his job. Come and put some make-up on. We all look like shit."

The somber beginning of the Doors' "The End" floated over the airwaves.

"Eleven forty-one," Ariella announced, the song's running time. We rushed to her bathroom.

We came out a few minutes later, presentable again. Todd fed us questions.

"What are you going to do now that the station is gone?"

"Spend more time with my son," Cat said. I could swear she was flirting with him when she said, "And enjoy being single."

"I'm going to take my severance and buy an around-the-world ticket," said Ariella. "With any luck, I'll breathe my last breath in India."

"Spend a lot more time with Ree," I said. "A *lot*."

"Aren't you mad he's not here?" Todd asked.

"Not at all. I completely trust him."

"Even when another woman answered his phone?"

"I'm sure it was staged." I smiled into the camera, knowing I was right.

"One minute to go!" Ariella popped open a bottle of fine champagne, pouring us each a flute. No point in being a bunch of depressos for the camera.

"To a hot rockin' past," she said. "And no more wigs!"

"To an even better future for all of us," said Cat. "Whatever it is."

"And to our special bond," I said. "No one really knows what it's like to be a female DJ except another female DJ."

"And to no more filing those damn CDs and commercials," Ariella said.

Shane's low voice filled the room.

"This *is* the end, my friend, of the best rock and roll station New York has ever known. Thank you for coming along for the ride."

He'd crafted a montage of the history of WBRR, starting with a young Maxx signing on:

"We've got the brand-new release from the Beatles we've all been waiting for and we're going to play it in its entirety with no commercials. Here it is, *Sgt. Pepper's Lonely Hearts Club Band* in static-free frequency modulated *stereoooo*."

There wasn't a dry eye in sight as Shane's aural masterpiece took us through the psychedelic '60s; glam-rock, punk-rock,

Bruce Springsteen and Southern Cal '70s; Live Aid, rise-of-U2 '80s that started with a bang, literally: the assassination of John Lennon. Then on to the grunge '90s, and the World Trade Center disaster in 2001 — all mixed with rock stars promoting the station, many no longer alive. It ended with snippets from Dick and Dork, the Barenaked Radio Ladies, Ariella, Chopper, and back around to Madd Maxx with his signature sign-off.

"Catch you on the flip side. Till then, keep rockin' in the free world, New York."

A dramatic silence.

Then a sexy female voice said brightly, *"Esto es Lolita noventa nueve effeh em!"*

31

To Ree or Not to Ree

I slept for ten hours.

When I woke up I was disoriented. Oh, right. *Montauk. Ariella. No more WBRR. No more Karl. Donna doing okay. Ree partying with Mo'.*

Future unknown.

Ariella and I sat in her back yard watching a pair of swans glide on the pond behind her house while sipping robust freshly ground Italian dark roast coffee.

"That was the best night's sleep I've had since I moved to New York."

"I hear that a lot from my city guests."

I remembered Cat leaving soon after the station flip, an attentive Todd on her heels, saying with a wink, "I'm taking *full* advantage of my son not being home tonight."

"You were right about Cat having something to hide. Not Hispanic and broke? Didn't see that coming."

"Nor that she took a pay cut."

"Another reason she felt they wouldn't fire her," I said. "They were getting a deal."

Ariella let out a light sigh. I knew a playful barb was coming.

"Joan Rivers once told me, 'If you walked into a room and saw everyone's troubles hanging on the wall, you'd still head straight to your own.'"

She was probably right.

"Cat sure inherited her parents' moxie," I said. "Wonder what I've inherited from mine."

"Maybe your parents' obesity set you up to accept extreme behavior?"

I hadn't considered that. "But why was I drawn to radio?"

"I know why I was. I came from a big Catholic family of eight kids. My voice was lost in the crowd. I spoke so rarely I was called the Mute Murkowski. The moment I talked into a microphone all that changed."

"It gives you permission to speak," I said. The swans floated closer to each other.

"I'm amazed by how ill-suited many people are for their chosen profession," Ariella said thoughtfully.

"What do you mean?"

"Take show business. It's one of the most unpredictable, brutal careers you can have, yet it draws the most insecure people."

"Or makes them insecure."

"There's something fascinating about radio, though," she said. "You can see it when you meet someone and tell them what you do."

"Yeah, they get that *look*. Like, *Wow, how cool.* Cracks me up."

"The human voice is incredibly powerful," she said. "It soothes. Destroys. Manipulates. If the eyes are the windows to your soul, the voice is what's beyond the window, what's really there. A lot of people in radio become their voice, like Madd Maxx. Would you believe he stammered as a kid?"

"No!"

We talked about another part of the equation: power. You're fielding calls from adoring listeners. Sliding faders and punching buttons like you're flying an airplane.

"But there's a lot of non-power in it, too," she said. "I call it the Cocoon of Imaginary Control. My show may appear to be mine, but other people determine whether I have one and when it runs.

Do you think I *like* being on in the middle of the night? Do I pick the songs I play?"

"It's really a hip assembly-line job," I said. "I don't have eleven years of radio experience. I have the same year repeated eleven times."

"Jaz, *every* job is an assembly line in some way. Every single one of them."

"Even being a veterinarian?"

"Yep. The paperwork, regulations, and heartbreak of watching animals you love die would get to you, I'm sure. Not to say you shouldn't go for it. But you don't seem the vet type." She touched my forearm. "You're *really* good on the radio. Don't ever forget it."

I clasped a hand over hers. "Thank you."

"You should have your own show. The Barenaked Hoochie Mamas was a gimmick that couldn't last."

We drank more coffee in companionable silence. I'd been so ready to leave radio. She was pulling me back in.

"Look, Ariella." The two swans had joined foreheads. "Could they be kissing?"

"Yes. Swans are monogamous."

I turned to her. "I know I asked you this before but I felt like you gave me a stock answer. Do you regret not having children?"

"Deeply. But it didn't hit me until much later in life, so I probably wouldn't have been a great mother. I mentored a lot of people in radio instead."

"You said you were married."

"Briefly. He wanted me to stop working, stay in New Jersey, and have babies. No way was I ready to give up being the goddess of WBRR."

"No one else came along?"

"Oh, sure. There was always something that killed the romance. One wanted me to convert to his religion. It didn't feel right. I was still that Catholic girl from Joisey. Another guy had three rotten screwed-up kids who couldn't stand me. One was horrendous with money, another horrendous in bed. Another wanted me to move to India. I love India — to visit." She shrugged. "I'm too independent and work crazy hours."

I told her about Ree's proposal at St. Peter's Basilica.

One hand flew to her chest. "How romantic! Totally from the heart. Nothing staged."

My smile vanished. "He's staging it for the show. We have to give it that Hollywood happy ending."

"I'm sure it'll be just as special. I'll say this. You'll never feel that kind of love again."

"Never?"

"There's nothing like our first love. I have an excellent tarot card reader I can—"

I waved my cup-free hand frantically. "No, thanks. *I* know what I have to do. Marry the man I love, start a family, and stay in radio. Why are you shaking your head?"

"If only love conquered all."

I suddenly had to leave. I loved Ariella, but I couldn't take another minute of seeing life from the perspective of someone old and regretful.

She held out an arm to stop me when I stood up. "I need to ask you something, Jaz. Did you and Marcie talk about addiction?"

"You mean Ree's? Yes." I saw her expression. "What?"

"Who has an endless battle with food?"

"Who doesn't? And look at me. I'm thin now."

She paused before saying, "I've known plenty of addicts in my life and dealt with my own struggles." Her voice was grave. "Addicts love addicts."

Driving back to the city, I tried to push away my anger. It wasn't just at Ree. I was angry at Ariella, too. Why did she have to rain on my parade?

32

Squeaky Clean

When I got back to the Manhattan loft, Joe Lumas and a cameraman were waiting for me.

Sensing trouble in paradise, he was like a hyena with his sights set on a newborn wildebeest. He looked like he'd slept in his clothes.

"I'm not angry with Ree," I said to the camera. "I *have* been wrapped up in my own drama lately. Now with the radio station gone, he's my top priority."

Without a job, I wasn't lying.

I prepared for Ree's arrival: fresh flowers, clean sheets, woodsy-scented massage oil. I had all the things he loved to eat and drink on hand, like plump strawberries dipped in dark chocolate, delicate rice candies we could only get in Chinatown, and $100-an-ounce jasmine tea.

All complimentary. Freebies that once had been a thrill now felt like scamming.

Joe yawned repeatedly.

The sun fell lower in the sky. Still no word from Ree.

At one point I was curled in a fetal position on the couch when the cameras caught me crying over the horrible way some jerk treated a cat and her kittens on *Animal Cops*. (I knew Joe would edit it so it would look like I was crying over Ree.)

It was like this years ago, I reminded myself. It wasn't just this conflict-driven reality show. I'd wait him out, fuming, until he showed up and we fought. Soon he'd say or do something super special or funny, or I would. I couldn't bear the thought of cutting our umbilical cord. Then we'd have incredible sex.

When Ree called, my worst fears were confirmed in just two words.

"Hey, baby."

His cool attitude and hoarse voice meant he'd been binging on drugs.

"Heeeeeey!" I sounded even phonier. "Where are you?"

"Richmond. Hadn't been home in a long time."

"Let me get this straight. Krazy Karl died, Donna was seriously injured, the station went under leaving me without a job, and you had to see a house you haven't seen in a while?"

"You sounded like you needed space to hang with the station people. I thought you'd be happy I didn't stay up all night partyin' and gamblin'."

Was I going to have to embed an electronic homing device in his brain? Keep him under house arrest? We hung up and I stormed toward the bedroom.

"Cut! Fabu!"

Joe lingered after the crew left.

"Everything okay, Joe? You seem pretty wound up."

He ran his hands through his oily hair. "You really want to know? My wife is having an affair with her yoga instructor because I'm never home. And when I am, all I talk about is this stupid fucking show!"

"Oh. I'm sorry to hear that."

"I could *really* use a Percocet." He held out his hand.

"Haven't got any."

"I gave you a whole vial!"

"I flushed them down the toilet."

He pulled on his hair so hard I couldn't believe it didn't come out in handfuls. His expression terrified me. I was alone with this crazy mofo.

"Almighty fuck!" he said, "you really are Miss Squeaky Clean Pure As The Driven Snow White."

"What does that mean?"

"Maybe you'll see. Maybe you won't." He took off without another word.

Pure as the driven Snow White? Squeaky clean? I posed for *Penthouse!* I got blasted on Maui Wowie. I loved to drink.

Joe had to be losing it because his marriage was a disaster. His life was a disaster. All that promise as a filmmaker and he'd been reduced to this inane show. I couldn't wait for it to wrap so Ree and I could live a normal life.

Well, normaler. And be married.

Ariella scheduled her surgery for the following week. The doctor had a cancellation, she told me over the phone.

"I want to get this over with."

"I'll be there for you," I said. "The show's about to end, and not a moment too soon."

"What's wrong?"

"I just know Ree's being a bad boy. I have to stop thinking like this."

"What kind of bad? Women or drugs?"

"Not sure."

"We all crave a man other women want. And let's face it, a man can be weak, no matter how much they love you. But drugs, that's a problem."

I had given a lot of thought to what she had said back in Montauk that had pissed me off. My very reaction was a tip off that she was probably right.

"Maybe we should both be in addiction therapy."

"I'm not commenting. This is why I wouldn't have made a good shrink. I interject too much. Where's Ree now?"

"In Richmond."

"Jazmyn! Get your ass down there, love that man, get therapy, do whatever you have to do to grab spectacular TV ratings and milk your gravy train for all it's worth!"

"But your operation. I said I'd help. Cat can't afford to help you, no matter what she said."

"I can hire a private nurse. I've got a helluva severance coming my way. Just don't end up like me, Jazmyn, saying shoulda, woulda, coulda."

I was on the road within fifteen minutes.

33

HOME

There's nothing like six hours on an interstate highway to clear your mind. I tried to see myself at Ariella's age. What would I regret the most?

The TV show had twisted everything in ten different directions at once. All reality shows purposely pushed your buttons, as a viewer and a participant. But we had just reunited after seven years. We were crazy to jump right into it. Like my therapist said, life often doesn't sync to our timetable.

I was not going to let this TV show ruin the love of my life.

As for radio, who said I shouldn't have to pretend I was naked and that I should have my own show? Ree. He'd seen the best I could be even when I couldn't. He believed in me.

And I believed in him as much, if not more, than I did when we met a decade ago.

I couldn't wait to see him. It was all I could do to stay anywhere near the speed limit. I called him as I drove to Richmond.

"I'm done with New York, Ree. I really am."

"Me, too."

"I'd *like* to go to college if I can get in, then have kids. But if we're parents sooner, we'll cope."

"Whatever you want to do, Jaz, you should do it. As long as it's for you, not me."

"You can be such a feminist sometimes, Ree," I said, unable to hide the smile in my voice. "I want to do what's best for *us*."

Pause. "So do I. But no one should bring a kid into the world if they're not ready."

"We'll do our best, Ree. What's important is we'll never regret it."

He took so long to respond I asked if he was still there.

"We'll talk more when you get here. Drive safe."

Of course. This conversation should have been in person, our final taping. He was going to propose. *Don't give the performance in the dressing room!* I never wanted to hear that again.

My eye drifted to my left hand as it rested on the steering wheel. I pictured a sparkly ring. Not huge, not small. Euphoria overtook me as I drove, blasting the radio, cranking it up when Ree's song came on. I'd lived my dream and was moving on. With my man. Forever.

I reflected on the full circle of leaving Richmond almost eight years ago and finally reaching the Big Apple, only to find it wasn't as sweet as I thought it would be. It hadn't been terrible, far from it. I was delighted I had the experience.

I just loved Ree more.

I could see our life together, our children, what a great father Ree would be, how our lives would change for the better once kids were the focus. So he'd done some partyin' with Mo'. He could be a bad boy once in a while. Maybe I'd get high with Ariella sometimes. We all have to let loose now and then, with and without our partner.

Maybe we could have our own pirate station and disguise our voices with some electronic gizmo, like Shane had done. On second thought, hadn't I said enough? Just play music. All kinds. That's what had drawn me to radio in the first place, the love of music. The power of talking into a microphone came later.

As the big green signs on I-95 counted down the miles to Richmond, I grew more excited about my new life back home. I could help my parents as they aged. They could help with the kids; spoil them.

I stopped at a rest area at the halfway point to call them. They had their own big news. "After your TV show came and interviewed us, we got a call from *The Biggest Loser*. We're going to get in shape come hell or high water."

"That's fantastic!"

Another item in the plus column of *Ree-ality TV*.

I checked my phone for messages before I left the rest stop and went right to the one from Shane.

I didn't hear the station sign off. I was holding Charlie when he left us forever a few hours later. At least it happened now instead of when I was commuting. I feel like a zombie. Half-dead. I know it'll get better in time. Hope you stay in New York.

That cute little boy just gone. It wasn't right. What unbearable agony Shane must be in. I reached his voicemail.

"Shane, I'm devastated. I can't imagine how you and Charlie's mother must feel. You were the best dad. Let me know where the service is. What a kid. I'll never forget him. Or you. I'm driving to Richmond now. Looks like my New York days are over."

Somewhere in Shane's grief there had to be a sense of relief. Charlie's rough road had come to an end.

I listened to classical music the rest of the way home.

Home.

Ree's house was a three-story 1904 classic revival brick beauty that took my breath away. I stood on the stone path to the front door, observing its perfect white trim and columns, the beautiful accents on each window.

Two white rocking chairs on the porch.

The door opened and Todd pointed a camera at me. He sure got here fast from the Hamptons. Did Cat kick him out yesterday morning or did he flee?

I threw my arms in the air. "I'm home! At last!"

I ran to Ree's waiting arms. He hugged me so tightly I almost couldn't breathe.

"That's quite a welcome," I said. I practically skipped around the house exploring it. "It's perfect, Ree. I love everything you've done. You're absolutely right about living here."

He seemed subdued. No, sad almost.

"Check out the garage." He nodded to a door at my left.

I opened it and looked in. It was filled with empty boxes from a moving company.

"What's going on?"

He looked down at his clasped hands, deep in thought. He said quietly, "I'm moving to L.A."

I grabbed the doorjamb to steady myself.

He looked up with moist eyes. "I was offered a part on a cop show. I have to expand into acting, Jaz. The music biz is more frustrating and unprofitable than ever."

A pounding pulse in my throat was all I could feel.

"You didn't say *we're* moving to L.A."

He looked at his hands, then back at me.

"Jazmyn, a part of me will always love you. This just isn't going to work with us. I need a woman who can trust me. We want different things. I want a family. Now."

"What did I say on the phone? I'm ready for whatever happens."

He held up his hand, palm out. "I want a woman who wants to talk to me more than she wants to talk into a microphone or study a textbook."

A metallic taste rose in my throat. One camera pointed at me, the other at him.

"If I'm less of a man for wanting a woman who doesn't have a job that consumes her, so be it. But it's more than that. A lot more, Jaz. The same problems we had before are still here. Yes, I was a train wreck on drugs then. Not now. I'm faithful, but you think I'm not. I can't feel like I'm always being watched."

I clasped my hand over my mouth, tears welling. I refused to utter one more word for that cold round camera eye. Not one.

"I know this show hasn't been easy," he said. "You may think it manipulated the truth. I think it sped up the truth. "

Ree had one parting gift for me. Was it for the camera to save his image?

"If you love this house so much, you can have it. It's all paid for. I owe you a lot."

Fuck you and your house, I wanted to say. I picked up my car keys. The cameraman followed me out. I flipped him the bird and kept walking. And that was my elegant exit from my fifteen minutes of fame.

When the show aired, I learned what I didn't know that day, as I watched Ree talk privately about his uncertainty over our future.

"We have such different upbringings. I can't change that ... She'll always think she's unattractive, which makes her insecure ... She worries too much ... Her father will never approve of me. That's not good for our kids, our marriage."

I was doing similar questioning about him. I was right to worry. I'd known deep down that it couldn't work between us, that my father was right. Or did it become a self-fulfilling prophecy?

Reality TV shows do show the truth. If only the participants could see everything that the camera saw. It was clear Ree and I weren't going to work to everyone but us.

34

THE GINGER ROOT AND MAGICAL TATTOO

It was now a month since Ree dropped the bomb on me. I was living with Ariella in her Montauk home. Her surgery recovery was excellent, though she still tired easily. Fall was in full force, the leaves brilliant gold and red. Frequent blasts of cold wind reminded us winter was around the next bend.

"There's never a shortage of melancholy in autumn," Ariella said as I drove us to a supermarket one morning.

"I'm worried about Shane," I said. "He's in a cave. I can feel it."

"His voice-over work reinforces it. He's literally in a cave. All day."

"Night, too." He had recently told me his wife had moved in with her boyfriend. He had no interest in dating. "I wonder if they would have stayed married if Charlie had never been sick?"

"I met his wife once," Ariella said. "I could tell they were mismatched. Shane told me they were about to separate when she found out she was pregnant. He's wanted out of the marriage a long time."

Charlie's funeral had been small and private. Respecting Shane's wishes, I didn't attend. No matter how heartbroken I was over Ree, it was nothing compared to Shane's loss.

I told Ariella he'd invited me to see his pirate station. "I'm afraid. I think he likes me. It might take the wrong turn, if you know what I mean."

"Maybe it's the right turn."

I shook my head. "I'm not feeling it."

"It's too soon. For both of you," Ariella said. "It's going to take time for Ree to be out of your system."

We split up the grocery list. By the time I'd made my way back to her, Ariella was checking out a good-looking man who was picking out shallots.

"I've had my eye on that guy for a year," she whispered. "Name's Patrick. Wife died, he retired from a big job at NBC, sold their summer home out here, downsized and moved to a place not far from me. And look, he cooks with shallots. That's a good sign. He's moving over to the ginger roots. Another good sign. I wonder what he's going to make?"

"Why don't you ask him?"

Her cheeks reddened. "Oh, no. I can't."

"Isn't ginger root on our list?"

I moved across from him by the lemons, watching as Ariella and Patrick reached for the same root at the same time.

"Oh, sorry," she said. "You can have it."

No trace of embarrassment. She was "on" now.

"No, no," he said, "I insist you take it. You're Ariella, aren't you?"

"And you're Patrick? Welcome to living in a small town. What are you going to make with ginger?"

They were soon having a lively discussion about the health benefits of ginger and who had the freshest fish locally.

"I had a heart attack six months ago," he said. "They put in a stent. It was a wakeup call."

"I just had surgery for an abdominal aneurysm," she said.

"That's serious."

"So is a stent."

"I'm glad it happened," he said. "I feel like I have a new lease on life."

"Me, too."

There was a moment of awkwardness.

I stepped in. "We'll gladly accept your offer to take that ginger root if you'll accept ours to come to dinner and enjoy it."

Ariella was blushing again.

I extended my hand. "I'm Jazmyn."

He studied me while we shook. "You're the one with the rapper, aren't you? You changed your hair."

Was, with the rapper, I thought. Though I was contractually sworn to silence, the rumor mill was churning that Ree and one of his beautiful co-stars on the cop show were seen getting cozy at a club. If Ree thought an actress wasn't going to be insecure, was he in for a shock.

"Will you come to dinner?" I asked.

He readily agreed.

As we walked to the car, Ariella gave me a hard nudge. "I'm getting you back for that."

"Right, for helping you move on with your life." I nudged her right back.

"Can you get that?" Ariella asked me when the doorbell chimed that night. "I'll uncork the wine."

I opened the door and there stood Shane. We fell into a long hug and a longer grin.

"Welcome to the Bungalow of Bliss," I said.

"I've heard it has magical powers. I'll take all the help I can get."

Soon Patrick arrived, and the wine and conversation flowed. Ariella proposed a toast.

"Here's to new friends and new beginnings."

Patrick added, "Here's to those we've loved and lost. Let us always remember the good times and look to the future."

I glanced at Shane. He seemed on the verge of losing it.

I rubbed his back while Ariella explained to Patrick. "His five-year-old son just lost a brave battle with cancer."

Stricken, he said, "I'm so sorry. So very, very sorry. I lost my wife to cancer, but a child. I can't imagine."

Shane took a sip of water. His shoulders stooped as though lead weights were on either side of his ears.

"It's time for me to make big changes in my life," he said. "I make more money than I ever dreamed of but I sit in a dark room saying the stupidest stuff you can imagine. I miss connecting with real people. I just received a love letter from the FCC telling me to shut down my pirate station. If that's not a sign to get out of that house and move on ..."

"Do you miss being on the radio?" I asked.

"You know where there's great radio?" he answered. "Santa Fe. There's a phenomenal small company there that's the antithesis of Sonic Broadcasting. I can do my business from anywhere. I'm thinking of moving there and getting a little weekend show. I loved reading to the kids at the hospital. No way am I ready to do that again."

She touched his hand. "Above all, give yourself time to grieve."

"Shane, I'm not sure if this will be of any help to you," Patrick said, "but I know a man who lost his daughter. He was inconsolable. He stayed like that one year, two years. Then he got a tattoo of her face on his left arm." He pointed to his bicep. "Every time he missed her, he patted his tattoo and it was like she was still with him. He came right out of his funk."

"Really?"

"I know a woman with breast cancer who tattooed a big rose where her breast used to be," Ariella said. "Six months later she was dating a much younger man. I considered doing something similar."

"Dating a younger man or getting a tattoo?" Patrick inquired with a grin.

"I'd go a *little* younger."

We'd already Googled him. He was five years her junior.

I glanced at my half-tattoo, remembering how when I was away from Ree I'd rubbed it all the time, like I was trying to conjure up a genie. Since we'd broken up, I'd stopped.

"I want to remove mine now that Ree's history."

"He is?" Shane asked. I couldn't quite read his tone.

"It all blew up on camera. He's living in L.A. now."

"I think you should *finish* your tattoo," he said.

"Why?"

"As an act of solidarity to yourself. You're complete as you are. You never needed Ree to do that."

Without thinking, I kissed him on the cheek. He smiled, ducking his head.

"Let's not rule out another person to *complement* us," Ariella said.

"Look at the time." Shane was suddenly nervous. "I need to be going."

"What? You haven't finished dinner," Ariella said.

"It's a long drive back."

"You can stay at my place," Patrick offered. "I have a guest room and I'd enjoy your company. I insist."

The rest of our meal was filled with laughter and no more tears. An image zipped through my brain of trapeze artists flying through the air, locking hands with a partner. We all had landed from a freefall.

Momentarily.

35

ONWARD

When a station flips formats and plays a song like "Macarena" or "Gangnam Style" nonstop for several days, it's to get the word out fast that the old station is *fini* and something new is coming. It's called "stunting." This time it was Todd Rundgren's "Bang the Drum All Day."

I was back at the Gramercy Arms waiting to see if ROCK 106 would stick to the wall like another flung bowl of radio spaghetti, and if so, for how long, with me as one of the main ingredients: afternoon drive. Solo!

The station had sprung up quickly after the demise of WBRR, proving there would always be an audience for *rock and roll*. It was now perfectly acceptable to use that term.

My stay in Montauk had stretched to over four months. Ariella and Patrick were practically inseparable. At first it made me miss Ree even more, until it hit me that we'd never had the same ease that they had, so wonderful to watch. There was always an underlying tension between us, a constant battle.

Ariella summed us up perfectly. "I've never seen two people so right and so wrong for each other."

She did talk sense into me regarding Ree's offer to take his Richmond house.

"You'll sell it and use the money as your down payment on a *modest* New York place," she said. "Don't get carried away. You could be out of a job tomorrow."

I was closing on the sale of Ree's gift in two weeks. It had amounted to almost half a million dollars. I still felt weird taking it. Ariella's reaction?

"You'll get over it."

When I wasn't helping at the local animal hospital I had plenty of time to walk on the beach and contemplate my future. I took college prep classes online, worked on applications. All my choices were in New York City or close by. Whoever accepted me would determine where I'd find a place to live. Then I'd get a pet or two. If there were no takers, that would be my answer about going back to college.

For now, thanks to that ridiculous TV show, I had a staggering salary plus bonuses, and the time to go to school part time if that worked out.

If ROCK 106 tanked, Santa Fe or Montauk here I come.

It felt great not to be so wrapped up in the radio life and *having* to be in Manhattan. There was life beyond both. Balance did not mean boredom, as I learned in therapy.

I had gained a lot of insight with Marcie. For one, she pointed out the significance of the nightmares I'd had as a child about the Church Hill Tunnel tragedy in Richmond. Not only did I feel trapped at the time from being mercilessly teased, when I met Ree, wasn't *he* trapped too by society, his race, and his circumstances? I wanted to rescue him. And I did. It was a powerful attraction. Add raging hormones and the seductive recognition fame bestows and you have quite a lustful bonfire.

When drugs trapped him again, I rightfully surrendered. There was nothing I could do to help him. I felt unyielding guilt and grief about it, though.

The day before my first show on ROCK 106, Ree called. It was the first time we had spoken since we broke up.

"I owe you an apology," he said.

"For what?"

"I *was* doing drugs again. VTV wanted to do another season of *Ree-ality*. I said no and went into rehab instead. No cameras. I wanted to be clean as a whistle for my acting career."

I felt a mix of emotions: vindicated, sorry for him, proud he could admit he had a problem and do something about it. But he cleaned up for his career, not me. And for how long?

"I see."

"Addicts are great liars," he said.

No kidding.

"I knew I couldn't get away with doing drugs around you. I wish I'd never said what I said for the show. The last thing I wanted to do was hurt you. I justified it by thinking it was okay to jack up the drama. If the show was a success, I'd be a success. It was my last shot, Jaz, at any lasting happiness for us. For *us*. It was the drugs talking. I needed my freedom to do *them*. I never stopped loving you. I asked you to marry me! And you said yes. I wish that TV show had never happened. I was also crazy to think I could handle being a father right now."

It took a moment to respond to his confession. "A lot of good came out of that show."

"It wasn't worth our breaking up. Let's get back together, baby. *No cameras*. Just us."

My answer this time was quick and sure. "I'm happy you went into rehab, Ree. That's a huge step. I'll always care for you deeply. Here's the problem. You're in L.A., I'm finally getting my dream job in New York City, and you don't want a career girl."

"That was the drugs talking, I'm telling you! I was so proud of you doing afternoons in New York. I thought you should be doing it alone, didn't I? And now you are. Radio and TV shows come and go, Jaz. True love doesn't."

He really knew how to say the right thing at the right time. "If only love conquered all."

"What does that mean?"

"Something's shifted inside me, Ree. I feel the best I've ever felt."

"That's great, baby. So do I. I'll be in New York soon. Let's have dinner."

He couldn't see me shaking my head. "I'll call you if I change my mind, but I doubt I will."

"Baby, don't do this to me."

"Ree, can't you see? We're just drugs for each other. One moment we feel really good and the next really bad. I don't think that's going to change."

"Jazmyn, wait."

"Goodbye."

My radio debut was off to a good start when Mother Nature dumped fifteen inches of snow on the Tri-state area. Nothing like a crisis to ratchet up the spirit of a community. A crisis in New York took it to another level. Schools and most businesses were closed. A *lot* of people would be listening.

Radio is an instantaneous outlet for people thrown out of their daily routine. For the most part, this one was fun. I saw a car buried under snow sporting a warning sign to would-be thieves from the tip of its barely visible antenna: *No Sound System or GPS*. I knew I'd get great, visual phone calls from listeners and not the usual "Play ZZ Top."

I trudged to the station in my Uggs and puffy parka, comfortable in my new look: touches of faux fur and my natural brown hair color with caramel highlights. I still favored turquoise nails. Best of all, I wasn't skinny anymore and didn't care. Men were coming on to me all the time. I could tell most had no idea I was the platinum blonde DJ on *Ree-ality* that had just finished airing. It wasn't because I was unrecognizable with the weight gain, I hadn't put on *that* much. My whole look and vibe was just different.

Ariella said, "Confidence is the ultimate catnip, and girlfriend, you've got enough now to send the station's signal all the way to Canada."

Bouncing up Fifth Avenue, I couldn't stop smiling. The city felt different as the usual horns, traffic, and crush of people were replaced by near-empty sidewalks and an occasional snowplow scraping past. It was the perfect quiet atmosphere to reflect on how what I did for a living wasn't just spewing a bunch of inane patter. I helped people get through their day in a better mood, sending positive ripples out into the universe. What's wrong with that?

Shane had just put his house on the market. Once it was sold he was moving to Santa Fe. I'd miss him terribly, but knew he had to follow his heart.

In one way he wouldn't be far. He was going to be introducing my show every day. Linda Walker, my new boss, had wanted to hire a monotone guy as the "stationality" voice. I insisted Shane could change his. She was dubious until I played something he'd put together.

We wrangled again over my first song. She wanted something new. I wanted something classic that had special meaning to me. The station would have been on the air since midnight, making it clear the format was new rock mixed with classic rock. She said she'd think about it. I didn't push it. I'd learned to pick my battles.

When I entered the state-of-the-art studio, the midday jock, Lizard (who was discovered on the Internet), gave me a warm welcome. Used to doing his show out of his dorm room at Rutgers, he was blown away by how "corporate" the station was.

"The rules, man. I thought this was going to be free-form."

Unless the steady paycheck and benefits changed his mind, he wouldn't be around long.

"You sure have a lot of fans." He nodded toward the flower arrangements and gift baskets covering a table for guest interviews. He put his headphones on, wrapping up his show as I inspected the gift cards.

The biggest flower arrangement was from Nigel.

Bang on! You're right where you belong — at the top. If there's anything you need, just call. Love, Nigel and the MGX family.

Paid for by the record company. Good. We were back to our previous professional friendship. I also heard he was seeing Olivia.

Cat had sent an arrangement almost as large. After she'd come clean that she wasn't a Latina, she'd ended up hosting a new TV show that was part *Amazing Race,* part *Jackass.*

Donna, now teamed up with Long Island radio legend Donna Donna for the Donna Donna Donna morning show, sent me a card with fifty dollars in it.

I'll never forget all you did for me, including the bucks you gave me for helping out at Bayonne BMW. Pass this on to your next producer.

And where was he? All I knew was his name was Paul and he had a burning desire to get into radio. No need to pull music or commercials and put them in neat stacks like at WBRR. Everything was on computer. He'd help answer the phones, edit calls, find content, and do background research for interviews.

I had become a female Madd Maxx. Without the gold-trimmed headphones and $10,000 microphone, thank you.

Ariella had sent a beautiful arrangement in the vase from Taos that I'd admired. Her card said:

Enjoy every minute and save your money!

There was a nicely wrapped gift, a little bigger than a tissue box.

By the time this blooms you'll have the number one afternoon show in New York. Stay tuned and "have fun with it." Shane.

Inside, an oriental ceramic dish held a bulb that would turn into a brilliant red amaryllis in about a month. I loved it.

Ree's gift was an exotic display of orchids, birds of paradise, and bamboo.

Congratulations, Ms. Brown. Let's follow our dreams, live right, and see where it takes us.

I'm always there for you. Love, Ree.

I would probably never again be as intoxicated by a man as I had been with Ree. Nor did I regret getting back together with him. It led me to where I was, and who I was, today. But I was now on the Ree wagon, hoping never to fall off, hoping the craving for that high with him would fade forever.

My boss stuck her head in the door. "Your producer will be here any minute. He was delayed by the weather."

"No problem."

Ten minutes later I heard Shane say in my headphones in his way-sexy natural speaking voice: "And now ... breaking all the rules ... the unpredictable ... unforgettable ... and fully clothed ... *Patty* Brown."

Aerosmith's "Back in the Saddle" began its ominous, slowly escalating guitar, drums, and bass intro. Picturing Shane's funny dance to it my first day on WBRR, I couldn't stop smiling. 100,000 watts zapped through my system, blasting me into another dimension like a NASCAR driver approaching 200 mph on a raceway. The most amazing feeling ever! My words spun around the music better than a silkworm.

"Hey there, New York. What a day to kick off a brand-new radio station. Jet skis have taken over Manhattan. Central Park is full of snow angels. Call me at 1-800-ROCK106 and tell me how you're dealing with it, how you're liking your new station, what you want to hear. Stick around for the best rock and roll and *front row* tickets to *U2* on Rock one ... oh ... six."

"I'm BAAAAACK!" screamed Steven Tyler.

"Yes!" My first break on my new show and I'd hit the post perfectly.

Linda Walker reappeared. "You sound awesome. Need anything?"

"Some speakers OSHA hasn't screwed with that I can blast all the way?"

"Sorry. Can't turn back time." She brightened. "Think of how you'll save your hearing. You know you're going to be doing this forever."

We held our smug grins a bit longer. A woman doing afternoon drive on a rock radio station in the number one market with another woman at the helm was a groundbreaking moment to be savored.

"And here's your new producer, Paul."

In walked Shane.

"What?!"

He extended his hand. "Paul Randall. Nice to meet you, Ms. Brown."

"I thought you two would make a fantastic team," Linda said before ducking out.

I rushed over, giving him a tight hug.

"If you're going to use your real name," he said, "so am I. And every time you hit the vocal post, I'll be saying 'Yes!' with you."

"You scoundrel. How could you not have told me?"

"I wanted to see the look on your face."

"And?"

"Priceless."

I checked the time left on "Back in the Saddle" and reached for the volume control.

"We only have two minutes left on *our* song," I said.

"Blast it."

I cranked the speakers as far as they would go.

It was still plenty loud.

Props

My gratitude extends to everyone I ever worked with in radio, and to those who would not hire me nor give me any encouragement whatsoever. Oh, the power of the word "no" to a headstrong woman. For all the radio air talents with careers spanning decades who make every show sound easy and fun, I hold you in the highest regard. This book is my homage to you and the radio profession. May it thrive far into the future.

BOOK CLUB CENTRAL

I love to Skype or call into book clubs. Reach out to me through my website or social media. Here are two sets of discussion questions. Mix, match, and *have fun with it!* — Jo

MUSIC/RADIO QUESTIONS

1. What was the first work by a musical artist you ever purchased and in what format was it?
2. What was the first musical act you saw live and where?
3. How has your taste in, and consumption of, music and radio changed over the years?
4. What role does radio play in your life? Do you still listen to AM/FM stations? Satellite or stream? What are your P1s (the preset buttons in your car)?
5. Did you ever have a radio show in college or want to be a DJ? If you did have a show, talk about it. (And please share any great stories on the Facebook Jo Maeder Author Page!) If you ever miss it, a lot of college stations will let non-students have their own show. Inquire at one near you.
6. How did you view DJs before reading *NAKED DJ* and how do you see them now, particularly female DJs?
7. What recording artist or radio star would you spend a lost weekend with — and would your significant other forgive you? Who is their Fantasy Fling?

1. *NAKED DJ* doesn't only refer to Jazmyn pretending she's naked on the radio or posing nude. In what other ways does she peel off (and put on) layers of psychological armor?
2. The decline of the radio DJ is a definite sub-theme of *NAKED DJ*. We know how Jazmyn feels about it. How do you? Should she follow in the footsteps of Ariella or change careers?
3. Say you (or your daughter) had been asked to do the *Penthouse* shoot. How would you react? To what do you attribute the increase in people exposing themselves, literally and figuratively, when control over our privacy is rapidly decreasing?
4. Have you known a Nigel, a man who says and does all the right things but is masking deep flaws?
5. Jazmyn says she doesn't have 11 years of experience as a DJ but the same year repeated 11 times. Ariella says all jobs are assembly lines in some way. Do you agree? If so, how do you keep a job interesting?
6. Jazmyn lost a lot of weight and Ree had a rough upbringing. How do you get past your past?
7. Jaz and Cat eventually reach an understanding (or at least a separate peace). Have you worked with someone you thought should be fired but could do no wrong in management's eyes?
8. Jazmyn tells her parents that Ree "completely changed." Her father's response? "I'm more worried you haven't." Could Jazmyn have done anything differently the first time around with Ree? The second time? Do you think she'll ever cut the "umbilical cord" with him? And how much does parental approval affect a relationship?

Jo Maeder began her radio career at age 16 out of spite when the student program director of her college station told her, "Chicks can't do Top 40 radio." She went on to DJ on South Florida's number one hit radio station, Y-100, New York's WKTU, classic rock K-ROCK (following *The Howard Stern Show*), and Z100, America's most listened to music radio station. She is now a writer and author of the bestselling memoir *When I Married My Mother*. For more on Jo, visit JoMaeder.com or find her on social media.

Sting, Chris Jagger, Jo Maeder. Jones Beach, NY

JO'S GREATEST HITS

OPPOSITES ATTACK: A Novel with Recipes Provençal

Alyce flew 4,000 miles to learn French, sophistication,
and inspire jealousy in her ex-boyfriend.
Enter the *très* different, exasperating Jean-Luc.

"A fun, rollicking tale with an enchanted setting, the kind of book you want to share with your dearest friends. Do yourself a favor and don't miss this one!"

—CASSANDRA KING

"Sparkles like fine champagne and feels like a Truffaut romantic comedy."

—RICHARD GOODMAN

"Merci for taking me back to the deliciousness of Provence! I wish my first stay in France had been this delightfully wicked."

—TERESA ENGEBRETSEN, The Sabbatical Chef

"This wonderfully entertaining novel will have you booking that trip to France you've been promising yourself for years."

—CHARLES SALZBERG

"Jo Maeder writes the kinds of books you pick up and all of a sudden it's getting dark in your living room. 'Where'd the last three hours go?' you wonder. This book will have you hooked."

—KAREN SOMMERFELD/JUNE GARDENS

"Filled with gutsy good humor and fantastic characters that made me laugh out loud. Armchair travel at its best!"

**—KIMBERLY DANIELS, The Country Bookshop,
Southern Pines, N.C.**

WHEN I MARRIED MY MOTHER:

An irreverent New York City DJ braces for disaster when she moves to the Bible Belt to care for her estranged, doll-obsessed, hoarder mother. What unfolds in this best-selling memoir is a hilarious, heartbreaking love story that sees eldercare and making peace with the past in a most unexpected way. Bonus material in the print version: Q&A, Mama Jo's Favorite Cookie award-winning recipe, caregiving tips, discussion questions. The ebook links to the trailer and film "The Doll Dilemma" by Jacob Rosdail. They can also be viewed on YouTube.

"This book is important to every mother and daughter, and to every woman who wants to be one."

—MAYA ANGELOU

"This generous gift of a book explores the mystery of how doing the right thing can become infinitely more."

—TOMMY HAYS

"Hilarious, heartbreaking, and real."

—NANCY GILES

"A wonderfully told love story for everyone."

—JULIE KLAM

"Two stubborn spirits come together in a shocking burst of love."

—SARAH KERNOCHAN

"Hilarious, poignant, utterly relevant. And her mother!! I adored this book."

—HOPE EDELMAN

"A wise, funny, and honest memoir. I couldn't put it down."

—NELL SCOVELL

www.ingramcontent.com/pod-product-compliance
Lightning Source LLC
Chambersburg PA
CBHW070537120726
47909CB00007B/2165